LITTLE GIRL X

KIT WITEK

OHB

Cover design by Dar Albert at Wicked Smart Designs

Published by Oliver-Heber Books

0 9 8 7 6 5 4 3 2 1

CONTENT WARNING

To the child you used to be,
and the adult you had to become to survive.
You were never broken.
You were healing.
Kit

CHAPTER 1

Fourteen Years Earlier
Dalton — Survival

Pain.

I couldn't open my eyes it was so intense. Muffled voices conversed around me. Foreign? Or merely distorted by the intense discomfort, I wasn't sure. The strength of the sun I honestly never thought I'd feel again, heated my exposed skin. I inhaled slowly the earthy humidity, instantly feeling beads of moisture on my forehead and upper lip. Was I being carried on a stretcher? Each jostled movement made me want to scream in agony, ask what the hell was going on, ask for water, for answers...but I couldn't find my voice. Once my tongue brushed against dry, cracked lips, pieces began to fall into place.

How long had I been out there?

The last thing I remembered was an almost paralyzing fear when the oxygen gave out, and my fight through the dark abyss before I finally breached the surface with lungs on fire as I prayed the trail of blood from my wounds wouldn't bring a shiver of sharks to the area.

One by one, I gently moved the fingers on each hand against the material beneath me. A smile tugged the tightened skin around my mouth when I successfully counted all ten. Light turned to shadow across my eyelids as all movement stopped and I was lowered. When a firm surface contacted my back, a stinging sensation burst through my torso and upper body.

On impulse, I attempted to bolt upright and assess any damage done by a shark attack I had no recollection of. As punishment for expending more energy than I had to give, the sound which emerged from my throat was more of a guttural growl. It not only startled me, but those around me, too.

"Mister! Mister!" someone cried out.

"Doctor! Doctor! Come!" another voice called.

Many hands met my chest, while others held my shoulders, guiding me back to a prone position. My eyes still refused to open as pain ramped its intensity in answer to my movements. Puffs of breath left my mouth as I tried to control the spasms within my body and the now burning pain.

Is this what death felt like? Hellfire eating you alive from the inside out?

"No, No, No." The English-speaking voice was female. My eyes opened to slits, but the image was still a blur. "I'm Dr. Jenny Weston," she said. "Can you tell me your name?"

"Dalton," my voice croaked.

"Well, Dalton, I'm going to need you to lie still."

I pinched my eyes shut, then forced them to slowly open wider, until the young blonde woman wearing a white coat came into full view. I know she had to be close to thirty if she were a doctor. Too old for me, not that I had anything to give a woman like her anyway. I breathed in a faint blend of orchids and coconuts as she rested the flat of the stethoscope against my chest.

All business, just the way I liked it.

"Lungs are clear," she said to someone over her shoulder. "I want to give you something to help you feel comfortable. From the size of your wounds, someone knew what they were doing. Were you attacked by pirates? We still see that from time to time here in the Caribbean."

Caribbean? Pirates?

"They've been known to trick people into helping them," she continued, while bending to shine a light into my eyes. "And then steal their boats, often killing the owners on board in the process."

A vision of the luxury catamaran appeared in my mind's eye.

Shit.

"The girl," my raspy voice broke the brief silence. I swallowed, failing to produce more moisture in my mouth. "Where is she?"

"You were alone when they found you." The doctor reached out a hand to someone behind her. "Can I have that cup of water, please." With a free hand, she supported my neck and brought a paper cup of water to my lips. Fresh, clean, not salty. She waited until I finished drinking before carrying on. "I did hear over International News a couple days ago that a Coast Guard ship found a young girl, eleven years old they said, floating in a life raft off the coast of Florida. Poor girl, she has no memory of what happened and is so traumatized she's not speaking. They don't even know her name at this point and are calling her Little Girl X. I guess they're still waiting for a relative to come forward." The doctor's blue eyes widened at me in surprise and her next words tumbled out. "Oh my God, is she yours? Give me her name, and I will notify the authorities immediately."

"No, not mine," I ground out through another round of pain which I hoped disguised my sudden anxiety. I couldn't let this doctor tell anyone I even existed. Not until I figured things out. I knew exactly what happened. I also knew if the girl placed me at the scene, I'd be doing jail time for murder. I wasn't about to let that happen. "How long have I been here?"

"A fishing boat found you four days ago. We did surgery to remove a bullet from your shoulder and another from your side, which is why I figured you were the victim of a pirate attack. No internal organs were damaged, but the fish did a number around the wound sites. I tried my best to stitch you clean, but unfortunately there will be raised scar tissue. You've been unconscious since the surgery, and we've kept you heavily medicated to give you time to start healing. Vitals were much stronger today, so we transferred you here to the recovery hut."

Four days on some unknown Caribbean Island with Dr. Jenny meant I had somehow survived three days on my own in the ocean. No doubt thanks to my guardian angel. I was in no condition to travel home. Based on current information from the good doctor, home wasn't the smartest idea right now for many reasons.

I closed my eyes from another rush of pain, but also to avoid the curious gaze from Dr. Jenny. A trained professional such as herself would be able to spot the truth hiding in my eyes. A truth that for now, I was the only one who knew.

There were three survivors that day, and three innocent lives taken.

I breathed through the pain and realized I needed to heal, get stronger. I'd made a deal with a dying man. No matter how long it took, I'd see it through.

"Let's give you something for that pain now. You still need to rest." She left my side and returned before I could speak. "Start counting down from twenty, please." The pretty doctor said as she slipped the needle into my arm.

"Twenty." I felt the warmth rush through my veins. "Nineteen. Wow, that's fast." I blinked a couple times as she came in and out of focus. "Eighteen." I prayed I wouldn't say anything incriminating while under. "Seven…teen…."

"See you when you wake up, Dalton. Tomorrow, we'll get you out of bed and moving," Dr. Jenny said, her beautiful blue eyes smiling down at me.

Blue like the Caribbean Ocean.

Blue, like the eyes of Samantha Taylor.

CHAPTER 2

Cavelli barbecues across the river in Jersey City were always a favorite summer event. Dalton Riley surveyed a group of kids playing in the large sandbox, while parents and friends competed in the different lawn games spaced out around the cozy backyard of their corner brownstone in Bergen Hill. Once it got dark, he knew from experience the backyard would be transformed into tiki torches and twinkling lights. Adults could continue the fun while kids would be ushered into the house for movie time and treats.

Tony and Bianca went all out, making their parties festive and family friendly since they had children of their own. One day, Dalton hoped for a family. Right now, he was content with being the Cavelli kids adopted uncle. He had a job to do, and until that was over, he couldn't risk losing anyone else.

"I like mine medium rare," Dalton said as he slid a beer in his detective partner's line of vision. The smell of Tony's secret seasoning made his mouth water.

"Hey! Glad you and your sorry ass could make it." Tony

Cavelli stepped away from the grill, his wide smile gleaming against his tanned, olive skin. He reached for a one-armed bro-hug, stopping short of making contact with Dalton's shoulder. "How's the recovery? Tell me you're coming back sooner rather than later."

"PT is hell. Probably another month or two before I'm cleared for active duty. Your new partner not working out?" Dalton nodded toward a thin man in a Yankees ball cap, chatting with some women by the nacho bar.

"Richie Jameson? He's a rookie, D. The kid means well, but he's over the top helpful. I didn't even want to invite him, but Bianca insisted."

"I've heard good things about RJ. Transfer from Trenton. He'll settle in."

"Well, he can do that with someone else. Hurry up and get back to the team." They raised their amber bottles.

"Wait." Dalton pulled back and broke into a toothy smile. "Should I call RJ over?"

"Just for that, your steak will be burned like your bad sense of humor." Tony tapped the neck of his bottle against Dalton's.

Dalton angled his chin upward in challenge. "Think long and hard about that, brother, if you still want me to watch your kids in a few months while you and the Mrs. go frolic in the sands of Hawaii." A small arm wrapped around his waist from behind and he startled, turning to gaze into the dark brown eyes of Tony's wife, Bianca.

If Barbie ever had doll competition, her name would have been Bianca. The woman should have been a model. Black hair down to her tiny waist and athletically fit all over. Tony met her at the gym, and after a standoff at the leg machine, she was the one who asked him out.

"I still don't know what you see in him." Dalton bent down to place a kiss on her naturally tan cheek.

"Whatever he said to you, I apologize," she said. "And baby, cook the man's steak the way he wants it, please."

"Yes ma'am." Tony returned his focus to the grill with a shake of his head and a deep chuckle.

"Where's Nicki?" Bianca asked, taking a sip of her margarita, and scanning the backyard where a dozen other friends had gathered.

"Dalton…." Tony warned as he flipped a sizzling sirloin.

"How should I know?" Dalton shrugged and took another sip of beer to avoid Bianca's brown-eyed scrutiny.

"C'mon, both of you *always* know where the other is at. The three of you have been thick as thieves since the academy. I know Tony invited her."

"And I told you she declined." Tony raised his BBQ fork as he lowered the lid to the grill. "She said she already had plans."

"Doing what? Her main attraction is right here." Bianca all but beamed at Dalton as she swept her free hand from his head to his feet.

"Her job, maybe?" Tony countered before placing the bottle of beer against his heavily mustached lip and taking a sip. "She's with a different unit, remember?"

"CSI, yes, I know. I haven't connected with her in a few weeks. I thought maybe she'd been reconnecting with tall, dark, and handsome here."

"That was a long time ago." Dalton drained his beer, his eyes pleading with Tony for assistance. What he received was a cop-out when Tony raised his palm and returned to the grill.

"I'm staying out of it."

"Chicken," Dalton said, shooting him a *c'mon* expression.

"Don't give me that line, Dalton Riley." Bianca looked up and pointed a finger at him that didn't quite reach his chin.

"She's one of my best friends. I know you two still have something going on."

"Wait, she told you?" He placed the empty bottle on a nearby picnic table, trading it for a fist full of peanuts.

How could she? We made a pact when things got weird.

"Sucker...." Tony said from behind his basting brush.

"Thank you for confirming." Bianca saluted with a Cheshire cat grin and her glittering nails wrapped around the stem of her glass.

Dalton silently cursed. "Bianca, we're still friends. We get together...occasionally, that's all."

"Of course, you do." She pressed her lips to the glass and took a sip of the frozen concoction.

"It's not what you're thinking," he tried to explain, but the knowing smile she displayed after lowering her glass told him her mind was made up. He tracked her motions as she scanned the yard, not sure what exactly she was looking for. Nicki had informed him a couple days ago she wouldn't be coming.

"Come with me," she said and grabbed his hand. "There's someone I want you to meet."

"I tried to warn you," Tony called, and Dalton wondered if he'd walked into an ambush.

Bianca never changed course and yelled in a voice Tony called her *mom* voice, "Anthony Geraldo Cavelli I'm going to need you to—"

Dalton managed to stop her long enough to ask, "Geraldo?" His brows raised and he glanced back at Tony.

"Shut it, Riley. You tell anyone, and RJ gets a permanent spot in the shotgun seat."

"Come on!" Bianca tugged while shaking her head and continued her mission across the yard. "Oh, I wanted to thank you for the recruitment referral." She slowed her pace and released his hand, turning all business. "Samantha has done a fantastic job in acquisitions. As a matter of fact, our company is up for an award due to her efforts over the last six months. I'm going to bring her to the Top Performers Gala and have her accept alongside me."

"Wow, that's great."

The words barely registered. Of course, Samantha would be here. He'd known the moment Bianca said her name — known before he saw her, before the yard blurred and the past rushed in.

He'd never intended to interact with her. It would be too risky. A million thoughts raced through his mind. He'd worked too hard to keep her life moving forward without him in it. He hadn't realized he'd blocked out Bianca until she had to repeat herself.

"I said…You never told me how you know her."

Here it was. The lie.

"I don't, really." He shrugged. "She worked at a bank I used to go to. I always thought she seemed bored, like she wasn't being challenged. When Tony said you were looking to hire, I thought she might be a good fit. I asked my account manager if he thought she'd be interested, and if so, would he mind facilitating the opportunity. I'm glad she's working out for you."

It wasn't the truth, but it was close enough to pass.

The real reason had nothing to do with her resume. Truth was, he'd wanted her close. Close meant visible. Protected. He knew Bianca would recognize good talent. And if Samantha was on her team, he'd be able to ask questions, quietly fill in gaps, make sure the world wasn't circling back toward her without ever letting her know he was watching.

"Working out? Oh, she goes above and beyond with everything. This young lady is on the fast track to moving up.

I can't wait to be the one to promote her. We should pay you a finder's fee. Great idea to work in the condo rental as part of her hiring package. I really think that sealed the deal. She was very excited to finally have her own place — leave Long Island and Oyster Bay behind and start her life on her own terms."

"That's good," he replied, gazing curiously at the umbrella table they were approaching. He recognized a couple people from previous Cavelli events, and —."

"Here is my superstar," Bianca boasted as she placed a hand on the blonde's shoulder. "This, is Samantha Taylor, one of our youngest senior acquisitions analysts." The young woman stood and gave her boss a hug. "Sam, this is Dalton."

"Nice to meet you." Sam extended her hand, and he shook it out of reflex, staring into a pair of blue eyes that haunted him for the last fourteen years.

"You, too." He slipped his hand away, grateful for the phone vibrating in the pocket of his jeans. Pulling the phone free, he checked the ID then looked from Bianca to Samantha and said, "Sorry, I need to take this."

Bianca turned her attention to the table with Samantha as Dalton stepped away to answer the call. "Perfect timing."

"Uh-Oh, what's Tony got you doing now?" Nicki Morgan's voice asked with a hint of humor, well versed in how he and his partner operated.

"Not Tony, Bianca." Dalton stole a glance over his shoulder, catching the woman in question studying him. He waved and she returned to holding court with her team. "She's up to something."

"She's always up to something." Nicki laughed. "Remember the time she made us both go on that dating app just to show us we were compatible?"

"Yeah, how wrong was that app?"

"Hey!"

"Sorry, Nicole." Dalton rubbed his weary eyes. Now was not the time to discuss their relationship. "What's going on?"

"Working late where the fun never stops. I've got some information on the Patrone family. There's a big meeting taking place within a week. Lots of product coming in from Florida and something about a merger."

"Florida? Who's down there that the family would want to deal with?"

"I'm working on it, love."

"Keep at it. I'm going to put a call in to CeCe, make sure Louie's aware of what's happening." Dalton could almost hear the gears in her brain working at the same angles as his.

"You think it's his brother or nephew trying to make a move?" *Bingo*. It was eerie, sometimes, how they seemed to share a brain.

"Not sure. CeCe will tell me straight up." He dared to turn in time to see Samantha laugh at something, her smile reminding him of a time when—

"Have you let Tony in on this?" Nicki's voice broke through his foggy brain. "Does he even know CeCe Patrone is your informant?"

"No, and before you lecture me, the less he knows right now, the better. I'll get him involved if there's a need."

"If you say so." Her tone was indifferent, and Dalton was about to end the call when she spoke again. "Why don't you stop over after the party, you know, for a nightcap?"

He grinned, never able to refuse his auburn-haired Irish firecracker. "I'll let you know when I'm on my way."

———

AFTER FINISHING A ROUND OF LADDER GOLF, SAMANTHA POURED another frozen margarita and decided to make a move. She'd been curious about Dalton since shaking his hand and gazing into the deepest green eyes she'd ever seen. After their brief hello, he hadn't been near enough to talk since stepping away to take a call. She'd watched him interact with Tony, Bianca, and a couple others, even catching him looking in her direction. Every time she'd get the nerve to approach and have a conversation, several co-workers wanted her attention or wanted to play one of the many games sprinkled strategically around the yard. With the evening wrapping up, this was the perfect opportunity. He stood by himself next to the outdoor bar while Tony and Bianca said good-bye to some guests.

"Well, hello there," Samantha said as she approached, setting her glass on the bar top and hooking her thumbs into the beltloops of her white denim shorts. He seemed surprised at first, and it took an uncomfortable moment before he visibly relaxed.

"Hi," he responded and pointed at her half-empty glass. "You know, you need to finish that. Tony doesn't like good alcohol wasted."

"No problems there." The warm summer night had melted her frozen drink enough to make draining the glass a breeze. She tipped it up and watched his eyes grow large when she finished. She had a hard time holding back her laugh long enough to swallow without choking.

"Well done." He clapped and she bowed at the waist. She'd been so nervous, and he seemed so relaxed now. To think she missed out most of the evening without getting to know him better.

Not that I'm looking for a relationship right now, but damn I'd be willing to give you a shot, she thought, then blinked several times realizing that was the tequila talking. Before she could stop, she found herself tequila-talking out loud.

"I saw you looking." The words rushed out and she saw the confusion register on his handsome face.

"Excuse me?" He leaned back, frowning as he brushed a

hand through his thick, brown hair. She could see the outline of muscle underneath his thin t-shirt. Sam had to bite into her lower lip to keep herself in check. The twinkling lights around the bar reflected in his eyes and she was mesmerized.

"Tonight. I caught you looking." She forced herself to look away as she played with her empty glass during the awkward pause. Feeling the confidence from a night of margaritas, she made eye contact once more and continued, "It's okay. I felt bad we didn't have a chance to talk. I hope everything is all right."

His eyes narrowed as if he didn't remember.

"Your phone call. I hope everything is okay."

"Yeah, the call." He shook his head as if to clear it and his hair fell forward again before he swiped it back again. "It's fine. Work." He still kept a watchful eye on her, and a warm feeling pooled in the pit of her stomach. He was extremely sexy and likely way out of her league, but she was ready to make an absolute fool out of herself over this complete stranger. There was something about him that made her want to know more.

"Do you work with Tony in the department?"

"I'm his partner. Out of commission for a little while longer. Rotator cuff surgery." Dalton gingerly made a circle with his shoulder, his muscles playing off the snug t-shirt material. "Took a bullet during a raid."

"Oh my!"

"Hazard of the job. And I saw you looking, too." He cleared his throat, looking like he wanted to say something more.

Her cheeks must have been eighty shades of red judging by the inferno creeping up her face. She would have given anything for another ice-cold margarita, or a cliff to jump off.

"Don't be embarrassed." Dalton's voice reassured.

"I didn't think I was that noticeable." She couldn't even

make eye contact now, second guessing her desire to make the first move. Samantha never did this kind of thing, and it must be obvious to someone like Dalton.

"I'm a professional and you still caught me." He held up his hands and they both laughed. His eyes were constantly taking in his surroundings, and he pointed toward the gate where a group of people were saying goodbye. "Hey, do you have to go? I think your boyfriend is leaving."

She looked up and waved, and a young man waved and smiled back. "Oh, wow, you're observant, but he's not my boyfriend. That's just Matt from the fourth-floor audit offices."

"Not your boyfriend?" Dalton let loose a low whistle. "Does *he* know that?"

"Matt and I are just friends. He did ask me out once, but I told him no. I just don't see him in that way. He's like that best guy friend from work every woman needs to have." She enjoyed hanging out with Matt, but that was all. Now a guy like Dalton…

"Nice to see the two of you getting acquainted." Bianca appeared next to Samantha.

"I know," Sam stated, thankful for the interruption. She didn't like discussing her personal life. For some reason Dalton made it too easy to reveal her emotions. "And now." She cocked her head and shot Dalton a sad face. "The night is over." He arched a brow and they both burst out laughing.

"Not so fast." Bianca interrupted, making them straighten up. "You missed catching a ride with the rest of the crew, and I don't want you going home alone at this hour."

"It's fine, Bianca, I can call an Uber."

"You're not getting in an Uber alone. Dalton, make sure Samantha gets home safely."

"That's not—" Samantha started before Dalton cut her off.

"I can't I have—"

"Neither one of you are going to win." Tony draped an arm around each of their shoulders. "Trust me on this one."

"And you should know better." Bianca pointed at Dalton.

"Yes ma'am." He glanced down at this watch. "C'mon princess, let's get you home before midnight." He shook Tony's hand and gave Bianca a kiss.

Sam hugged them both and hurried to catch up to Dalton. "I'm not a princess."

"And I'm sure as hell no prince," he muttered half beneath his breath, but she heard him.

The mood between them had definitely shifted to almost a big-brother vibe. Samantha didn't like being a burden to anyone, and she didn't know what Dalton thought. He was so hard to read, but the Cavellis had been so insistent. She'd planned on taking the Uber with everyone else and could have very easily taken one alone. She'd never intended for Dalton to have to watch out for her. She could do that on her own, too.

"Listen, I know you weren't planning on this so you're free to go. I can take the Uber myself."

"I appreciate you relieving me of my duties, but that's not going to happen. The Cavellis are right. If you were with another woman even, it would be better than being alone this time of night."

"I do it all the time," she lied. To be honest, she'd only ridden home alone in an Uber once, and on the subway train twice. All three times she had been nervous, but after that she'd made sure she went out closer to home so she could walk and not worry about the train. Not that she had much of a social life, but there was a part of her that wanted Dalton to find her independent and interesting.

"Not this time." He pointed toward the corner. "That's our car."

They slid into the back seat of the Uber and returned to

New York in silence. Close to home, Sam caught Dalton glancing down at his watch for the second time since leaving the Cavellis. She wondered if he had somewhere else to go, which would explain the change in his mood upon being told to bring her home. The margarita still swirling in her head begged her to change his mind. The car stopped at the light by Washington Market Park and Sam suddenly needed air.

"Can I get out here? It's literally a few blocks." She placed her hand on the door handle. "I feel like walking."

"Sure. Hold up, buddy, we're getting out here." Dalton stepped out of the car first, then reached in to help her out. "Let's go." He placed his hand at the center of her back, guiding her down the sidewalk. "I take it you had a good time tonight. You must have had around what…five or six margaritas?"

"You were counting?" Samantha stopped short under a streetlight with a sassy, hands-on-hips stance. "Who counts a stranger's drinks?" She bent forward and eyed him with a squinty glance. "Should I be worried you didn't take *the out* when I offered it?"

"Not at all." He pulled his phone from his pocket and stopped as if he were going to send a message.

"Really? Because I'm feeling things are about to get interesting." She started walking fast, and it was his turn to catch up.

"Wait up. You could trip and get hurt." Genuine concern laced his words. "Interesting, how?" he asked with a suspicious look.

She appreciated that he still had the phone in his hands, making her next move a lot easier.

"Like this." She stepped in front of him and for a moment became lost in a sea of green eyes. When she felt herself sway forward, she recovered and swiped the phone from his hands, jogging out of reach.

"Hey!" He caught up fast, and she dodged his every move to get the phone. Thank God it was late, and the usual pedestrian foot traffic was non-existent.

"There. All done." She grinned triumphantly and set the sleek black object into his awaiting palm.

"What did you do?"

"I texted myself from your phone."

"To get my number?" He shoved the phone back into his pocket, no amusement at all on his face. "Why didn't you just ask?"

She shrugged as they continued walking. "We just met. I wasn't sure you'd give it to me."

"You should have asked." His tone continued to be stern, and she wondered if she'd somehow read him wrong.

"Admit it, this was more fun." She winked, hoping amused Dalton would return instead of this serious one. "Look, here we are!" Samantha quarter turned with her arm raised toward her building when her heel slipped out of her wedge sandal. In an instant, she was balancing in Dalton's arms instead of hitting the pavement. "Whoa, thank you," she said, a bit breathless as he stood her straight.

"Of course." He released her, but she kept her palms on his chest feeling the beat of his heart beneath the soft navy-blue cotton.

"Would you like to come upstairs?" She knew how forward that sounded and was totally out of character for her, but touching him seemed warm, *familiar*, and she found herself wanting more time with him.

She never should have had that last margarita.

"How about a raincheck." He gently removed her hands and before he could let go, she used them as leverage to balance on tiptoe and kiss his cheek.

"Thank you," she said before turning and rushing up concrete steps lined with pots of colorful flowers as the doorman opened the large, glass door. She didn't need Dalton to see her die of embarrassment a second time. There was no misreading his signals this time.

He'd definitely just put her in the friend zone.

Sam wasn't sure how she felt about that.

CHAPTER 3

ouie Patrone sat in an overstuffed leather armchair, puffing on an equally stuffed Cuban, with his favorite Italian opera playing softly in the background. His lovely wife of thirty-four years would never let him smoke in the house. Building an extension onto their garage where he could play cards, watch a game, and smoke to his heart's content was the best decision. Even better, when he was underfoot, she would banish him to the 'game room'. He made sure he was in her way more times than not. But all she had to do was smile, and he was like a little puppy all over again, chasing her around the house.

Cecelia was his reason for living.

Today, she was entertaining some ladies from church. He gladly banished himself. His brother, Rocco, sat in the other chair nursing a scotch and sending what he'd been told was an urgent text message. His younger brother had called saying he had something very important to talk about.

"Are you done?" Louie asked, blowing smoke toward the open window. "You say you want to talk, but you seem to be more interested in your phone."

"Sorry." Rocco slipped his phone into the pocket of his cargo shorts.

The man was a Patrone, yet he dressed like a slob. Louie didn't expect the younger generation to dress in suits, but he did expect them to respect the family name and dress accordingly. Sometimes, he had his doubts about his brother.

"Are you going to tell me what the surprise visit is about? You saved me from listening to all the woes of the church, but you never said what was so important." He puffed the cigar again, drawing in the flavors of spice and leather. In dealing directly with Mexico, he'd built trustworthy connections for his favorite cigars. He returned the favor by sending fine wines from Italy and his wife's homemade sweets.

"I've got a friend who's giving me a shot at running my own crew."

"What?" Louie sat up and placed his cigar in the ashtray. "What friend? We are your family. You have a place here at the table."

"You don't let me lead, Lou. I want my own crew. I can handle it, and you don't give me a chance."

"I gave you a chance, Rocco. How can you forget what happened?" He waited for the recognition in Rocco's eyes and then nodded his agreement. "We lost product. I had to be accountable to our distributors and their customers."

"You've never let me forget it." Rocco downed the remainder of his drink and rose to pour another. "If family means so much to you, brother, let me lead."

"May I remind you, *brother*, you let those responsible off the hook, with a tip that I would be coming for them." Louie walked to the bar cart and poured a glass of Chianti. "How could I not let you forget that." His voice held a venom he saved for his enemies. While Rocco was his brother by blood, he did not completely trust him. "I gave you responsibility to me, to our family business, and you strayed Rocco."

"It was an error in judgement. I thought they would make good on the debt. I believed them when they told me as much."

"But you never tried to fix it. You just let them go." Louie elevated his glass as if it were floating away.

"What was I supposed to do?" Rocco slammed his glass down on the table.

"Be loyal to this family. Take care of business." Louie took a sip, watching his brother for any signs of betrayal.

"This new opportunity will bring business in, more than we've ever imagined."

"There will be no opportunity, Rocco. I forbid it."

"You can't do that! You don't even know what it is!"

"Tend to your duties in this family. Prove to me you are worthy of more and dedicated to the livelihood of everyone in this family, not just yourself. You do that," Louie said while raising his glass, "and I will promise you a bigger role."

"I am loyal to you. Why don't you believe me?"

"The proof is in your actions. My Cecelia has tried to tell me I'm being too good to you. But you are my blood, and I love you, my brother. I want nothing more than to share everything with you and Enso. You must be ready, and I fear you both have so much to learn."

"I am ready, Lou. I am." Rocco seemed eager, as if he thought Louie would give in. For once, his gut was in line with CeCe's. This, he would not ignore.

"Show me. You get nothing until I see and feel your loyalty to this family."

"Lou, you—"

"Leave, Rocco, before I change my mind and our conversation takes a turn you're not ready for." Louie stared hard into his brothers' eyes. He was done giving handouts to family who didn't understand the meaning of the word.

"You don't mean that, Lou. Don't listen to CeCe. She's trying to turn you against your blood."

It was blood that boiled in Louie's veins at the mention of his beloved wife. He stalked Rocco across the room like a lion hunting a gazelle. He was the boss of this family for a reason, and he would be respected, especially by blood. In a flash he had Rocco's throat in his grasp and pinned him against the wall. Rocco's glass shattered as it hit the floor.

"You will never speak lies about my wife. Do you understand," his voice finally releasing the venom he needed to put the fear into Rocco.

Rocco violently nodded as he rasped, "Yes, Lou, yes."

"Do not speak with me again of your crazy plans. If you break my trust once more, you leave this family in a box." He released Rocco, catching him before his weak knees buckled. "Get out." He gave him a shove and watched his brother stumble through the door without another word.

———

DALTON ROLLED OVER AND BRUSHED A SOFT RED CURL OFF Nicki's cheek, making way for his lips to trail kisses across her smooth skin. She stirred as his lips moved to her tan shoulder and the pale skin saved from the sun by the bright yellow bikini she'd worn two weeks ago, for an annual girls' weekend at the Cape. He'd burned that photo to memory the moment she'd sent it.

Sliding an arm across her waist, his hand moved to cup one of her full breasts. A soft moan sounded from her sweet mouth, and she wiggled her butt closer against him. He kissed down her back then skipped to her ribs.

"Dalton...what time is it?" she asked, her voice filled with sleep.

He smiled when she flopped another pillow over her

head, fighting him when he tried to remove it. He'd arrived at her studio loft on the east side later than expected last night, but she'd been awake and ready for him. It had been weeks since they'd seen each other. Last night's sex had been so hot, he was ready to go a few more rounds.

"Shhh…it doesn't matter."

He moved over her, placing kisses up her stomach to her breasts. By the time he was done teasing each one, the pillow hit the floor and she cradled his whiskered face in her hands and kissed him. He felt her need as strong as his own in that kiss. As soon as he settled over her, her long legs wrapped around him. She arched her back, pulling up against him.

Dalton kissed her hard and she responded in kind before he sat back on his knees to spread her thighs and gaze at her gorgeous body. He couldn't wait to get inside of her. Those marigold-colored eyes stared at him with such passion he had everything he could do to retain control. Sex with Nicki was a pleasure to be taken slow, enjoying every inch of her, bringing her to the peak of ecstasy. And he planned to do it all again.

"Touch me," she breathed, and he enjoyed all too much the rise and fall of her chest as he brushed his fingers along the inside of her thigh until he reached her wet center. He watched her expression change, and her eyes grow heavy with desire as his fingers stroked deeper and deeper. He'd been rock hard just looking at her, but once he touched her, the throbbing ache between his legs demanded release.

"I'm going to do more than touch you."

Nicki sucked in a breath when his tongue replaced his fingers. He smiled before continuing his onslaught. She rocked against his face until he held her hips in his hands, encouraged by the writhing and panting going on above him. Her legs hooked across his back, and he drank from her like it was his last. Her heels thumped against his skin as she pressed harder. He pulled away and she cried out only to moan when he rubbed his swollen cock against her.

"Not yet, baby," he said in a husky drawl as he took his time sliding inside her until she had every inch of him buried deep. He moved slowly, feeling her body cradle his. "Does this feel good?"

"Yes."

"And this?" He bucked hard against her, drawing her out of the soft sensuousness and preparing her for the animal he was about to unleash. He began to rub her with his thumb as his cock dove in and out, creating a rush of wetness. His thumb rolled across her swollen bud and hovered there creating small, light circles until she screamed, and he pounded against her. Their skin glistened with sweat, neither ready for it to end. The highs became higher and for a moment he thought he would black out from the sheer rush of passion burning like a fuse between them. He worried he might be hurting her as hard as their bodies were crashing together, but she never asked him to stop.

"Dalton...." Her voice rose in pitch as she hit a frenzied high. He had no breath to answer her. Every ounce of him was vested in this pleasure, in their taking and giving of each other. He was so sensitive to her heat he could burst. She tilted her hips and the renewed sensation drove him over the edge. His hands immediately anchored her to him as he thrust repeatedly, recognizing her cries of desire until he roared with complete satisfaction and pulsed fully inside her.

As he lay spent on the tussled sheets beside her, he asked, "Are you okay? Did I hurt you?"

"I'm more than okay." She smiled and trailed her glossy pink nails across his chest. "I could get used to this."

"Oh yeah?" He turned his head, returning her smile.

"Yeah…." She inched up and kissed him softly on the lips before settling skin-to-skin and pulling the sheet over their bodies. "I could."

Dalton stayed silent, enjoying her afterglow. They were a great team, in and out of the bedroom, but things were complicated. He had unfinished business she knew nothing about, and he wanted to keep it that way for her own safety.

"Dalton—"

"Shhh…We're fine."

"Are you sure?"

"You don't ever have to question that." He stroked her hair. To prove his point, he pulled her on top of him and kissed her with all the emotion he felt but couldn't express or promise. She kissed him back, and he prayed that was her way of saying she understood. He broke the contact at the jarring vibration of his phone against the bedside table.

"Don't," Nicki said, and tried to stop his arm. "Not now."

"It could be work." He stretched until his fingers had control of the device, holding Nicki against him with his other arm. "What the hell?" His eyes bulged at the screen.

"Who is it? Is it CeCe?" Nicki propped herself up to look at his screen.

"No, it's her."

"You mean the girl you chaperoned home?" Nicki's features registered the same confusion as his.

"Yeah. Why on earth would she be calling me?"

"Why don't you answer and find out, love." She slid off him and bent to pick his t-shirt off the floor. She pulled it over her head and walked away saying, "Don't keep her waiting. I'm making breakfast, and I expect details."

Dalton sat with his legs hanging off the side of the bed. "Hey, what's up?"

"I'm sorry to bother you, but I felt awful about last night. Sorry for anything I said or did. The night's a little fuzzy."

Samantha laughed, but he could hear her embarrassment. Her voice sounded so young through the phone. If he hadn't seen her with his own eyes, he'd think she was still that little girl.

"I'm not sure what you're talking about. Everything was fine last night, no worries." He glanced over at Nicki slapping some bacon into a large pan at the stove.

"No, you shouldn't have had to bring me home like my personal babysitter. I should have stood up to Tony and Bianca. I'm a grown woman, though I certainly didn't act like it last night."

"I've known them a lot longer than you. They would have made you sleep over if I hadn't been there. Which, by the way, is actually a fun time with the kids, and Bianca makes some mean empanadas." He tried to lighten the mood.

"Regardless, I wanted to call so you didn't think I was part of any Cavelli conspiracy."

"Wasn't thinking that at all." He smiled, casting an appreciative glance toward Nicki, remembering all too well being victim of a Bianca conspiracy. "No worries, okay. Enjoy your weekend."

"Wait!" He caught the nervous quiver in her voice. "Let me at least treat you to dinner as a thank you for putting up with me and my mucho margaritas. I do love a good one or two."

"It was more like six." Dalton chuckled. "But I wasn't counting."

"Is that a yes?"

"Samantha, that's not necessary."

"I want to. And if you think Tony and Bianca are a tough crowd, you haven't tangled with me. I can be stubborn."

"I'm starting to sense that. So, I guess it's a yes," he conceded, and shrugged when Nicki sent a curious glance in his direction before cracking some eggs.

"Great! I can't wait. Uhm…should I pick you up? I can take an Uber to you."

"Since you took my number, text me the address of the restaurant, and I will meet you."

"Right, sorry about that too." She paused briefly. "I'll text you later. Six o'clock work?"

"See you then." He ended the call, tossed his phone aside and fell back onto the bed. Maybe there was a way he could get out of it. Spending more time with her was a risk he wasn't sure he was ready to take just yet. What if she remembered….

"Trouble in paradise?" Nicki stood at the side of the bed, moments later, balancing a bamboo tray with a plate of bacon and eggs and two cups of steaming coffee.

"Very funny," he said while sitting up. "You have no idea." She joined him on the bed with the tray between them.

"You played right into Bianca's hand. Did you really think you could make sure the girl got home and never hear from her again?" Nicki shoved a piece of bacon into his gaping mouth. "Never mind. That face says it all."

"Listen," he said with his mouth full and reached for the coffee to wash it down. "I never really thought about it. I just wanted to make sure Bianca was getting a quality candidate."

"Oh, I have no doubt that's true. But you know our friend Bianca. She loves to play matchmaker."

"I didn't think it would matter. Aside from an occasional house party, I don't see or talk to Bianca that much. The girl is way younger than me. Trust me, she's more like a kid sister."

"What did lil' sis want?" Nicki blew across her cup in an overly exaggerated fashion, the brown flecks in her marigold eyes swirling with curiosity.

"*Samantha*, asked me to dinner tonight." He was quick to raise a hand. "As a thank you for what she called babysitting her last night."

"And you said...?" Nicki waited expectantly, fork in hand, so he chose his words wisely.

"I told her it wasn't necessary but, in the end, I lost the argument."

"Since when are you such a pussy?" Nicki stabbed a fork full of eggs. "Do I need to be jealous?"

"No, are you?" He quirked a brow, taking the fork from her hand to scoop up some eggs of his own.

"Hell no." She re-crossed her legs and tucked a thick wave of hair behind her ear. "I've more important things to do."

Dalton watched the playfulness in her eyes shift to something darker. He knew she'd never admit she was jealous, but the change in her expression was enough to remind him their connection wasn't exactly rock-solid. He stabbed another serving of eggs and fed them to her, their eyes renewing a mutual unsaid understanding.

"You mentioned the Patrone family last night. Do you have more news?"

"I do." She took another sip of coffee, cradling the mug in her hands. "Rocco Patrone has been making new friends with connections in Florida. It's rumored he's waiting to receive some extra special cocaine. And by that, I mean fentanyl."

"How did Rocco make a connection in Florida? Louie has always held him back because he made too many mistakes. He'd never let him travel that far." Dalton offered up the last piece of bacon. When she declined, he took a large bite.

"I'm still digging into the connection. From what I've found on Rocco, he's never even been to Florida, so it must be someone who frequents New York."

"Interesting." Dalton paused, feeling the connective energy with Nicki. "Rocco's trying to make a play?"

"Seems that way." She smiled in recognition. "Baby brother Enso sticks tight to Louie so he's no threat, unless Rocco flips him."

"Nah, Louie has always watched out for Enso, that would never happen. But I can see Rocco trying though. He's never been one to think things through." Dalton drained his cup. "Is he stupid enough to try to take out his own family? Or is this just a side gig? Louie has always run a clean ship. He'd never condone fentanyl-laced product."

"Unless he doesn't know. Did you ever call CeCe? I think Louie needs a heads-up."

"I ended up taking Samantha home and came straight here. I'll text CeCe right now."

"I don't think that's a good idea."

Dalton froze with his hand over his phone. "Why not? She can clue Louie in without implicating any of us." As he turned his head, Nicki was stripping out of his t-shirt. He perused every inch of her, his cock stirring to life.

"Because love." In one shove, the tray and remaining contents hit the floor. She crawled over to him, easing him onto his back and tossing the phone over her shoulder. "I do believe it's my turn."

She traced her finger around his mouth, then planted the softest of kisses on his lips. Her tongue teased and entered his mouth to dance with his. His hands found her waist, becoming lost in her kiss as a fire ignited within. He stroked her legs, growing harder with each thrust of her tongue in his mouth. She ground herself on top of him, rubbing against him and teasing his cock with her heat.

"Nicole...." He reached under her to position himself for entry.

"Ah-ah-ah..." She moved his hand, sliding herself down his body until it was her mouth wrapped around him, her tongue teasing his tip, licking his length before sucking so hard he groaned with each sensual tug. When she released him, he looked up as she licked her lips and held his stare.

In one smooth and sensual swirl of her hips, she was

seated with him fully inside her, riding him into a full-blown climax. Dalton couldn't even think straight as sheer lust took over. He sat up, holding her inside of him before gripping her hips and guiding himself harder into her. She whimpered, and he growled as she pushed him backwards. Regaining control, she used her hips once more to swirl around his shaft before sending him deep inside over and over again until the frenzy of their building crescendo caused her to lean forward to leverage the giant headboard. He thrust hard one final time sending them both to heaven.

"Did you like that?" she panted after she collapsed on his chest. He could feel her body shaking.

"Yeah." He cradled her tight, breathless, and spent.

"Good." She raised her head, flashing him a wicked smile which made him shiver in a good way. "We've got the rest of the day. When I'm through with you, all you're going to think about at dinner tonight is getting back here to me."

CHAPTER 4

Dalton waited outside the seafood restaurant at South Street Pier. He'd texted CeCe on the way, but she hadn't responded. Maybe she would have some insight on the fentanyl. He knew that wasn't Louie's style. The possibility of Rocco being involved made sense, and that didn't sit well with him.

Back before Dalton straightened up his life, he had seen Rocco as a wild card. He always had a better way of doing things, and it didn't matter what anyone else had to say. Most of the time, his ideas failed, and Louie would come down hard on him in front of everyone. But using Rocco as an example only made him more of a schemer.

After all these years, could Rocco really have found someone to align with him against Louie?

"Hi!" Samantha's voice startled him from behind. "I wasn't sure you would be here."

He turned to see her wearing a pair of cut-off shorts and a simple white blouse, her hair pulled back in a single braid down her back.

"I told you I'd meet you." Saying those words made him

feel a little awkward, like he was on a date with his sister or something. He tossed the feelings aside, pushing the truth that he was there as a favor to her to the surface. Everything would be fine as long as she didn't recognize him.

"I know, but you didn't sound like you really wanted to." She shrugged. "I'm glad you came."

"Me too." He smiled to ease whatever trepidation she was having. He still didn't feel a thank you dinner was necessary when he would have done it for anyone if Bianca had asked. It was a little tricky being around Sam, but it was interesting seeing a little of who she had become now that she had grown up. "I haven't been down in the Seaport area in years." *A whole lifetime ago*, he thought.

"What did you used to do here?"

He looked anywhere but at her face. "Trust me, you don't want to know."

"Try me," she stated with a little quirk of her mouth as she made it a point to be in his face. Her attempt at being bold reminded him how innocent and inexperienced she was. He didn't want to be the one to darken her view of the world.

"Let's just say there were hazards to the job. Hazards that made me become a cop."

"Oh." Her eyes widened at his implication. She'd never figure it out. All she had to understand was it had to have been a crime. "It's good then, you got into a career you like."

"A career I needed, and one I like on most days." He shrugged, brushing off the feeling of setting himself up for more questions. "Some days it's a struggle."

"I hear you there." She sighed. "Don't get me wrong, this job with Bianca's firm is amazing. I love dealing in acquisitions. I'm busy every day, which is great, but I haven't quite found the balance with my personal life."

"You mean that guy Matt."

"No." She held her hands up to stop him from saying

more. "Matt and I are just friends. You seem to think there's more, but there isn't. I'm just socially awkward *and* a workaholic, not necessarily a good combination if you're trying to meet someone."

"What are you all of twenty-four?"

"I'm twenty-five."

"Come talk to me when you're thirty-four. I'm sure by then you'll have it all figured out."

"Like you?"

Her inference was harmless enough, but it struck a chord deep inside Dalton. "No." He shook his head and chuckled. "Far better than me." Life-changing events happened all the time to people. Dalton felt the familiar pressure in his chest and pushed the thought away before it could settle. "This is a busy place. Hope you made a reservation."

"Of course, I did." She smiled when he opened the door.

The large wooden bar was packed a row deep. Mirrored shelves stocked with every liquor imaginable ran the length of the wall. Fishing nets hung like garland from thick beams while buoys and stuffed fish were anchored to the walls. He kept his hand at her elbow as they made their way to the hostess station. Within moments they were seated on the back deck with an amazing view of the Brooklyn bridge. A server stopped and took their drink orders before disappearing back into the restaurant.

"This is one of my favorite views." Sam pointed toward the bridge. "No matter where you look, its breathtaking skyline."

"One of your favorites? What are the others?"

"Top of the Empire State Building for sure. I know, it's so touristy, but on a clear day a person can get lost in their thoughts. I go there when I need to work through things." She paused as if she had something else to say, and Dalton waited patiently, but she blinked a couple times and didn't elaborate. "The one I don't see often enough is the view from the water of Lady Liberty." Samantha placed a hand over her heart for emphasis. "She gets me every time I think of her."

"She is a beauty," Dalton said as the server set down their drinks. "I'm surprised, no margarita?"

"No. Those tend to get me in trouble." She laughed. "I'm still a tequila girl, just taking it with soda and lime tonight." She raised her glass in salute.

"Don't worry, I won't be counting." He winked.

"Last night was a party, and I got lost in all the fun. Tonight is…different."

"Again, this wasn't necessary." He recognized that distant look in her eyes and felt the immediate need to ground her back to reality. "But thank you." It was his turn to raise his pint of his favorite summer IPA. To be honest, he felt a gentle tug toward her for totally different reasons, and he wasn't about to lead her on for a free meal.

"No, thank you for indulging me. It's not a bad thing that I enjoyed your company."

"It's not." He agreed and took a long draught from his glass. He watched her carefully as she met his gaze, searching for any sign of recognition or trouble in her blue eyes. Whether she understood what he'd been saying, or not, she finished her drink and motioned to the server for another round.

Conversation with Samantha continued over their surf and turf dinner and two more rounds of drinks over the course of the evening. He noticed the way men looked her over as they passed by, then back toward him as if he were some lucky bastard. She never stopped talking, oblivious to their hungry eyes. The trained detective in him went on high alert even though nothing looked wrong.

Only there was, and she had no idea.

"Are you all right?" Her hand resting gently on his wrist brought him out of his daze.

"What?"

"Where'd you go just now? I was talking about Tony's pool table, and you were literally in a zone of your own."

"Sorry." Dalton pulled his wrist free and scanned the outdoor area, suddenly feeling as though they were indeed being watched. "Ready? I could use a little walk after all this food." He stood and reached for the bill on the table. Sam quickly pulled it from his fingers.

"My treat, remember?"

"Force of habit."

"Are you sure you feel okay? You seem a little anxious."

"I'm fine. Thinking about my list of calls for tomorrow. Some of them won't be nice."

"Wow, I was boring you that much, huh?"

"No, not at all." He followed her out to the street, relief setting in the farther they walked from the super crowded restaurant. "Work tends to run my life every once in a while." Dalton breathed deep, clearing the ever-present shadows from the past.

"It's still kind of early, want to check out the Fulton Market or find a bar toward my place and get another drink?"

"How about something more fun than that?"

"Like what?" She perked up at his suggestion.

"Why don't we do one of those evening harbor cruises. If you want a drink, we can have one on board while we enjoy that view of Lady Liberty you love so much."

Samantha slowed her walk until she came to a complete stop. She appeared deep in thought, yet he swore he caught a glint of fear in her eyes.

"You can say no, I won't be offended. I thought it would be a nice ending to the evening, and a way for me to thank you for the company. You've brought the best back to the Pier for me."

"I'm so glad. And you have no idea how much I want to say yes, but there's a reason why I need to say no."

"Okay?" He cocked his head, knowing there was more coming. "You don't owe me any kind of explanation, really."

Her mouth slanted, and she bit her lower lip before deciding to speak. "I'm sure you'll find this hard to believe after everything I've said, but I'm not a fan of boats in general. I don't like the rocking of the water, and I hate the sound of it slapping against the side of the boat." She hugged herself as her entire body shivered. "I've only seen that view once. I wanted to do the tour with some friends, only I threw up the entire ride and was a sobbing mess by the time they carried me off. I've never done it again."

"I'm sorry it was such a horrible experience." He put his hand on her shoulder realizing that trauma must have remained with her all these years.

"But I saw her, and she was more beautiful than any picture. I keep that vision close, because even though I had a major melt down, it was a special trip."

"You don't think you'd want to try again?"

"No." She paused. "Well…maybe, just not tonight."

He patted her shoulder in a reassuring gesture and said, "Sometimes you just have to ride the tide." Dalton froze when Sam sucked in a breath and took a stutter-step backwards.

Dalton remained still and silently cursed. He hadn't meant for the phrase to come out, it was just his natural response. A phrase he and his brother had shared. A phrase he'd only used one other time.

"What did you say?" she finally managed to get out.

Now, as he stared at her bewildered expression, he couldn't help but wonder what was going on inside her head.

He couldn't find his voice as his mind whirled with how he should even think of responding. Everything he'd worked so hard on, things he'd kept close, could all come crashing down with one wrong answer.

"My dad used to say the same thing," she continued when it was clear he couldn't find his words. "I've never heard anyone else say it."

"Your dad?" Dalton forced a swallow, grateful in a way for her mixed-up memories.

"Yes, he used to take me fishing. I remember tossing bait fish to the seagulls and screaming when they would swarm the boat."

"Did you fish a lot?" His eye twitched, and he hoped she didn't notice.

"I only have a couple memories of it, but they make me happy when I think of them. My parents died when I was younger, in what I've been told was a boating accident."

"I'm so sorry." He could feel himself perspiring as an urgent need to change the course of the conversation overtook him. "Maybe you'll fish again someday."

"Maybe. I was raised by my aunt and uncle, and they did their best to keep me away from the water." She looked at him as if she were seeing him differently. "Why don't we go for that drink?" Their eyes locked, and the innocence he saw reminded him of the promise he'd made. Reality punched him in the gut. He had a job to do, damn it, and needed to stick to the plan.

"I think we've had enough." He started walking and motioned her to follow. "Better we get you home."

The words sounded like a lie.

———

"How was dinner, Lover Boy?" Nicki cooed when he walked through the door of her east side studio flat.

"It was fine. She's a nice girl," Dalton answered.

"You're home awfully early. I thought for sure Party Girl would keep you out late."

"She tried." He grinned, and Nicki swatted his arm. "Hey! I said she tried. I pretty much spoiled her plans, I think."

"So, my evil plan worked." She nuzzled against his shoulder, kissing his neck until she reached his lips. "I hope you saved room for dessert."

"Always."

His mouth devoured hers before she could speak a saucy comeback. It was so easy to get lost in him, and she knew he felt it, too. He backed her against the wall, sliding his hands underneath her cropped sweatshirt. Movement halted when he realized she wasn't wearing a bra. His impatient groan against her lips made her tingle as he flipped the material over her head and tossed it on the floor.

"Damn, woman," he growled at her exposed, bare breasts.

When she hooked a leg around his hips, he supported her by cupping her backside and forcing her closer. His lips left hers to suckle each one of her breasts, gently tugging at a nipple until she moaned and entwined her fingers in his wavy brown hair.

She couldn't think straight. Didn't want to think straight.

They'd been doing this for so long it felt as normal as it was exciting. Every time was as intense as the first, as if they couldn't get enough of each other. Nicki tried not to think too much about it, she'd never been a dreamer. But Dalton Riley made her want the dream.

The attraction started during the academy, where neither one of them had been ready to put a label on what was going on. It wasn't until Tony and Bianca got married that suddenly they were under scrutiny to move to the next level. Bianca had gone so far as to force them to sign up on a dating app, where they proved they were indeed a match. After one month of trying, they collectively agreed that owning the label of *couple* was too much pressure.

They never verbally set rules for their relationship. Things just organically happened, and she was fine with it. She believed the times they were together were even more special because of it.

"You need to get out of these clothes," she said between kisses when he hoisted her other leg around his waist.

"I can't stay." He uttered before kissing her and sliding a hand into the waist of her sweatpants to squeeze her bare bottom. "Nicole, what the hell are you doing to me?"

She smiled against his lips. She'd been prepared and had to admit she enjoyed making him crazy. Only this time she saw a definite struggle in his sexy green eyes. She dropped her legs to the floor, feeling a change in their vibe.

"The same thing you do to me. But if you can't stay, you can't stay. That's fine."

"But I always stay." His hand cradled her cheek and she turned away from it even though he still held her captive against the wall. This wasn't how she'd expected the night would go.

"You don't have to, plus you just said you can't. It's not like we've never done this before." She ducked under his other arm to retrieve her sweatshirt and quickly put it back on. He followed her over to the sofa.

"I want to, Nicole. I wouldn't be here at all if I didn't want to be."

"I know, sorry. Maybe you shouldn't have stopped by." She sat down and turned on the television, scrolling for a distracting movie.

"Hey, don't be this way." He sat next to her, and out of reflex, she leaned into him. "I have a lot on my mind that I don't want to burden you with, and an early morning meeting with Tony."

"I understand. This was on me. For whatever reason I didn't plan on tonight being a *'thanks for the sex but I gotta go'* kind of night. We haven't done that since the very beginning." She sat up straight to look him in the eye. "I agreed to help you find your brother's killer, on my own time. There's nothing you could say that would ever burden me. I've always got your back, Riley."

"And I've always got yours. I'm trying to process this information with the fentanyl. CeCe has gone dark and that worries me. She's always returned my calls or messages. And this added distraction with Samantha I—"

"The girl is a distraction to you? I honestly thought you had better willpower than that." She tried to read his mind. "You really are a pussy, aren't you?" She broke into a smile when his jaw dropped and slapped her palms on her thighs. "This changes everything."

Nicki felt it now, this surreal connection she'd never felt with anyone else but Dalton. It was like an energy flowed between them, reminding her they truly were on the same wavelength. The conflict she'd seen moments ago had nothing to do with her, but the culmination of his many demons past and present. With Dalton, she knew he couldn't look toward a future until he'd taken care of a past that haunted him. She also knew there were things he held back, and when he could tell her he would.

"Come here," he said and pulled her onto his lap. His arms held her tight, and her head rested against his. "The only pussy around here is yours, and right now, *that's* a distraction."

"Dalton!" She sat up and saw the passion glowing in his eyes. Her body immediately ignited.

"Baby, I'm sorry if what I said earlier upset you."

"Shhh…it's okay. Sometimes I need to be put back in check is all. No worries, love." She planted soft kisses on his lips and repeated his words from that morning, "You and I are just fine."

"I never doubted that." He slipped his tongue between her lips, and she felt every muscle relax into him. She broke the contact as her heart began to race.

"Does this mean you're staying?"

"I'm going to set the alarm, and no funny business when I have to leave in the morning."

"No funny business." She shook her head and crossed her heart even though her smile was anything but innocent.

"Then let's get you over to the bed so I can make sure *everything* is back in check."

He kissed her again and carried her to the bed. Every kiss, every touch held the promise of the passion they shared. One day, she'd get her wish. Today wasn't that day, and she was okay with that.

CHAPTER 5

Dalton knocked on Tony's door, thoughts of Nicki still troubling him even after their night filled with mind-blowing sex. While they appeared to be free agents, he'd always considered himself exclusive to her and he assumed she was the same. After last night, she basically confirmed that, and he sensed her need for wanting stability.

He also knew she understood he couldn't give it to her. She'd needed to vent, and he'd let her, which was why he ended up staying. Knowing they were going to be up most of the night, it was important to her that he be there, and he would be, with no question.

But would she still be there if she ever knew the truth?

If she knew the things he'd done before he ever met her, all the using and dealing of drugs and the violence which came along with it. Would she be able to forgive the young, headstrong, misled boy and still love the man he'd changed into? He wanted to be that man for her, but he also knew the risk of keeping her in the dark for too long. Once they found Justin's killer, the truth would come out and everything he knew about faith would be tested.

"Morning, D." Tony greeted him at the door. "You missed breakfast, but Bianca left us a couple cinnamon rolls, and I made fresh coffee."

"Appreciate you being free." Dalton followed him in. He knew he wasn't cleared yet for any real work, but he needed to see what Tony might know about the Patrone's and specifically Rocco. CeCe still hadn't responded to his messages. Something wasn't right, he could feel it in his gut.

"You seem like a man with something on his mind. Everything okay?" Tony's voice brought him back to the moment before he took the steaming mug his partner offered.

"If you're referring to Nicki, I plead the fifth." He eyed Tony. "Bianca put you up to that, didn't she?" He set the mug on the granite breakfast bar and reached for a cinnamon roll.

"Not necessarily. But she was a little upset at the barbecue. She thought for sure she'd see you two together."

"I know she means well. But Nicki and I are...different. We like where we're at." He hoped like hell after last night she still felt the same way. He just needed more time.

"I know. And that's your business. But as far as my wife is concerned, she wants her two good friends happily together."

"Nicki aside," Dalton said, "I need to get your input on something."

"Sure, what's up?"

"I have a source that says someone is bringing fentanyl-laced cocaine into Louie Patrone's territory."

"I'd say that's something all right."

"They think Rocco might be trying to make a move on Louie. I have feelers out to someone close to the family, and I'm hoping to hear back." He hated keeping Tony and Nicki in the dark, but he didn't know what he'd be up against. If something went wrong, he'd never forgive himself, so it would be better not to take the chance.

"Dalton, you're not supposed to be doing anything other than processing paperwork and physical therapy."

"You know I can't do that. There's a lot of mixed messages circling out there, and I feel like I'm close to finding out the truth." The truth for a lot of things he couldn't let Tony in on.

"I need you at one hundred percent when that happens. Let me and RJ work your leads."

"No."

"Dalton, we're partners, but you're under orders until medically cleared."

"I'm telling you, I'm fine to be digging where I'm digging. If I turn up something solid, I will let you know and then we can handle it together."

"Somehow, I have a feeling you're running your own rogue mission. Tell me that's not true."

"I'm just fishing, Tony. Casting the line, that's all."

"That better be all." Tony paused and leaned in closer. "I have a lead of my own that says there are some wealthy Venezuelan men hiring handlers here in the states to traffic young women."

"Venezuela? Are they involved with any of the Mexican cartels?" This was news to Dalton and maybe Rocco was getting involved with all the wrong people.

"Not sure. They are making contacts in large tourist cities. New York is one of them. They all run in similar circles. Hard to tell if they are connected in any way."

"I'll check with some of my sources. I'd hate to think we've got more to worry about than the doctored-up cocaine coming in from Florida."

"Me too, my friend. This city has enough problems."

"Let me know if you find anything more about the Venezuelans being connected to this fentanyl."

Dalton had a very bad feeling about this. If Rocco was making some kind of move to overtake his brother, there seemed to be a lot of players in this game. Which meant Rocco was in over his head and probably had no idea.

"Will do." Tony refilled his mug. "Have time for another cup of coffee?"

"Off to PT. You know, I'm under orders." He shot Tony a sarcastic expression and set his cup in the sink. "I'm taking my cinnamon roll for the road. I'll let myself out."

As he drove to his appointment, the Patrone takeover fought for airtime in his mind. There had to be something more at stake, and he was damn sure Louie was purposely being kept out of the loop. If that were the case, then Louie, CeCe and possibly Enso were sitting ducks. Dalton parked the car and sent one more message to CeCe, praying she'd respond.

Urgent. Must meet soon. Potential threat to family.

Deep in the recesses of Dalton's mind, Billy simmered in the background. The man was out there somewhere. Dalton wouldn't stop looking because one day the guy would mess up. And when he did, Dalton would be there to seek his vengeance.

———

SAMANTHA WALKED INTO BIANCA'S OFFICE WITH A STACK OF files and her Chinese takeout. They'd agreed upon a working lunch to set up the next round of mergers and acquisitions for the fourth quarter. She was very excited to see some of her clients returning with new projects and business solutions.

"There's my rock star!" Bianca closed her laptop and reached into her desk drawer to pull out a small lunch box and a shaker bottle full of protein powder.

"Another salad? You're going to waste away to nothing."

Sam pointed to the small salad Bianca had pulled out of her cooler bag and the plastic sports bottle.

"Nonsense. This is exactly what my body needs. I haven't had time to hit the gym lately, and I'm feeling sluggish. Nothing like a good detox."

"I guess so." Sam shrugged. She hadn't set foot in the gym for the last month since she'd picked up more clients. Too many late-night meetings with lawyers had her too tired to even think about working out, or dinner for that matter.

"I was contacted the other day by Victor Perez. He was referred to us by Greg Maddox."

"Really? That's great."

"He has plans to build a posh resort property along the panhandle of Florida, with a sister property in Baja California."

"Beautiful choice of location, too. How exciting for BCA."

"You've got a great future here, Samantha." Bianca pointed at the files. "I can't believe how much you've learned and how many new clients you've picked up. Therefore, I'm putting you exclusively on the Perez Account."

"What? Bianca, thank you. Surprising enough, half of these files are repeat clients."

"Well done!" Bianca clasped her hands together. "Let's take a look."

"Before we do, can I ask you a question?" Sam divided the folders and slid a stack toward Bianca.

"Sure. Hopefully I'll have an answer."

"It's about Dalton."

Bianca set the fork back into her salad. "What about him?"

"I can't stop thinking about him since he took me home from your barbeque, and we had dinner."

"You had dinner?" Bianca's expression changed to surprise.

"It was my idea, and I was so glad he said yes." Sam paused

and could still picture his smile and how it made her feel. "I don't know how to explain this, but I feel a connection with him."

"Sam…."

"I know it sounds crazy because I don't even know him, but I feel like I do, and on some weird level he understands me more than any other man I've ever been with."

"And how does he feel?" Bianca watched her carefully.

"That's just it. I can't get a good read on him. He seems a little guarded and just when I think I see a spark of some kind, he douses it out before I can act on it."

"How and what were you thinking of doing if he didn't?"

"I'm not sure, but I want to explore things more. I think he does like me, but for some reason he's holding back. I want him to know that he doesn't have to."

"Dalton leads a very complicated life."

"I know. He's hinted to some things in his past, and I don't expect to know exactly what they were, but I can put enough of the pieces together. I know he's older than I am, but I don't care about that either. Love has no age limit."

"Love?" Bianca leaned forward and placed both palms flat on her desk.

"*If* we were to fall in love. I'm just saying it would be okay. I don't care that he's older. I just want to explore this attraction, our connection."

"What exactly has he been doing?"

"Being a perfect gentleman. It's not like I haven't tried… I've invited him up to my place both times he's seen me home, and he's declined."

"I'm sure he has his reasons." Bianca seemed to relax. "You don't know what you could be getting into."

"All I'm saying is I'm okay if I don't know. I only want a chance to get to know him. I swear, he feels this weird connection between us, too, but then he turns away from it.

He even said a phrase I remembered my dad saying to me when we'd fish. I mean, if that's not some sort of sign from the universe, I don't know what is."

"Be careful with this one. There's a lot about Dalton you don't know. Don't get me wrong, he's a great guy. The man would literally lay down his life for my family. But there are things about him Tony doesn't even know, things Dalton doesn't like to talk about, and we respect that."

"I will respect that, too. Bianca, he's the first man I've ever started to know who eases my anxiety. I've never felt safer than when I'm near him. I say this out loud, and it sounds even more crazy, but I can't help how I feel. There's something between us, and it could be everything I've ever needed."

"Or your undoing," Bianca pointed out with a sigh. "With that being said, and because I was young once, too, I know that you're not going to let this drop."

Sam shook her head with a smile, knowing Bianca was seeing things her way.

"I don't want you to embarrass yourself by continuing to push for something that might not be there. Why don't you invite Dalton as your plus one to the award ceremony in a couple of weeks. If he says yes, then take it as a positive. If he says no…you gotta leave him be."

"That's an amazing idea! Why didn't I think of that?"

"Because you're too busy obsessing." Bianca laughed.

"Nothing wrong with that, is there?"

"Just promise me you won't get too far ahead of yourself. The man has a lot going on and takes his work seriously. He will tell you this, and it's the truth."

"I just need to see this feeling through. I know if he gives me a chance, he'll want to do the same." Sam's heart swelled with hope. Now she had a reason to contact him and hope-

fully a date for the event. Dalton would have to say yes...
wouldn't he?

"I'll be picking up our tickets next week. Give the man
enough notice. I do think he should be there to see you accept
the award."

"Oh, I will, and I can't wait."

"Do me a favor?"

"What's that?"

"Don't lose focus on your future." She pointed once more
to the stack of files. "You've found your niche with me, and
there's nowhere to go but up. I want that for you."

"Thanks, Bianca. I love it here, and I won't do anything to
let you down."

"Good. Then let's stop talking and start creating strategic
plans for these clients. You stand to make a hell of a lot of
money over the next two years if we can get them all closed
in Q4."

Samantha dove into her stack, having a hard time concen-
trating on anything other than Dalton Riley. She forced
herself back into the files—

But the feeling that something had already shifted
wouldn't leave her.

CHAPTER 6

Dalton sat inside the small diner with his half-eaten BLT and fries, waiting for CeCe. She was late, and he wondered if he should be concerned. She'd canceled before, and the fact that he hadn't heard from her was unsettling. He flipped his phone over to see if he'd somehow missed a call when a shadow passed by and sat across from him.

"Forgive me for being late," the older woman said while grabbing a plastic menu.

CeCe Patrone must have been in her sixties by now, but her thick, dark hair and flawless skin kept her looking ten years younger. She carried herself like a true matriarch, in her suitcoat and pants complete with designer leather bag. A little out of place in a greasy spoon city diner but he'd chosen the location so she wouldn't be seen with him.

"I was getting worried." Dalton took a sip of his large soda and glanced out the window at the waiting black SUV and very muscular driver.

"Louie was needy. You know how that goes." She tilted

her head, her perfectly lined red lips forming a sassy grin. "Satisfy the man, and the woman gets to do what she wants."

"Ah, so that's how it works." Dalton smiled back. He always enjoyed the warm banter with CeCe from the first moment they'd met, back when he was a troubled teen hanging with the wrong people. "And what does he think you're doing now?"

"Spending his money. What every woman wants to do." They shared a burst of laughter before Dalton became serious.

"How much time do you have? Not that this will take long, but I don't want you to get into trouble because of me."

"Dalton, you have nothing to worry about. Louie loves you as much as I do." She paused, her eyes scanning the room behind him. "Your message has me worried. I didn't want to say anything to Louie until I understood more."

He folded his hands on the table. "It's about Rocco."

"What's going on?" Her eyes narrowed. "I don't like that look on your face."

Dalton cleared his throat and motioned for the server to bring a cup of coffee for CeCe. "I have some intel that suggests Rocco might be dealing with someone outside of New York in order to make a move against Louie."

"Ugh! That slimy man. I've told my dear husband many times his brother is no good. Yet my darling Louie gives him chance after chance and never thinks blood will betray him." She sighed. "Are you sure?"

"Not a hundred percent. I'm still putting the pieces together. Have you noticed anything odd with Rocco, his behavior, any new friends, or contacts? Is he spending a lot of time out of town, and where does he say he's going."

"Now that you mention it, he has gone away a couple times. Says he's seeing some old friends, but he never says where he goes."

"Hmmm...anything else? Any idea who this friend might be?"

"Well, I didn't want to think this could be true, but if what you're saying is accurate then it possibly could be...."

"What?" Dalton saw the worry seep into the woman's eyes and a knot worked its way into the pit of his stomach. "What's going on CeCe?"

"I heard Rocco talking to some of the cousins, after Sunday supper a few weeks ago, saying he's talking to someone powerful. Someone with connections."

Dalton's mind raced. This could be the opportunity Dalton had been longing for.

"I didn't hear too much detail." CeCe continued, "But the man Rocco mentioned and how they were hanging out, doing the drugs, it reminded me so much of young Billy."

"Is there anything else? Where did Rocco stay? Is he going to see him again?"

"I don't know where he stayed, but I do know they will see each other again. He said this friend is coming to New York soon."

"Then I guess we'll find out who Rocco's friend is. For your own protection, you and Louie need to amp up your security and pay attention, maybe even take a vacation but don't tell anyone where you're going."

"We're Patrones." She sat up straight. "We're not afraid. Louie has made sure we have excellent protection."

"Trust me, CeCe. Something doesn't feel right. Whoever this guy is, I believe Rocco will use him as leverage to take out Louie."

"Maybe I need to have Louie talk to Rocco again. Get him to see the light so they can compromise on whatever it is Rocco really wants."

"He wants it all, CeCe. Rocco isn't going to stop until he's in charge, but he's not smart enough to do this alone. He's going to align with whoever has the most power, or use whoever else that person knows, to make the takeover happen."

The normally strong, put-together CeCe Patrone displayed a glimmer of genuine fear for the first time since he'd met her. "Dalton, you're scaring me."

Truth was, Dalton was a little shaken himself. For all the years he'd been tracking and searching for any sign of Billy, this was the first solid lead. Having CeCe as a source had finally paid off.

He'd been nervous coming back to New York as a detective and reaching out to them. He'd explained their absence by telling them the boat sank and Billy went down with the ship because he was too high to swim. Dalton had been rescued, finally taking their advice and cleaning himself up. What he didn't tell them was he believed in his gut Billy survived and would someday return to settle a score. Working a deal with Louie and CeCe was the only thing he could think of to stay in the family loop in case Billy ever decided to reach out to old connections.

"There's no need to be scared," Dalton reassured her. "Like you said, security is tight, and Louie is a smart man. Let him know what you suspect, but don't let him make a move of his own, not yet. I need to verify all this information, and it may take a few days."

"Of course. Let me know what you find out. I'd be happy if Rocco left New York for good. He's nothing but trouble, always has been."

"Until you hear from me, please be careful."

"I don't like that look in your eyes, young man. I want *you* to be careful." Her brown eyes grew moist with tears. "When we lost our only son, God brought us you. We've always thought of you as the son we never got to watch grow up." She smiled the loving smile which warmed Dalton's heart every time. "A mother knows when her boy is thinking of doing something crazy."

Dalton laughed. She always had a soft spot for him even in his darkest days. CeCe had been the one constant, whispering in his ear he could do better than working with Billy, he could change and do something to make a difference. How many times had she and Louie told him he was a good person even when he didn't believe it himself? The relationship with his own parents started to mend once he'd cleaned up and went to the academy. Some tensions remained, and he was fine with it. He called occasionally and went home to visit now and then, but they realized his job was all consuming. If they only knew the truth of what really consumed him, they would probably disown him.

He hoped one day he'd be able to tell the whole story, and for once everyone would understand who Dalton Riley really was.

"In case I've never told you, CeCe Patrone, I'm grateful for all the faith you and Louie had in me, even at my worst. I love you for it. You were the mom I didn't have at a time when I needed one the most. You know I will do anything for you and Louie."

"I know. I've always known. That's why I help you." She patted his cheek before giving him a kiss. "That's what mothers do." She walked out the door without looking back, and Dalton made a promise to himself to stop by and see the Patrones more often than just when he needed information.

When the black SUV pulled away, Dalton grabbed his phone and called Nicki. Even though he didn't have visible proof, he felt in his gut CeCe's intuition was correct.

"For what do I owe this afternoon delight?" Niki's voice teased, but Dalton was all business.

"You're never going to believe it, but I've finally got a lead on that sonofabitch."

SAMANTHA HAD PROMISED HERSELF SHE WAS GOING TO HAVE FUN tonight.

No backing out. No excuses, and no letting fear dictate every decision. So, when Kelsey had texted about a low-key bonfire at Crescent Beach with a handful of coworkers and friends, she'd said yes before she could talk herself out of it.

And at first, it had been nice. The wind was mild, the fire warm, and the soft hum of guitar strings mixed with laughter and the distant roll of waves. It was the closest thing to normal she'd felt in years.

"You know," a voice said beside her, "I noticed you the second you walked down the beach."

Samantha glanced up to see the guy from earlier—tall, easy smile, dark hair kept a little too long. Drew. She'd caught him looking more than once but had brushed it off as friendly curiosity. Now, standing this close, his eyes held something bolder.

"You did?" she said, managing a small laugh.

He handed her a fresh drink. "Figured if I was going to spend the night by a fire, I might as well do it next to the prettiest girl here."

The line was cheesy, but it didn't feel gross. Not yet. "You're laying it on pretty thick."

"Hey, when you're impressed, you're impressed." He grinned. "Come on, walk with me?"

Her instinct said no. Stay by the fire. Stay where the noise is, where the light is. But she'd promised herself she'd try. Be normal for once. And normal girls didn't flinch away from compliments or isolate themselves in the dark.

"Okay," she said, and accepted his outstretched hand.

They walked along the waterline, shoes in hand, surf lapping at their ankles. For a few minutes, it was…fine. He asked about her job, her favorite movies, and how she liked the city. She answered. She even smiled.

They stopped near a washed-up log at the edge of the beach, far enough away that the fire was just a faint orange glow in the distance. Drew sat down and gently tugged her hand, pulling her down onto his lap.

"Whoa," she said, laughing nervously. "Bold move."

"Sorry. Couldn't help myself." His hand slid around her waist.

She shifted slightly, intending to stand, but his grip tightened. "Don't be shy," he murmured, lips brushing her ear. "I like a little teasing."

"Drew—"

"Relax." His other hand grazed her thigh. "I'm not gonna hurt you."

Her heart stuttered, and for a moment she forgot to breathe. That sentence. *I'm not gonna hurt you.*

It detonated something deep inside her.

The firelight, the music, and the laughter—it all vanished. Suddenly she was somewhere else. A hand, not unlike Drew's, holding her still as the world tilted. A door slamming. Cold water rushing under it. Shouts from somewhere farther away.

"Stop," she whispered. "I want to go back."

"You don't mean that." His voice was heavier now, slurred from all of the drinks he'd had. His grip tightened as he held her to him. "You've been flirting with me all night. Don't act like you don't want this."

Her pulse surged, loud and insistent. Her breath came in sharp, useless bursts. She pushed harder, panic flooding her limbs. "Let go of me!"

"Don't be a tease."

Samantha hurled the rest of her drink into his face.

"Damn it!" He recoiled, wiping at his eyes, loosening his

grip long enough for her to bolt. Sand sprayed beneath her feet as she ran—toward the fire, toward light, toward *anywhere* but here.

Only he was faster.

His hand closed around her arm, yanking her back. She screamed, stumbling as they both splashed into the shallow surf. Cold water soaked her jeans, clinging to her skin. She kicked, twisted, every nerve screaming *no no no no no* as memories exploded one after another—

The door.

The water rising.

A voice saying, *"Be a good girl."*

The sound of the lock turning.

"Let me go!" she screamed. "I need to get out of here! Let me out!"

She fought like an animal, clawing at his chest, slipping in the water as her mind shattered between past and present. Her shriek carried down the shoreline, ragged and desperate.

"What the hell is wrong with you? Drew shouted, backing off, eyes wide. "You're one crazy bitch!"

Samantha collapsed into the wet sand, chest heaving. Her body trembled so hard she could barely stay upright. In the distance someone was shouting her name. Kelsey. Blurred images of others were running toward her. Kelsey's boyfriend, Ben, scooped her up but she barely felt it. Barely heard Kelsey say, "You're going to be okay."

The firelight grew closer. Warmer. Safer. A towel dropped around her shoulders the moment she was lowered to a chair. Arms, familiar and firm, helped steady her as Kelsey knelt beside her, her voice low and soothing.

"I'm sorry," Samantha whispered. "I-I didn't mean to. I don't know what happened."

Drew stood a few feet away, rubbing his jaw and watching her like she was a live wire. With a muttered curse, he turned and stalked off into the dark. A couple of his friends followed, asking questions.

Samantha barely noticed.

All she could feel was the water around her ankles…and the certainty that somewhere beyond the glow of the fire, someone was watching.

CHAPTER 7

The night before still clung to her skin like salt and smoke. Samantha had barely slept, the crash of waves echoing in her ears long after she'd left the beach behind. She hadn't told anyone—not her friends, not her therapist, not even herself—what really happened. It was easier to pretend it was just a bad night. A misunderstanding. Drew had been drunk. She had been overreacting.

But Dalton wasn't Drew.

He never made her feel trapped, or second guess her instincts. With Dalton, it felt easy, safe. Standing in the office breakroom, she poured a second cup of coffee and told herself it was just a call. Just an invitation, a way to move forward.

Moments later, she drummed her fingers on her glossy, cherry desk and stared at Dalton's contact number in her phone. She'd called him before, but this time she was more nervous than ever. He seemed to have a good time with her at dinner. What if he told her no?

But what if he tells you yes?

Without further hesitation, she pressed the call button, her fingers still trembling. It seemed to ring forever, and she was expecting to hear his voicemail when he picked up, sounding breathless.

"Hey, Sam, what's up?"

"Hi. Are you okay? You sound winded?"

"Sorry, I got some really good news today on a case and decided to go for a run."

"That's an odd way to celebrate."

"No, that comes later. I just had this burst of energy, you know? Plus, running helps me clear my head, so I've been thinking of my next steps."

She heard his pace slow and could just picture him jogging. Sam visualized him in a pair of nice fitting athletic shorts and a tank top. If his legs were anything like his arms....

"So, what's going on?"

"What?" She blinked a couple times, but the picture of a glistening Dalton stayed front and center.

"Sam, you called me."

"Oh, right, sorry. Someone just dropped some mail off, and I got distracted." She was distracted all right, but no one had come into her office.

"Whew! Man, I haven't run five complete miles in a long time. Nice to know I still have my cardio, but my legs are going to be dead tomorrow." She heard a couple groans before he said, "Sorry, I gotta stretch before I head back. What did you need?"

"Need?" Sam took the finger she'd been chewing out of her mouth. "Tickets. I have tickets. I mean, I *will* have tickets."

"Where are you going?"

"Bianca is giving me tickets to the Top Performers Gala in a few weeks. The company is up for an award, and she wants me to attend with her."

"That's great! Congratulations. I told you she was proud of the work you're doing."

"I'm so thrilled. She's even giving me a new account she just acquired."

"Well, that's a huge accomplishment. Bianca is a tough cookie. I can tell you for certain, she wouldn't give it to you if she didn't have confidence that you could handle it."

"Thanks. That's not why I called." She took a slow breath to calm her nerves.

"Oh. What can I do for you, then?"

"Be my plus one to the event." There, she'd said it. There was silence on the line except for street noise coming through his phone. She panicked. "I mean if you're free of course. I had so much fun the other night at the pier, and I thought you did, too, and I don't really have anyone else to take. Hey, it's free food and drink and I promise I won't bore you or scare you with my phobias." She slapped her forehead, hating it when she babbled.

"You have phobias?" His voice held a teasing tone which put her immediately at ease.

"Many."

"Mmm, can I think about it?"

"Oh, sure." She tried to hide the disappointment she was feeling when he started laughing.

"I was just joking. I'm sure I've got a phobia I don't even know about yet." He paused and their laughter subsided. "I had a nice time at the pier, too."

"I'm glad." Sam was literally dying inside. She didn't want to push him, but she wanted an answer so bad.

"I would very much enjoy going with you to the gala."

"Really?" she squeaked, her feet tapping under her desk.

"Of course. I always like supporting my friends when I can. Send me the details, okay."

Her heart dipped a little, but hey, many romantic relationships started as friends. She decided to focus on that. "For sure, yes, I will."

"I gotta run, literally, another five miles back home. Next time I get the idea to go for a run, I'd better hit the gym instead. We'll talk soon, okay?"

"Yes!" she said with a bit too much excitement. "Yes, okay. Bye."

Sam hung up and squealed as she spun around in her chair. Dalton was going to be her date, her plus one. Friends with *many* possible benefits. She felt giddy with anticipation. Thank goodness she had time to prepare. She needed something special to wear, and nothing currently in her closet was acceptable. First the good news from Bianca and now to have Dalton easily say yes.

"Well don't you look exceptionally joyful," Bianca said when she poked her head in Sam's doorway.

"He said yes. Dalton said yes!" Sam left out the part about supporting friends.

"Wow…that's great news."

"I'm over the moon! We were laughing, and he didn't even have to think about it. He just said yes." She paused to catch her breath. "I need to go shopping, make an appointment at the salon, and a mani-pedi. I hope these weeks fly by. I can't wait to see him! I wonder if we'll get together before the gala?"

"Whoa, slow down." Bianca held her hands up. "I'm happy for you, but remember you have clients who need your head to be out of the clouds." Bianca's smile was sincere, but Sam could tell her eyes were warning her to be cautious.

What could possibly go wrong?

———

THE CEMETERY WAS NEARLY EMPTY THIS TIME OF NIGHT, JUST THE way Dalton preferred it. A handful of cars lined the gravel loop

AT THE EDGE OF THE PROPERTY, HEADLIGHTS WINKING IN THE dark, but no one lingered among the rows of markers. The world had gone still—only the faint hiss of grass beneath his boots, soft and uneven. Each step pressed into the earth with a muted crunch.

Moonlight pooled in the hollows between headstones. A breeze stirred the leaves overhead, brushing against his collar like a breath. He stopped at the far end of the path, where the headstones thinned and the earth sloped gently toward the stream. Justin Riley, the engraved marble read, as if the name belonged to a stranger.

He slowed as he reached it. The final few steps felt heavier, deliberate. His standard issue boots made no ceremony of arrival. Just a final press into the grass, a pause, and more silence. Dalton stared down, hands shoved deep into his coat pockets, breath catching in the night air.

"Hey, Jus," he said quietly. His voice felt too loud here, too real. "It's been a while."

He lowered himself to a crouch, his fingers brushing a dead leaf off the base of the marker. Someone—probably his mom—had left a small arrangement of roses. They were brittle now, edges browned by the daily sun and lack of water. Justin would've hated them. He'd always joked that flowers at a grave were like balloons at a funeral—"too damn cheerful for death."

Dalton smiled faintly at the memory, then let it fade.

"I don't know why I keep coming here," he admitted. "It's not like you're listening. You always gave advice when I didn't want it. Now that I could use some..." his voice trailed off. "Yeah, well, you know."

He swallowed hard. The wind carried the faint scent of wood smoke from somewhere beyond the trees. It reminded him of the bonfire nights they used to sneak out for as teenagers—cheap beer, bad decisions, and Justin always looking out for him. Always pulling him back before he went too far.

"You were the smart one," Dalton murmured. "You were supposed to make it out clean. And I was supposed to be the screw-up. That's how it was supposed to go, right?"

The silence didn't answer. It never did.

He tilted his head back toward the stars, blinking against the tightness behind his eyes. "I'm still trying," he said. "To make it mean something. To make *you* mean something. And maybe, to make up for what I couldn't do back then."

The breeze shifted, cooler now. Dalton's thoughts drifted to Samantha—the tremor in her voice when she called about the gala, the way her laugh still carried that unspoken question beneath it. He'd told himself that protecting her was about keeping a promise. That it was about justice. But it wasn't.

It was about a guilt that wouldn't die. About ghosts that didn't stay buried. About the ache of losing someone once— and the terror of doing it again.

"I couldn't save you," he said, the words catching in his throat. "But maybe I can save her."

He rose to his feet and gazed down one last time.

"Watch my six, would you?" he whispered. "Feels like everything's about to go sideways." Silence pressed against his chest and made it hard to breathe. "You always did."

The faint smell of rain and something darker beneath it hung in the air like trouble looming just beyond the horizon. Dalton shoved his hands deeper into his pockets and turned back toward the car, boots shuffling across the grass. Something made him pause halfway to the car.

A shadow moved just beyond the wrought-iron fence at the far end of the cemetery. Barely there, maybe nothing. Maybe the wind catching a branch or a deer slipping through the underbrush.

Dalton's gut tightened.

There was a car parked across the road. Not one of the usual mourners or staff he'd become accustomed to seeing. This was a dark sedan with tinted windows and the engine off.

Just sitting there. Watching.

Dalton lingered, gaze pinned on the vehicle, his hand brushing the grip of his Glock holstered beneath his coat. He didn't make a move toward it. Whoever was inside would see that as a challenge. He didn't need confrontation, not tonight.

His jaw flexed. "Rocco?" he said under his breath. "Or someone worse?"

He continued toward his car, back straight, pace steady, as if nothing was off. But the feeling followed him—hot eyes on his neck, the whisper of danger just beyond reach. Whatever game was being played, it had just shifted.

And he wasn't the only one keeping score anymore.

CHAPTER 8

The Yankees were in the fifth inning as Greg Maddox grabbed his wife's hips, keeping her on her knees at the edge of the bed. He loved having sex with the tv on. He could watch the game and listen to his gorgeous wife moan with pleasure as he slid in and out of her. What could be better? Doing her for four more innings, that's what. He grinned before leaning over her back to cup her breasts.

"Pace yourself, baby." He tweaked her nipples, and she cried out before he continued his rhythm. They had a great sex life, so he wasn't concerned about his own stamina. It was hers. She could be a tigress when she wanted to be, and if he kept that tamed, she could go forever. She'd hate him after all the teasing and multiple orgasms and he'd probably have to let her sleep the rest of the day, but so be it. He'd take the kids fishing or something fun like that. It would be well worth it.

"You know what I like…." She purred from below him.

In answer, he slapped her ass and reached down to stroke her with his finger as he pumped in and out of her.

"Yes, Greg, give it to me."

His phone rang, temporarily breaking his stride. He

glared at the screen wondering what could be so urgent on a Saturday morning. He pulled out, much to Becca's dismay. She collapsed on the king-sized bed but rolled over to continue pleasuring herself which almost made him lose it. She was used to the many interruptions that came with his job, and she knew he wanted her to stay in the mood.

"This better be important," he said into the phone.

"Sorry, boss," came the reply. "I think there's a problem with our special guest."

"What kind of problem? Can't you handle it?" He gazed at Becca and moved the phone away from his mouth. "Easy now, don't get there without me."

"Sir?" the voice on the other end of the phone questioned.

"Not you, asshole, I was talking to my wife." Greg licked his lips in anticipation of what was waiting for him. "You'd better start talking."

"I'm sending you security footage. I think you need to see this."

"It can't wait until normal business hours?" Greg grumbled and pulled the phone away when a video attachment came through. He watched in disbelief as the image on the screen killed his erection. "I want this piece of shit video confirmed, do you understand me? *Confirmed!*"

"Yes sir."

"Don't sir, me. I paid good money to replace that system so our tenants can feel safe. You can barely make out the person's features." Greg paced, feeling his blood pressure rising. "I don't care what you have to do, whose dick you have to suck, but I want someone out there to replace the entire system today! Got it?"

"Of course. I'll let you know as soon as the new system is installed, and I'll find someone who can enhance this image. I know a guy."

"I don't give a shit who you know. Do the job I hired you

to do and get it done." He hung up the phone, tossed it across his corner desk before going into the bathroom and digging through drawers for his anxiety medication. That fucking pissed him off the most. He hated feeling weak. He hadn't had to use it in years, but this…this was a nightmare coming back to haunt him.

"Greg…," Becca called from across the room. "Are you okay?"

"Just work." He walked out to join her and sat on the edge of the bed, then brushed the hair away from her face.

"Is there a problem?" She tried to sit up, looking serious and concerned. He gently eased her back.

"Nothing for you to worry about." He kissed her softly, the contact making him come alive again, ready to pick up where he left off. "The only problem is, I'm not inside you." Her eyes burned with desire and her tongue found its way into his mouth to tangle with his in a heated kiss which seared him to the core.

"Then you'd better get there." She wrapped her hand around his erection and stroked. "I'm ready for you."

In an instant she was on top of him. Settling herself over him and easing down in a slow motion which was his undoing as her wetness surrounded him. She'd done well while he was dealing with a potential crisis. She moved faster, sending him to the erotic place he loved to be with her. Much better than thinking about the phone call.

This was just her opening act he knew all too well. Becca created an appetite within him that was insatiable. It surprised him sometimes that they only had four children, then again, he'd been a messed-up jerk at the beginning of their relationship.

Two years of his life he'd never get back, but he'd done more than make up for it. He'd started his own business and once he knew everything was working out, he went looking for her and the baby. One look into that little face and dark brown eyes and he knew that little girl was his. He'd felt foolish for doubting Becca. She'd forgiven him and they got married.

He continued to provide the perfect life for his growing family, a life he deserved after all the hell he'd gone through. A life he could never imagine not living. This was where they belonged, on top and living the high life.

Becca moaned, reaching behind to massage his balls, snapping him back from the clutches of the past. He grabbed his wife's hips and forced her to move faster against him. Becca screamed, hitting her climax first before he flipped her to her back, hell bent on exercising his demons.

"Let them come! Let them all come!" he grunted before losing himself deep inside her wet, spent body. "Damn it!" He collapsed beside her as something dark and foreboding drifted over him.

If the person in the video was who he thought, then he could stand to lose everything.

CHAPTER 9

Fourteen Years Earlier
Dr. Taylor — The Bait

"Tell me how this happened, Mister....?"

"It's Billy. Just Billy," the young man told me, keeping his gaze fixed on the grey tiles of the emergency room floor.

"I'm Doctor Taylor." I set the chart on the edge of the bed before donning a new set of latex gloves to examine his arm. I was coming off my second double, more than ready to spend quality time with my wife and daughter. While the wound was a little messy, it wouldn't take long.

"It's like I told the nurse. I had a little skirmish on my boat is all."

"This doesn't look like a little skirmish." My nurse had flushed the wound, and I gently inspected it for any other foreign material.

"You should see the other guys." His attempt at being flip made me pause and study his eyes.

Sure, he seemed a little jumpy when I first walked in,

which I'd blamed on adrenaline from the incident. But now, taking a closer look, his pupils were dilated, and the whites of his eyes seemed overly bloodshot. My first guess would be drugs, either cocaine or heroin.

I must have made him uncomfortable because he cleared his throat and focused on the jagged split of his skin. "That's why I'm here. Not enough thread in my med-kit to stich it myself."

"Of course. My apologies," I said, reminding myself I was here to heal and not judge. The man seemed harmless enough. Probably in the wrong place at the wrong time. I pushed the stool toward a stainless-steel counter, rolling back within seconds, holding a sealed package of instruments. "No police involved?" I ripped the package open, and dropped the equipment onto a small, towel-lined tray next to the bed.

"No."

"Keep your hand still. You're going to feel a pinch and some burning."

"Damn it!" He flinched at the momentary burn from the lidocaine injections, then relaxed as I re-examined the wound and prepared the instruments.

"Knife fight, I take it?"

"Yeah," he replied, sounding shocked that I knew. "Sono-fabitch took me by surprise."

I kept my eyes mostly on my sutures. "I'm guessing over a woman?"

Billy snorted. "She would have been a wild ride, but she wasn't worth fighting over. They tried to cheap out on my payment. I let them party their way up the coast, provided food, fishing gear, party favors, whatever they needed. I put up with their pompous bullshit like they were better than me. Then they think they can take what's mine."

I steadied his arm. "I'm going to need you to keep the arm still, or I'll have to call someone in."

Billy inhaled slow, understanding what that could possibly mean for him, then dropped his gaze once more. "Sorry. I work hard. Things like this piss me off. Not that a guy like you would know about that."

"I know more than you think." I paused until his eyes met mine. He was nervous. Probably thought I'd call the cops or the armed guard who continued to make his rounds along the floor. Honestly, I was too exhausted to want to deal with this kind of drama. I bent my head, resuming my stitching and said, "There's a price to pay if you want to make the money and be successful." I kept my tone calm and felt his arm relax. "Where do you run your charter out of?"

"New Bern."

"Outer Banks?" As much as I wanted to leave, the longer I kept him talking meant the more he might sober up and not get into any more trouble once he headed back to where he was staying for the night. Could I write a report? Call in the guard? Sure. Billy seemed like a smart man. In my book, everyone deserved a second chance. Maybe our paths crossed just for that reason.

"Yup. Born and raised and trying like hell to get out."

"Gotta be a thriving business, though, with all the tourists."

"Sure."

He sounded like he either didn't care for my small talk, or he wanted to leave. The wound needed a little more attention than I originally thought, not that a man like Billy would care about the size or shape of the scar, but I was a surgeon after all. I continued stitching, making sure to keep my eyes on my work and not on Billy.

"Being the captain of my own boat is number five on my bucket list."

"You don't say...." Billy's voice faded off and I dared to sneak a peek to make sure he wasn't about to pass out, although I didn't believe he was high enough for that to happen. If I focused hard enough, I could detect a slight smell of perfume and liquor. He wasn't kidding about partying up the coast. I decided to keep the talk about a safer subject.

"What kind of boat do you have?" My innocent question hit the mark as he snapped out of whatever haze had been trying to grab hold of him.

"Sixty-five-foot, twin keel catamaran."

"Wow, that's a big one."

"She's gorgeous. Cruises at eight knots with a max speed of ten."

I stopped my work and said, "Sounds like a beast of a machine."

"Oh yeah, it'll get your blood pumping, and when that adrenaline kicks in…." Billy whistled low and smooth, bringing a wide smile to my face.

"One day, Billy. I'll be living that dream." I knotted the final suture and snipped it with a pair of scissors. "You're all set. My nurse will be in to wrap it up and give you some antibiotic ointment to apply. The stitches will dissolve on their own but follow up with your primary if you suspect any signs infection."

"Thanks, Doc."

I left the nurse bandaging his hand and moved down the hall to my next patient. Two more and I could go home to my family for a long and much deserved weekend. I had no sooner left the patient's room when Billy bolted into the hall, waving his good arm to get my attention.

"Doctor Taylor! I want to talk to you about my yacht."

"What about it?" My gaze tracked to the clock on the wall then back to Billy.

"I'm getting ready to put her on the market but considering your interest, I thought I'd give you first crack at her."

"I appreciate the offer, Billy." I chuckled, feeling punchy from need of sleep. "I don't quite think I'm ready."

"You sure? You could make number five move up the list." Billy's eyes lit with an excitement, not caused by drugs. The man made an interesting point. "Once I get her back to the Banks, someone will snatch her up."

"I'm going to have to take my chances, sorry." I quickly came to my senses, gave him a smile and slight wave of my hand before turning toward my last patient's room.

"Take a chance and live your dream." Billy's confident statement caused my hand to stop on the handle of the door. "I'll be down at Cooper Park Marina the next two or three days while I take care of some business. Stop on down. Doesn't cost anything to look and I'll even buy you a beer… Captain."

That's all it took. He was right, there was no harm in looking. Once I got some sleep I could talk to Nina about the potential, then make a trip to the marina to settle my curiosity.

"I'll tell you what, let me see what I can do. You take care of that hand." I clapped him on the shoulder before giving a nod and heading into the next exam room.

Leave it to the love of my life to understand my passion for boats. Billy had reeled me in, and I couldn't stop thinking about what he said. I called Nina as soon as I'd clocked out, and we talked my entire drive home. I told her about the captain in the ER and how beautiful his boat sounded. I explained it could be everything I'd always wanted, and then some. She actually encouraged me to take a look, get it out of my system, and buy a damn boat if I wanted to.

God, I loved this woman.

———

THE NEXT DAY I BROKERED A DEAL WITH CAPTAIN BILLY, WHO was a totally different man than I'd seen in the ER. We put together the perfect test run, a three-week vacation to the Bahamas. I'd let the captain skipper us down, he said it would take about a week. He'd show me the workings of the ship while we stopped in different places along the way to enjoy the sights and culture. We'd then spend a week enjoying the islands.

If I was happy with things—and I couldn't imagine why I wouldn't be—I'd give him a down payment in cash, skipper us home and wire transfer the balance. I strongly advised the captain there would be no drugs on board. I wanted a clean run because I was pretty much planning on the purchase. He agreed, and we shook on the deal.

What a thrill to be doing something so spontaneous. Having our own vessel at our disposal to go where we wanted whenever we wanted. Hell, I could even hire a crew once she was ours. I couldn't wait for the girls to see it. We would leave in two weeks for the vacation of a lifetime.

All because of Billy.

CHAPTER 10

"Lou, what a pleasant surprise."

Louie Patrone turned in his overstuffed chair to see several men walk into his home as if they lived there and he was the intruder. One man, in particular, made the hairs on the back of his neck bristle, and he surged to his feet. He already knew this wasn't a social call, and he prayed Cecelia would stay in the kitchen until whatever this was... was over. He thought he'd seen the last of this troublemaker. The man had changed his appearance over the years, but Louie would never forget any man who betrayed him.

"What the hell are you doing in my house?" He squared off with the man, not falling for any intimidation tactics. This was *his* home. They would all have to answer to him.

"He's with me." His brother, Rocco, pushed the men aside until he was face-to-face with Louie. "We've got a business proposition to finish, brother."

"You know where I stand." Louie stood to his full height, dominating over his brother by a good four inches. "You thinking bringing *him* with you is going to change my mind?"

When Louie laughed, he could see anger glowing in Rocco's eyes.

"Tell him, Rocco," the man said stepping forward, obviously the puppet master. Rocco was a wild card, but he wasn't a loose cannon. His fault was being a follower, and he'd never had an ounce of good judgement. "You see, Lou, I'm here to support Rocco in his decision to do better for himself, be the leader you refuse to let him be."

"That's right, Louie." It was Rocco's turn to strut in front of Louie like some rabid rooster. "And you're going to let me run my own shit. I'll be making bank, and you'll be sitting here jealous that I'm living like the king you used to be." Rocco jabbed a finger against Louie's firm chest. "I'm going to do things my way, got it? Or—"

"Or what?" Louie roared, causing everyone to take a step back while he loomed over his brother. In a voice filled with all the disappointment and disgust he felt, he spat, "You're no leader, Rocco. You never listen. You'll be dead before you can enjoy any of your dirty money."

"Louie? What's going on in here?" Cecelia burst through the door, the curiosity on her beautiful face immediately turning to fear as two men grabbed her.

"Take your hands off my wife!" Louie took a step forward only to be met by two other men and their drawn guns. He took a deep breath, realizing he'd get nowhere with anger. "Remove your hands off my wife, gentlemen."

"Louie, who are these people?" She glanced from the men who still held her to everyone else in the room. "Rocco, are these your friends?"

"They are no friends, *Cara*," Louie said in the loving tone he always used to address his beloved wife. "Go back to what you were doing. I'll handle this."

"Sorry Lou, she's not going anywhere now," the man said

from somewhere behind Rocco. "She's going to be the reason you do everything we want you to."

"That's right! So, sit back down and listen to me," Rocco yelled, and for the first time, Louie realized maybe he should have listened to his wife. With that wild look to his eyes, Louie had a feeling his brother was consuming the souped-up drugs he wanted so badly to be selling.

"For God sake, Rocco, settle down," the man stated and Rocco appeared to pull back.

Louie focused only on the worried face of his wife. "Let her leave. I don't want her to witness what goes on here."

"But I do. And so does your brother." At the man's words, Louie glared at Rocco who stood silent, shaking his head as he'd been directed to do. Louie was ashamed to claim him as blood. "We're about to give you a little heads up on what's going to happen every time you don't comply." The man caught his attention, and with a snap of his fingers, one of the henchmen holding CeCe balled his fist and landed a blow to her ribs. The air left her lungs, and she dropped to her knees only to be hoisted to her feet where she was slapped across the face until she spit blood.

"That's enough!" Louie yelled, helpless with gun barrels only inches from his chest. His wife may be mentally strong, but she was no match for such violence. The gun in the side table drawer was enough out of reach that if he moved, they would surely kill him…or CeCe. "Tell me what you want, and do not touch her again or I will kill all of you myself. Starting with you, *Billy*."

"For all the ways you did me wrong, I want you dead." Billy circled Louie like a vulture.

"You screwed up that deal," Louie reminded him. "I told you the Colombians were not to be trusted. You didn't listen and used product that was not yours to begin with."

"Best damn cocaine I'd ever experienced, back then." He

paused as if reliving a memory. "But you wouldn't leave it alone."

"*I* had to pay for your error in judgement. You needed to learn from it."

"You took a hit out on me you bastard! That's not a lesson, but it's going to be for you."

"What is happening?" CeCe cried and tried to hold her head up to look at Louie.

"Shut her up," Billy commanded, and both men hit her.

Louie went into a rage. He grabbed the heads of the two in front of him and smashed them together, their guns falling to the floor. He wrapped his meaty hand around the material of Billy's shirt, but before he could choke the man, Rocco had picked up one of the guns and held it against his temple.

Billy removed Louie's hand. "You should have let me finish. As much as I want you dead, I'm not going to do it."

"Don't you touch my wife," Louie growled.

"I don't care what happens to her. But Rocco, here, is going to earn his keep and take what's rightfully his, and that's your motherfucking kingdom." Billy tapped Louie on the cheek and walked over to CeCe. "Get her up off the floor. She's the boss's wife, you morons," he ordered. "Open your eyes CeCe and say goodbye if you can. But before you do, I'm going to need you to remember to give our good friend Dalton a message. Can you do that for me?" Billy forced her head to nod in agreement, and Louie saw her wince in pain. "You tell him to stay away from that girl, got it?" Billy seethed close to CeCe's ear. When he propped her chin up, Louie gazed into eyes that would forever follow his soul to wherever the good Lord sent him.

"I love you, Cara." As soon as the words left his mouth, Billy drew a gun and pulled the trigger, dropping Louie to the floor.

"I think I'll put one in this bastard's black heart for good measure." Billy stood over Louie, the gun pointing down at his chest. "You screwed with the wrong captain. You should have known I wouldn't forget."

"You. Were supposed to be dead," Louie fought for breath with each word.

"You taught me to never underestimate my enemy. Guess you should have listened to your own advice." Billy adjusted the aim of his gun. Without warning, CeCe lunged free and pushed Billy just as he pulled the trigger. The bullet penetrated just under Louie's collar bone. Not that it mattered, he'd lost too much blood already.

"Louie, my darling Louie," she sobbed as she fell against his chest. He used what little strength he had left to wrap his arm around her. He should have known she wouldn't go down without a fight.

"I never deserved you," he whispered against her head, a tear falling from the corner of his eye.

"Stop talking, my love. You can't leave me, we have so much to do." She patted his chest. "Save your strength."

"Damnit, CeCe!" Billy bellowed, and Louie felt her startle against his arm. "Rocco, take care of this mess. I'm done here."

"What do you want me to do with CeCe?" Rocco asked.

"I don't care what you do with her. I have another appointment."

Through blurring vision, Louie watched Billy walk away. He gazed up at his brother, struggling for every breath and worried what would become of his wife. "You don't have to do this," his voice rasped.

"I do. And I know you'd do the same." He motioned for the other men to leave. "We're leaving her here. She can watch him bleed out." Rocco walked a couple steps then turned around. "Just so you don't get any ideas…." He fired a shot into each of CeCe's legs. When Louie tried to sit up, a bullet cut into his chest and his head hit the floor. "Goodbye, brother."

The last thing Louie felt was CeCe's head against his, her hands fisted into his shirt as if her undying love could keep him alive. Her sobs faded with every last beat of his breaking heart.

———

"BECCA! WHERE ARE YOU?" GREG MADDOX CALLED AS HE MADE his way through the house. He'd been gone all week on a very important business trip. Today had been a banner day and he couldn't wait to return home and share the news with his family. He proceeded through the large, marble foyer, noticing how the open floor plan made the enormous coastal home seem even more grandiose. Becca kept their décor tasteful and clean.

"We're out by the pool!" He heard her yell through the double screen doors that had been left open.

He dropped his keys on the granite island in the kitchen and paused to scan the mail which sat in a seagrass basket. There were a couple of marketing postcards, reminding him he would soon be sharing in these methods. If business continued this uphill trend, he would soon be extending his reach far beyond Miami. The smell of sea and salt tickled his nose as he breached the door to the patio. He paused to take in the vision of his children splashing and diving into the crystalline water of the massive infinity pool. An all-consuming smile spread across his face.

This. This was everything to him.

"Get over here woman!" He noticed her curious grin when he waved her over. She jumped off her chaise, adjusting her hot pink bikini top before hurrying to his side.

"What's the matter? Why are you looking at me that way?"

Greg knew he couldn't hide his lust for her even if he tried. Becca had curves in all the right places and had turned him on from the moment he'd met her. She still had that hold over him to this very day, which turned him on even more. They needed a solo vacation, and soon. Hot sex and no kids for at least a week, maybe two. He spanned her waist with his hands which felt cold against her sun-kissed skin and pulled her close.

"What do you think?" he said in a gravelly voice filled with need for her.

"I'm thinking a lot of things right now, but we have a pool full of children." She giggled and stood on tiptoe to kiss his cheek. "You're home early. This morning you thought you might be late."

"But I'm not." He brushed her blond hair away from her collar bone and kissed the sensitive spot. "Wanna know why?" he spoke against her skin, and she immediately pulled back.

"Oh my God, did you hear about the property?"

"I did." He continued to grin, keeping her close.

"And?"

"It's ours."

"Greg! This is wonderful!"

"And they threw in the smaller marina next door like I asked, so we'll have more than enough room."

"It's just what you wanted!" Becca launched herself into his arms and wrapped her legs around his waist. He cupped her ass, forcing her closer to feel his erection. Kids or not, they were celebrating in style tonight.

"I've got all I want right here. That marina is just extra icing on our cake, baby." He kissed her hard before setting her down and reigning in his desire. "Where's my lucky

Penny?" He rested his hand above his brows and scanned the pool. His daughter waved from atop the slide before shooting down the spiral into the deep end. "Come over here, princess." He watched her swim to the edge and climb out.

"Hi, Daddy!" She dried off her face with a towel and wrapped it around her dripping body.

"Sweetheart, remember the pictures I showed you? The ones I pointed out when we were on the boat the other night and I let you pick the one you liked best?"

She nodded, droplets of water rolling down her face.

"Well, Daddy put in an offer, and they said yes. Thanks to you, my lucky Penny, Daddy's going to expand our charter business down in the Keys."

"Yay!" She jumped up and down, the bright orange towel flapping as she clapped her hands. "That was the one on Penny Point, right?"

"It sure is. We're going to name it, Maddox Charters on Penny Point."

"I love it!" Becca joined them and he put his arms around them both.

"How come Penny gets to have her name on it?" Nick pulled himself up over the edge of the pool, reminding him of the surly boy he'd been at the same age.

"The area is called Penny Point, buddy. It's just extra special because it's your sister's name, too. That's all."

"And I picked it out for Dad," Penny added with a smug expression toward her brother.

"I want to pick out the next one," he added, so as not to be left out again.

"Don't worry, we'll have plenty of time and opportunity." Greg ruffled his son's wet head, feeling once again the swell of family pride.

"What's going through that mind of yours?" Becca said,

leading him away from the pool and toward their outdoor kitchen.

"Do you have any idea how great this expansion is going to be?" He walked behind the stone bar and poured them each a glass of red wine. "It's just the beginning, babe. That area of the Keys is booming. Within the year, we'll be ready to grow even bigger." He lit his cigar and sent a puff of smoke into the air.

"How big?" She sipped her wine, studying him.

"I want to go up the east coast." He stretched an arm into the air. "Why be limited to fishing charters? Let's add whale watches and maybe some overnight stuff."

"Whale watches? That would mean a whole different fleet of boats, wouldn't it? Why up the east coast?"

"Because that's where it all began for me…for us. We can come full circle and know we've led a great life, built our family legacy. I will never forget how happy I was when you came back to me."

"You're scaring me. Are you sick?" Becca reached over and felt his forehead, making him laugh.

"No." He lifted her hand away and held it. "But picture this. The outer banks, Jersey Shore, all high tourist areas. I know, there are some others up that way, too, straight up to the Long Island Sound! Think how great it will be to stroll back to North Carolina, to our hometown, as the successful millionaires that we are. I want to show you off, baby. You and the kids are my world. I want our parents to see how happy we are, and my low-down brother, who didn't think we'd last or that I'd ever make anything of myself."

"You have nothing to prove, Greg. You know I love it here in Florida with you. We don't ever have to return to North Carolina."

"It would only be once, for a grand opening. Then I'd hire a crew and management. But I'd want those nay-saying bastards to know how wrong they were. Greg Maddox made it when they didn't believe."

"I always believed, Greg. Even when you were going through those tough times. I knew you'd come back to me. Even when you didn't want the baby, didn't believe me when I told you. There was never anyone else for me but you."

"I will always regret being that kind of man to you. You didn't deserve it, and I don't deserve you." He kissed the back of her hand, looking into brown eyes he never wanted to lose.

"Yes, you do. You built this from nothing. You did it without me. We both struggled on our own until you came to Penny and me with the business already running and prof-itable. I never loved you more. You deserve everything you have coming."

"God, I love you, Becs." He rested his cigar on the edge of the bar, framed her beautifully tanned face in his hands and kissed her with every ounce of passion and love he felt.

Life as they knew it was about to change and nothing was going to stop him.

CHAPTER 11

Dalton walked through the antiseptic smelling halls of the hospital on a mission to get to CeCe's room. Tony had called to tell him Louie Patrone was dead, and CeCe had been badly injured. Dalton hated to think this had happened because of their meeting at the diner. When he reached the door, he nodded to the security officer and walked inside.

"God, CeCe, what happened?" he asked softly as he took a chair next to the bed, glancing at the machines keeping track of her vitals.

Tony had briefed him on her injuries, but nothing, not even all his years in uniform, could have prepared him for the vision of CeCe in front of him. The woman was like a mother to him, and to see her so bruised and weak, wrapped in bandages, shattered his heart in places he didn't think were possible.

He cleared his throat and swallowed the wad of raw emotion. "Did Rocco do this?" Dalton didn't want to believe it but based on what he and Nicki had talked about, his gut told him yes.

"He's dead, Dalton. My Louie…." A tear trailed down her cheek, and he brushed it away while trying to hold back his own.

Louie Patrone was what they liked to call an honest crook. He wasn't dealing in anything too heavy; he stayed within the bounds of the law as far as outside interests, and with the help of CeCe they passed along inside information on anything that wasn't on the up and up. And in turn, he was granted some form of immunity to continue his business.

"I'm so sorry," Dalton said, his chest aching with every word.

"There were six of them." She swallowed back a sob. "They came into our home. Our home, Dalton."

"Six? Did you recognize any of them?" He watched the fright return to her sad, brown eyes as she nodded. "Was it Rocco?" Dalton filled with fury thinking Rocco would sink to this level and injure CeCe in the process. The woman had been nothing but good to them.

"He was there, with my Louie. Then they hit me so hard." She pinched her eyes shut as if feeling the blows all over again. "I don't know if Rocco had anything to do with this."

"Come on, CeCe, he had to." Frustration surged and Dalton had to remind himself the woman was grieving. He took a minute to count to six and reground himself. "I'm sorry."

"You know Rocco has never been able to think for himself," CeCe spoke up, then stopped for a moment, and he could see her trying to catch her breath. Tony told him she had several broken ribs, and a concussion as well as bullets removed from her legs.

"There's no one else who could make a call like that stick." No one in the family had the balls to challenge Louie. But Rocco, he was cocksure to think his were big enough to try.

"There is." The words were barely audible over the drone of hospital equipment. Her eyes glassed over, and a knot formed in Dalton's stomach when she squeezed his hand. "And he had a message for you."

"For me? Who? Why?" She was visibly trembling, and out of reflex Dalton pulled the blanket up to her shoulders. "What did they want you to tell me?" He kept his voice soft as a feeling of dread seemed to settle over them in the small, sanitized room.

"Stay away from that girl." She pinched her eyes tight again and turned away from him as if reliving what had happened next. Dalton watched fresh tears fall, and if she wasn't so beaten, he would have scooped her into a hug.

"What girl? There is no girl," he said out loud, and she turned her head back to him. They stared at each other in silence until the knot in his gut tightened. Samantha had to be the girl in question. Only no one knew of his connection to her, not even Nicki or Tony, and certainly not CeCe. "Wait, you said you recognized one of the men. Someone other than Rocco?"

CeCe pulled her hand from under the blanket and rested it on top of his. Her eyes closed and when she opened them, she searched his face as if trying to find the right words. She exhaled a shaky breath and before she could speak, he knew she was about to confirm the only other person alive who would do something so terrible to Louie.

"Louie said his name and I didn't think I'd heard him correctly. I wasn't sure at first, he looked so different... bigger than I remembered, darker...but that was so long ago. Even his voice sounded smooth, not rough, and edgy like it used to. I thought...I had to be wrong, but...." She closed her eyes again as if fighting some bad dream, only it had been real, and Dalton was beside himself watching her suffer this way.

"It's okay, CeCe. Take your time," he encouraged by rubbing her hand.

"He, he told Rocco to earn his keep and take what was rightfully his." She inhaled sharply. "Oh, I hurt so bad. I could barely open my eyes to focus, but when he came close to give me your message, his eyes were still the same. They were dark brown, cold, and heartless. But how could it be?" A sob escaped her throat, as if everything that had happened was too much. "It was Billy Benning. He's still alive."

"You're sure." Dalton didn't want to believe it either. He'd been chasing a ghost for so long. Hell bent on a vengeance he'd never thought he'd find. "Billy is in New York?" The truth stared back at him in CeCe's tear-filled eyes. In that moment it was like Dalton's world had flipped upside down.

Revenge would soon be his for the taking.

"What will I do without my Louie? How will I go on?" CeCe squeezed his hand, and she seemed so lost. The bossy, proud woman had been replaced with a shell of her former self and the people to blame needed to be held accountable.

Dalton leaned over and kissed her cheek. "I'll find them, CeCe, and I'll make them all pay."

A nurse came to increase CeCe's pain medication, and Dalton stayed until she was comfortably sleeping. He hated to leave her, but the truth of what Rocco and Billy had done refueled his thirst for justice. He needed to go for a run, burn off the surge of adrenaline pinging through every cell in his body. He would have to have a clear head if he ever expected to find and take care of Billy Benning.

"No one enters this room without authorization from me or Detective Cavelli, got it?" he ordered the guard at the door. "The approved medical team and no one else."

"Yes, sir," the officer responded.

Dalton glanced once more at the door before taking the elevator to the street. He felt responsible. He should have done more to ensure CeCe and Louie's safety. Starting now, the hunt was on, and he wasn't going to rest until Billy paid for every innocent life he'd stolen.

Outside, Dalton stood impatiently on the pavement, bouncing on his toes and shaking the tension from his arms as he waited for traffic to clear.

What the hell?

His vision zeroed in on a group of three men, standing close together smoking. The smaller man looked oddly familiar. As he crossed the street, Dalton recognized him immediately and his blood pressure spiked.

"Hey!" he yelled, clenching and unclenching his fists with each step. The men jumped and moved away from the curb. "What the hell are you doing here, Rocco?" When Dalton got close enough, he shoved the man so hard he almost toppled his friends over. "I think you've done enough damage."

Rocco held his hands in the air, the cigarette bobbing between his lips with each word, "Dalton, whoa, settle down. I'm just having a little smoke with some friends."

"In front of the hospital? This isn't your neck of the woods."

"I'm here to check on my poor CeCe. I came as soon as I heard."

"Bullshit." Dalton narrowed his eyes, making contact with each member of the group. "She's already identified you at the scene. You're not getting anywhere near her."

"And what are you going to do about it?" Rocco dropped the cigarette and ground it out with the toe of his sneaker. "She's traumatized and confused. I wasn't there, and these guys right here can vouch for me." He pointed toward his buddies, and they nodded in agreement.

"Did you use your brother's money to pay them off?" Dalton spat. He wanted nothing more than to haul this bastard to jail, where he or Tony could break him. Alone, Rocco was a spineless worm.

"Family business is none of yours, Dalton. I don't give a damn how much my brother and his wife loved you. You're not in this family."

"You're testing my patience, Rocco. I suggest you and your so-called friends crawl back to your own part of town." Dalton stepped close enough to smell the stale beer and cigarettes on Rocco's breath. He could see fear in his eyes and the slight quiver to his lips. When Dalton spoke, his voice was deep and menacing, "You, or anyone associated with you, steps foot in that hospital... I will come back and do far worse to you than you did to Louie and CeCe. Do I make myself clear?"

"C'mon, Rock, let's go." The larger friend tapped Rocco on the shoulder.

"Yeah, this is a waste of time," the other muscle head said and started walking away. "We've got dope to smoke and whores to screw." After a couple steps, the larger friend left Rocco's side to join the muscle head.

"Fuck you guys!" Rocco called after them and then turned on Dalton. "And fuck you, too."

"Oh, I'm going to fuck you all right. And you're never going to see it coming. You're going to wish you'd turned yourself in."

"I told you I didn't do it. She probably had it coming anyway," Rocco announced and straightened his spine attempting to make himself taller. "I'm not afraid of you, Dalton."

"Maybe you should be."

He needed Rocco to lead him to the real mastermind. If Billy was in New York, Rocco knew exactly how to reach him. And when he did, Dalton planned on being there. He forced his lips into a sinister smile, never breaking eye contact with Rocco.

"You haven't seen the last of me Dalton," Rocco yelled as he turned away and slowly jogged after his buddies.

"I'm counting on it."

———

"Thank you for the invitation, Manuel." Greg had been surprised by the call but found himself eager for the new opportunity. "I've reviewed your proposal and I'd be happy to add Maddox Charters to your fleet."

"You have so much to offer, and I believe you will find this partnership to be a very lucrative investment," Manuel's smooth, Latino accent filtered through the phone.

"I'm always looking to diversify my portfolio." It was about time his personal charters got some attention. He'd been playing his cards right over the years, keeping the business lines separate, and it was about to pay off in spades. "Your numbers are impressive. I'm looking forward to the revenue stream."

"Glad to hear you say that. Your money may be flowing sooner than you think," the excitement was prominent in Manuel's voice as Greg pressed the phone to his ear.

"Tell me more, Señor," Greg said in anticipation. The world was becoming his playground and, boy, did he want to play.

"We have new merchandise ready for shipment. Why don't we make this Maddox Charter's virgin voyage?"

"I would like that. I'm eager to show you what my crew can do."

"With you at the helm, I'm sure this will be a trip to remember."

"Me at the helm?" Greg smiled and waved to his kids

kicking a soccer ball around the yard. "I will have to respect-fully decline. Unfortunately, I have other matters I need to attend to."

"You trust your crew alone?" Manuel seemed almost surprised. "You know this is very delicate merchandise and a package deal. Nothing must go wrong."

"I trust my people one hundred percent. If it makes you feel better, I will assign my top trusted associate to oversee the trip." Greg always ran a tight ship, which meant making sure he could never be connected to the job if something went wrong. He'd never had an issue and he never planned to. Everyone he hired understood risk verses reward, and he rewarded them handsomely for a job well executed.

"If you are secure with that decision, then I will be as well. My administrator will advise you when the ship reaches the port of destination. Upon successful transfer of the merchan-dise, full payment of ten million dollars will be wired to an account of your choosing. Does that meet with your approval?"

"Yes, it absolutely does." Greg felt the sweat on his palms. This had to be the easiest ten million he'd ever made. "Give me two days to put together my crew."

"I'll send you the trip itinerary and corresponding docu-mentation."

"May this be the start of a very profitable partnership," Greg said.

And with that, there was no turning back.

CHAPTER 12

"Are you having a good time?" Greg wrapped his arms around Becca and whispered in her ear.

"Of course, I am! We sure can throw one hell of a celebration." She turned in his arms, leaning back against his chest as they looked out over the sea of people who'd come to break ground and celebrate their new charter out of Penny Point.

The marina had been filled all afternoon with community members, families, and media. He and Becca had met some very influential people. Everyone they spoke with conveyed how thrilled they were that the run-down place was getting a major renovation and would supply additional jobs within their community.

And this was only the beginning.

"If you're tired, you can take the kids back to the boat. I won't have Cappie raise the anchor until after breakfast tomorrow. We'll be back in Miami by lunch."

"The kids are having too much fun. Don't worry about me, I'll rally."

"Hey." He spun her to face him. "You do a great job

looking out for the kids, but you need to stay hydrated, too." He worried about her because she tended to be obsessive about her figure and do some crazy fasting shit he couldn't comprehend. He loved her body as is, and she knew it.

"I am." She reached up and kissed him. "And I love how you worry."

"I'd worry less if you'd get out of this heat for a while. I don't think I've seen you eat at all today."

"Fine." She faked a pout. "Make sure you bring the kids back in time to watch the fireworks from the water."

"I will. I want to thank everyone for coming and supporting us, then I'll round up the kids."

"Should I be with you? I can stay if you need me."

"It's okay, babe. This heat is a bitch."

"No, I should be with you. I *am* the supporting wife after all."

He slapped her ass. "Be a good girl and we'll have a private post-firework show." Becca laughed and the space within his pleated shorts became agonizingly tight. She was sexy as hell, always had been. And to think he could have lost this was a thought he had every time he saw his family.

"Don't tease, me," she all but purred, the gleam in her eyes stoking the fire within.

"You know I will, and you'll like it." He leaned in to kiss her, and she devoured his mouth, reminding him of the vixen he could barely tame. He'd better knock off the alcohol for the rest of the night so he could keep up with her. Knowing his wife, she'd want to be fucking the entire way to Miami. His boner throbbed and she moaned, grinding up against it. "Easy now, not here." He laughed and peeled himself away. The heat in her eyes was undeniable.

"Then where? I can't wait." She licked her lips seductively and he felt his own heat on the verge of boiling over. "C'mon, Greg, just a little quickie somewhere. No one's around, I need you right now." Her voice carried the husky tone of a woman in desperate need, and he wanted to fulfill her every wish. He scanned their surroundings looking for a place to lay her down or bend her over.

"Mr. And Mrs. Maddox! I've been looking all over for you," a voice boomed from over his shoulder. Greg turned and brought Becca with him to shield his giant hard-on and took a sip of his water on the high table beside them.

"Mayor Shipper, we're glad you were able to come today." Greg shook his hand.

"Please, call me Paul," he said.

"Of course, Paul. I hope you've enjoyed yourself?" Greg leaned against the edge of a chair, shifting Becca so she was between his legs, and he had easy reach of her. Holding her right hand on top of the table, he slid the fingers of his left hand up under her floral sundress, squeezing her bare ass at the discovery of her lace thong and the easy access it provided. She stiffened briefly, then relaxed when he slipped between her swollen folds. She reached for his water glass with her left hand, took a sip and leaned forward on the table, giving him better entry.

My hot wife, he thought, wanting her even more.

"What's not to enjoy. You've done a wonderful job setting up the future of the marina."

"Thank you." He pushed two fingers inside his wife, and she squeezed his hand. She wasn't about to embarrass them in front of the mayor, but Greg felt like pushing her buttons. He'd bring her to orgasm right in front of Paul, and she'd have to keep quiet. His fingers skillfully moved inside her while he continued his conversation. "Still a work in progress. You know how that goes. I thought the 3-D model and architectural plans and drawings for the remaining space would be helpful. Plus, making it family friendly lets the community know we are here to support the infrastructure."

The mayor nodded and Becca shifted as Greg's fingers worked faster gliding within her hot, wet box. He kept his voice smooth, as his dick throbbed, and he fought the urge to let loose in his shorts.

"I'm expecting four more boats within the next couple of weeks, two of them will be for overnight fishing charters, with four cabins below deck and another on the main level."

"Excellent! You're doing great things to boost our small-town economy. I can't thank you enough for making Penny Point your new home."

"You can thank my daughter, Penny, for that. She's the one who picked this place."

"Well, what do you know! A Penny for a Penny!" Paul roared with laughter, obviously well-fed by the many tall boys he'd had.

Greg took full advantage and locked Becca between his legs, knowing she was about to orgasm. Her body tensed.

"Mrs. Maddox? Are you all right?" Paul asked and Greg inwardly laughed.

"She may have been in the sun too long." His fingers frolicked as her body exploded with liquid heat.

"Yes," she gasped as he removed his fingers. Grabbing the water glass, she quickly drained it. Greg stood taller behind her, wrapping his arm around her waist as her knees buckled slightly.

"It sure has been a hot one." Paul gave them both a curious glance.

"Very hot," Greg said and winked at her.

"Some of us more than others," she said. To Greg's surprise, the eyes of his wife continued to swirl with unspent passion.

"I, I think I should refill my beer." As quick as he came, the mayor waved toward someone and was off to socialize.

"Just wait 'til I get ahold of you later," Becca said against his ear and nipped at its lobe. Reaching down, she rubbed her hand along the ridge in his shorts. "Let's have another baby," the words floated as hot puffs against his skin. With all the good fortune in their life, Greg was more than ready to give her as many as she wanted.

"Then I suggest you prepare to get busy." He kissed her long and hard, probing his tongue the way his cock would soon be inside her. "We just need to sneak away from all these people."

"I'm ready when you are."

"Excuse me, Mr. Maddox?"

Greg turned and put on the brakes, staring into dark brown eyes of a woman rivaling his wife in the hotness department. Her black hair was swept off her neck with pieces falling in waves around her face. Her skin was naturally tan, and she wore a lilac t-shirt dress which clung to curves he'd pay good money to appreciate in person. He found himself wondering what it would be like to be sandwiched between this woman and his wife for just one night.

"Honey?" Becca poked his ribs before addressing the gorgeous woman before them. The hint of jealousy in her voice peaked his lust even more. "I'm sorry, you are?"

"Bianca Cavelli, your husband and I spoke a couple days ago. We handle your business acquisitions and loans." She extended her hand, and in a flash, he remembered their conversation.

"Of course, Bianca! I'm so glad you could make it to Florida. Please excuse my manners, this is my wife, Becca. We were so engrossed in our conversation you took me by surprise." He smiled and hoped he'd covered any awkwardness either woman may have picked up on.

"I ran into the mayor, and he told me where to find you. As I approached you did appear to be rather preoccupied." Bianca flashed a knowing grin. "I apologize for interrupting."

"No interruption at all. We were discussing making our rounds of good-byes, gathering up the kids and heading back to our yacht to watch the fireworks."

"You're welcome to join us," Becca offered, and Greg's balls ached thinking his amazing wife was going to make his fantasy come true. "I know Greg has been thrilled with the service he's received with your company."

"Yes, please join us." He hoped he didn't sound too eager.

"I appreciate the offer, but I'm meeting an old friend for dinner. After your invitation to the Penny Point opening, I wanted to stop by and personally deliver these." She reached into her purse and pulled out two gold-foiled tickets, extending them toward Greg and Becca. "Two tickets to our Top Performers Award Gala at the end of the month, in Manhattan."

"Tickets?" Greg took the small, golden vouchers.

"My company is up for an award thanks to you and your business projects. I'd also like to personally thank you for referring so many of your friends. It's only fitting you and your wife are there as our special guests, to celebrate with us. I'd also love for you to meet Samantha Taylor in person. She's my associate who has personally overseen your project from start to finish."

"I've heard wonderful things about her from my legal team. I look forward to meeting her."

"So, are we going to New York?" Becca asked, her voice rising with excitement.

"We're going to New York!" he confirmed. Becca jumped into his arms, and he nodded his approval toward Bianca. "We haven't been in a few years, this will make a nice getaway, thank you."

"Oh, honey, will this event interfere with your other meetings?" Becca's face lost a little of the excitement over the possibility.

"No, not at all. I will be there the week before. I'll send the jet to pick you up toward the end of the week. Don't worry, we'll still have our getaway." The spark returned to her eyes, confirming her love and trust in him. There was no way he'd fail her.

This invitation couldn't have come at a better time. Greg had a couple projects requiring some follow up. At night, they'd live like the king and queen they were, and Becca would love every minute of it. She was used to fending for herself during the day while he got down and dirty in the trenches.

He never had a problem rolling up his sleeves and taking care of business.

———

THE NEXT DAY AFTER SAILING HOME AND PUTTING THE KIDS TO bed, Greg was eager to plan his meetings in New York. There were several projects he needed to catch up on, and one of them was the security system at the condo. The new system was up and running, but Erik had yet to identify the person caught on camera with the old system. Greg decided to chalk it up as a lost cause at this point. He had his own hunches, which he planned to personally look into once he arrived in the city that never sleeps.

He sure as shit hadn't slept soundly since seeing that video footage.

"Hey, Becs, give me thirty minutes to make a couple calls and then we can watch a movie."

"Work, really? Honey, you've been on for the last two days. Take tonight off, please?"

"It's what I do, babe." He leaned down to kiss her, whispering in her ear, "I do believe I took off at least four times last night, you naughty girl."

"You had it coming remember, for what you put me through in front of the mayor." She laughed then fell back against the sofa, hugging a pillow. "Go ahead, do your work thing. But I'm picking the movie and you can't complain."

"Thirty minutes, I promise." He jogged toward his office calling, "And we're watching it upstairs. I feel like taking off again."

Greg sat at his computer and pulled up the new security camera footage. The extra money for the live feed was worth it. He'd been so busy he hadn't had a chance to download the app for his phone or even check on things since it had been installed.

About time Erik earned his pay, he thought. The doorman had done exactly as Greg had ordered and made sure the security on his building was updated immediately. The system included a personal camera with a pass protected link where Greg could drop in, at will, through the camera for a real time experience. It was the suggestion from Erik on where to mount the personal camera, which earned him the five-thousand-dollar bonus Greg had wired him.

Greg clicked the link and leaned back in his chair as the beautiful young girl appeared in a sports bra and yoga pants. Her hair was in a high ponytail, and he felt like a kid in a candy shop when he realized he could zoom in by using the track ball on his mouse. He was enjoying the show, watching her bend and stretch in a variety of positions which made his mouth water and his dick hard, when his phone rang. He recognized the number even though he purposely left the name out of his contact list. Safety was always a top priority, he understood that once he became one of the wealthy.

"Victor! How the hell are you?"

"Very well, Greg, thank you. I wanted to thank you for referring me to BC Acquisitions. I've talked in depth with

Mrs. Cavelli, and she has insisted I work with Samantha who she said also handles your accounts."

"She does." While Greg was happy many of his friends were hooking up with BCA, he didn't necessarily want to share Samantha. "I think you're going to be very happy with her. My legal team sings her praises. As a matter of fact, I'm going to be attending their award ceremony in a couple of weeks and will get to meet Samantha in person. I'll be sure to report back." Greg laughed, hoping Victor would take the hint.

"I hear from Manuel your charter will be transporting my special cargo."

"He never mentioned to me the shipment was yours." He pulled up his email ready to lambast Manuel for putting him in this position so soon in their partnership.

"I told him not to, although I'm sure his administrator will tell you when they send the manifest. My bride will be aboard your boat."

"Well congratulations." Greg hoped he could keep the agitation out of his voice. "Tell me her name and I'll make sure she has an extra special experience."

"That won't be necessary, Greg. She already knows she's special, and I don't want her treated any differently than your other guests. All the young ladies should be celebrating their new lives to come."

"Of course! I wasn't implying the others would be treated differently. Each one of them will receive attentive service during their journey, you have nothing to worry about." Victor's attitude was making Greg mad. He had plenty to worry about going into the next couple of weeks on top of dealing with this pompous jerk. He needed to cut this call short and make the proper arrangements.

"Manuel said your crew is one of the best you have."

"All of my employees understand the importance of their positions. They can be trusted."

"Glad to hear."

"If you'll excuse me, Victor, I'm due to be on another call. No rest for the wicked, am I right?" He faked a laugh, already tired of dealing with this man and hoped he wouldn't have to make other deliveries for him any time soon.

"Wicked," Victor laughed. "I like you, Greg. Manuel was right to suggest you as a partner. We are about to become wealthier men, my friend. I'll be in touch."

The line went dead, and Greg shrugged off Victor's pompous behavior. If the money poured in as easily as this first ten million, he could handle that asshole any day of the week. Pulling up his contact list, he decided to check in and make sure everything was set.

"Hey," came a sleepy voice on the other end of the line. "Everything okay? You never call on a weekend."

"Listen, I need to make sure you are one hundred percent up for this trip."

"Yeah, I am. I've been ready. You know I can handle this."

"I just got off the phone with Victor Perez. This shipment is his."

"Shit, really?"

"Yes, really." Greg tried not to sound as annoyed as he felt. "This is a clean run, do you understand? No one touches these women, not even if they beg to be touched. Hands off, got it?"

"Sure." There was a pause. "Then what are we supposed to do with them? It's kind of a long trip to Isla Margarita."

Greg slapped his palm against his forehead and bit back the words he really wanted to say. "Keep them happy. They are young, beautiful women. Let them sunbathe, play some dance music for them, or anchor for a swimming break. Give them the experience of a lifetime. But by no means will you bring out the drugs or have sex with any of them. Do I make myself clear?"

"Yeah, I get it, boss."

"I'm giving you this leadership position. Don't make me regret it."

Greg disconnected the call and sat at his desk with an ache deep in the pit of his stomach. His instincts told him he should be on that boat. But damn it, the chance of a lifetime was waiting for him, and there were preparations to be made.

CHAPTER 13

The water had a way of swallowing sound. Nicki Morgan crouched low behind a stack of overturned lobster traps, her breath warming the inside of her jacket collar. It was just past 2 a.m., and every instinct screamed at her that she shouldn't be there—not alone, not unarmed, not without backup. But instincts had never kept her from chasing leads before.

Her contact at the department hadn't even given her a name. Just a murmured warning that someone was using the marina after hours—cash drops, maybe more—and that if she wanted eyes on the Patrone thread, this was the time and place to look.

Nicki adjusted her grip on her phone, the camera open and ready. The battery was low, but the lens was angled toward the empty slip near the end of the dock where a fishing boat, *Sea Valor*, bobbed gently in the current.

Salt and diesel filtered through the cool evening air. In the distance, a buoy bell tolled, a hollow sound that seemed to mark the minutes until dawn. Her pulse thudded in her ears as she stayed motionless, waiting.

Then, faint footsteps on wood.

She tensed. Two figures emerged from the darkness, moving fast but not furtive—too casual, too confident. One was Rocco. She recognized his frame, the stiff-shouldered walk. The other...taller, hoodie pulled low, keeping to the shadows. They met at the edge of the dock near *Sea Valor*, where a dull metal case exchanged hands.

She snapped a photo.

Too blurry.

She tried again. Another click, flash off, but her heart jumped. Had they heard that? The hooded man said something sharp, voice low and tight. Rocco shifted uneasily. Money changed hands next. A thick envelope. She strained to hear.

"...Tell him it's done," the hooded man said. "He doesn't make the next call until I say so."

Nicki leaned forward. That voice—familiar? Or was it just the nerves playing tricks?

Wind off the water stirred the traps beside her, a hollow clatter that made her flinch. She stilled them with a gloved hand, but the hooded man turned. His head angled toward her hiding spot like a predator catching scent.

Damn it.

Nicki froze, every muscle tight. Her breath misted once, twice, before she held it completely. The men both turned toward the sound. Nicki ducked lower, breath caught in her throat. She didn't move. Didn't blink.

"Thought you heard something?" Rocco grunted, half mocking.

The other man didn't answer at first. He stepped closer to the edge of the dock, boots scraping the wet boards. The motion light above the bait shack flickered once, then twice, and then the dock was bathed in a wash of pale gold before it clicked off again.

The brief flash illuminated his hands. He wore black, leather gloves with a perfectly sized fit. Even wearing the hoodie, he wasn't a typical dock worker. Nicki pressed lower, resting her shoulder into the damp wood, camera angled through a crack in the traps.

She caught a fragment of dialogue, faint but distinct over the lapping of the water against the dock.

"Shipment's light," Rocco sputtered.

"Weight's right," the hooded man replied. "You counting ghosts now?"

"We can move more. You sure the route's clear?"

"Don't question how I do business. I make it clear and you do what I tell you."

A long pause followed, broken by the metallic click of a lighter. The hooded man lit a cigarette, the ember a small red eye in the dark.

"We're burning hot already," Rocco continued, unbothered by the man's bossiness. "If he's spooked—"

"He won't be," the man cut in. "He's too busy cleaning up his own mess. You tell him that."

Nicki's stomach lurched. *He*. Always a *he*. Never a name.

Her phone vibrated once, barely a buzz, but in the dead quiet it sounded like thunder in her ears. She slapped a hand over it, but the screen had already lit up. A soft glow spilled through the gaps in the traps, landing on the slick wood beside her.

The hooded man stopped talking.

Nicki's pulse rocketed. The glow dimmed as the phone screen went dark again. She forced herself to stay still. *Don't run. Don't breathe. Don't move.*

"You hear that?" Rocco's voice sounded uneasy now.

"Shut up," the other man grumbled. "Hold on."

A gull cried somewhere over them, and the hooded man turned his head sharply toward the sound. For a breathless moment, Nicki thought he'd seen her shadow within the traps until he flicked his cigarette into the water, the ember dying immediately.

"No one's here," he said, finally satisfied. "You're too jumpy."

Rocco grumbled something, but Nicki couldn't make it out. The men turned back toward the metal case. The hooded man crouched and cracked it open. She caught a glint of something inside. It appeared metal, shaped and packed tight. Could it be gun parts or something worse?

Snap. Her camera clicked again, quieter this time.

"Next meeting is inland, got it? Warehouse, not water." The man ordered.

"He's going to want details."

"Tell him to stop asking questions and leave the details to me."

Rocco spat into the water. "You talk a lot for someone who doesn't want to be found."

The hooded man's head tilted slightly, amusement or warning—it was hard to tell. "And yet, here we are."

Something in his tone sent a shiver creeping up Nicki's spine.

In the distance she heard the faint hum of a boat engine. Out on the dark water, another vessel's running lights glowed red and green as it eased closer to the marina. The men turned instinctively toward it.

Nicki used the distraction to crawl backward, slow and silent, retreating to the path that wound back toward the parking lot. Her heart thundered.

Halfway there, a flashlight beam swept across the docks from the direction of the harbormaster's shack. A night guard possibly, who called out. "Who's down there?"

Both men froze. Nicki pressed herself flat against the piling, the rough wood scraping her cheek.

"Get rid of him," the hooded man hissed.

"And say what?" Rocco spat back.

"Figure it out."

Rocco started up the dock, shoulders squared, calling out "Hey! Just me! Had to grab some gear. Bait order came late!"

The guard muttered something indistinct, his light wavering before he moved in the opposite direction.

When Nicki dared look again, the hooded man was gone. Vanished like the evening mist. Only Rocco remained, shaking his head as he took the metal case inside Sea Valor's cabin. The boat engine flared to life, loud and sudden. Nicki flinched but kept moving, faster now, boots silent on the gravel path.

She didn't breathe until the sound of the boat faded behind her.

At her car, she checked the photos. One was just shadows. One showed Rocco's side. The last…the profile. Not clear. Not identifiable.

But enough to raise questions.

Nicki stared at the grainy image. She didn't know him. But something about the set of his jaw, the cool stillness in his posture—it felt familiar. Or dangerous. Or both.

She hadn't told Dalton she was doing this. Hadn't told anyone.

And now she had proof of something. She just didn't know what.

CHAPTER 14

"How are you doing, love?" Nicki asked as she draped Dalton's tuxedo jacket on the back of the brown leather recliner. He'd been distracted and slightly short-tempered all afternoon.

Wood, leather, and basically bare walls...a typical bachelor pad. Not that she cared, they spent equal time at each other's apartments. One of these days she was going to make some of her things permanent here in Upper Manhattan, just to see if he noticed. Nothing too feminine, but something more than her shampoo and toothbrush to remind him of her when she wasn't here.

"He's here. The damn ghost of my nightmares is in my city, and I'm locked into attending some ridiculous award ceremony," he replied, "instead of combing the streets and calling in every favor I have."

"You can call off, you know." She stood behind him with her forehead resting between his muscular shoulders, breathing him in body and soul. She knew how important finding Billy and avenging his brother, Justin's, death was to him. A piece of his past he could finally close the door on.

With that, she hoped he'd be able to really start living, no longer for revenge but for himself. "She'll understand if you tell her, it's the job…which technically it is."

"I'm sure she would. But this is a big deal for her, and Bianca, too."

"Then how come I didn't get an invite?" Nicki moved to stand in front of him with her arms crossed. "It's because I snubbed the barbecue, isn't it? C'mon, you can tell me."

"I seriously doubt it." He smiled and walked over to his liquor cabinet "Pre-game?" He held up the scotch bottle.

"Of course! I can't let you drink alone." She joined him as he filled a glass and handed it to her. "Is there something else troubling you besides this ridiculous event? CeCe is stable, I keep checking in with the hospital."

"Thank you. She's still got security, right?" He looked up from filling his glass, worry clouding his eyes. "I want a team on Rocco, too."

"Already on it." Nicki sipped the scotch, the warmth of the liquid moving through her body. Her answer didn't seem to relieve his tension. She could bounce a quarter off him, he was wound so tight. Rightfully so. This was the closest to Billy they had been in years. This event was piss-poor timing.

"I don't trust Billy won't try to finish off CeCe. Rocco either for that matter." He closed his eyes, breathing deep the aroma of his drink before taking a long sip. "Dammit."

"Nothing will happen to CeCe. We'll find Billy. I'll round up my own favors while you're out having fun. Leave the woman to do the work, no worries."

"You're the best." He glanced at his watch, tossed back his drink, and gave her a quick kiss on the cheek. "I gotta run. Enjoy the scotch. There's Chinese takeout in the fridge."

"From last week?" She wrinkled her nose.

"No, from last night." He laughed. "And do me a favor?"

"Anything."

"Be here when I get back? We need to talk this through. This opportunity has me so high- strung. I can't miss it. I've got to find him."

"Of course." She watched him head for the door. "Dalton, wait!" Grabbing his jacket, she rushed to catch him. "Don't forget this." She held it open for him to slip his arms inside, then straightened the lapels while he buttoned up. "Maybe we can play double agent later?" She planted a firm kiss on his delicious lips. He pulled away, the spark in his green eyes heating her more than the scotch ever could.

"I'd like that," he replied, displaying a huge grin before closing the door. In half a beat she flung the door open, not allowing him the last word. She caught him right before he stepped into the elevator.

"You'll most certainly like it. Best be home before curfew!" she called and received a thumbs-up before the elevator door slid closed. God, she enjoyed messing with him, probably more than she should.

———

SAMANTHA STEPPED OUT OF THE CAB IN FRONT OF THE MASSIVE luxury hotel in upper Manhattan. Dalton waved and approached, looking amazing in his tuxedo. She loved black tie events. She'd been to enough charity dinners over the years, but nothing of this magnitude. She'd been anticipating this moment for weeks. There were times when she thought Dalton might back out. Looking at him now, she was so glad he didn't.

"You clean up pretty good, detective." She purposely eyed him up and down which made him laugh, his rich vibrato touching her deeply. Tonight had finally arrived, and this handsome man was hers for the evening.

"And you look gorgeous." He kissed her cheek and a warm feeling settled over her.

She'd chosen a red gown which dipped low in the back and the heat of his palm against her skin started a slow burn deep in her core. His compliment meant everything. She hadn't been able to stop thinking about him. More than anything, she wanted him to see her as something other than the friend-zone-vibe she'd continuously picked up on.

"Thank you." Due to their schedules, she and Dalton hadn't been able to connect since she'd asked him to attend. Tonight felt like an unofficial date of sorts, which she hoped would turn into the first of many.

His energy was contagious, and she couldn't stop herself from gushing as they walked into the grand hotel lobby. White lights wrapped every column within sight, and banners from all the attending firms hung in welcome. She felt so proud to be representing BC Acquisitions alongside Bianca, and even more proud to have Dalton on her arm.

"What's going on in that head of yours? You're absolutely beaming."

"I'm so glad you wanted to come with me. It's such a big night for Bianca's company. She's put so much faith in me, and I'm thrilled beyond belief she's happy with my efforts."

"You don't have to worry about a thing. Bianca sees you as her star. She's going to make sure you continue to rise and shine."

"Gee, no pressure." She paused, thoughtful. "Want to know the best news?"

"Sure, what's that?" He flagged the bartender once they reached the massive mahogany bar. The next thing she knew he was handing her a glass of red wine while he held a rocks glass containing what she assumed by its deep amber color, was scotch.

"I get to meet my client tonight." The words came out in a

rush of excitement. "Bianca invited Greg Maddox to the event because, thanks to his deal, we are getting this magnificent award."

"That's great." Dalton's hand once again found the small of her back as he escorted her away from the crowded bar to a high-top table adorned with a fancy glass floral arrangement in the center. "What kind of deal was it?"

"It's called the Penny Point Project, down in the Florida Keys. Once it's complete, it will be Maddox Charters at Penny Point. It's going to do so much for the surrounding towns and villages. He already owns a bunch of charters in Florida. He's starting with this small expansion for now but told Bianca he's planning to add additional boats and start scouting for other properties along the east coast."

"Interesting." There was a moment of awkward silence and Sam wondered if she was boring him when he asked, "What kind of charters?"

"I guess he's looking to do some deep-sea fishing and whale watch type cruises."

"That's good." Again, with the short answers. He suddenly appeared preoccupied as his eyes scanned the room in every direction but at her. Sam sipped her wine, trying to cover her anxiety. She'd anticipated this night for weeks, and they'd just gotten there. She couldn't bear to think it was going south so fast.

"Hey, what's going on?" She placed her hand on his forearm to get his attention. "You seem a little off all of a sudden."

"I'm sorry. It's just work." He shook his head, obviously embarrassed. While she felt relief it wasn't her, she also didn't want her date to be consumed with anything other than her company. He'd been so easy to talk to at the pier, she decided to keep the conversation going in hopes he would work through whatever was bothering him.

Nothing was going to hinder their evening together.

"I didn't think you were back on duty yet."

"Not officially." He air-quoted. "But even Tony knows I can't sit idle, and I'm not the desk jockey kind of guy."

"What do you do then if you can't be out in the field?" She had to ask, wanting to know as much as possible about him. Bianca had called his life complicated, and Sam needed to know why. He never mentioned a girlfriend, and she secretly hoped she could take that title at some point.

"Mostly follow up with informants for some of the cases I'm working on, along with a couple pet projects I'm trying to build cases for."

"Ohhh, that sounds so secretive." She took another sip of wine.

"It has to be," his gaze locked on her intensely, "so I'm trusting you not to say anything to Bianca or Tony."

"Cross my heart." She smiled when his eyes followed her finger as she made an X on her chest where the material created a diamond shaped cut-out, exposing her skin. "Looks like I've been doing all the talking, and you've been doing all the drinking." She reached for his glass. "Let me get you another."

He raised his gaze back up to hers. "I'm fine for a while. Why don't we catch up with Bianca?"

"Sure," she answered just as the heady scent of bergamot, sage, and cedarwood floated like an invisible mist in the air before her, causing her to stop motion and slowly breathe it in. She'd smelled it before, but when and where? She quickly turned her head from left to right in search of who might be wearing it.

"Sam, what's wrong?" Dalton's voice sounded far away, and she felt his grip on her arm tighten.

"Did you smell that?"

"Smell what?"

"It was right here." She breathed deep, but it had vanished. "Someone's cologne, I think. It smelled like bergamot, cedarwood, and sage. It seemed familiar and I can't figure out why."

"I don't smell a thing," Dalton responded. "The place is filling up. It could have been anyone." She watched as he, too, scanned the immediate area.

"Yeah, you're right." She shrugged, deciding to let the odd feeling go instead of hyper focusing on it. "If there's dancing later, will you dance with me?"

"Let's just say dancing is not my forte." His voice turned serious again, and she felt his wall being resurrected between them once more.

"Don't worry, I can lead." She shot him a hopeful glance over her shoulder as they weaved through the crowd toward the center table where Bianca stood, talking to other colleagues.

"I didn't say I couldn't lead." He kept his face neutral, but his words sent a trill of excitement across her skin.

His forearm grazed her shoulder as he pointed for her to watch where she was going, and she loved the intimate closeness of him. Hope blossomed in her chest once more. She'd never met anyone as mysterious and sexy as Dalton Riley.

CHAPTER 15

When Dalton and Sam reached the table, they were greeted with hugs and kisses from Bianca. Tony shook hands with him and kissed Sam's cheek. Dalton hadn't seen Sam in a couple of weeks and tonight she was stunning. He'd always known she would grow up to be a beautiful woman.

Her blond hair was styled in a braided twist at the nape of her neck, with loose pieces framing her face. She wore classy pearl earrings and a double strand pearl choker. The red-hot figure-hugging dress with its sexy as hell cut-outs made her runway model ready and worried the hell out of him. With an event of this magnitude there were sure to be predators everywhere.

He kept scanning the room.

Meanwhile, confidence vibrated off her. She appeared relaxed and in her element. He created some distance and stood next to Tony, remembering all too well the dreamy look in her eyes during their evening at the pier.

He didn't want to lead her on. His life was complicated and about to be more so, with Billy on the loose. He'd noticed other eyes on Sam since they'd arrived, and he didn't like it. He silently cursed. All the more reason for him to stay close, just in case any one of these strangers had come to watch her and report back to Billy.

The talk, of course, was centered around other prominent guests from the city and senior leadership from the parent company who continued to sing Bianca's praises for record third quarter numbers. Dalton observed Samantha taking part in conversations like she'd been with the company since the beginning. He was proud of her for stepping up to such a big role. She glanced at him and smiled. For a moment he wondered if she'd somehow read his thoughts. He returned the smile until something across the room caught his eye.

It couldn't be....

He placed a hand on Tony and Sam's shoulders and spoke softly as he prepared to exit the group. "Excuse me for a moment, I think I see someone I know. I'll get you another glass of wine. Be right back."

He worked his way through the crowd, searching for the blonde in the sequined black dress. She couldn't have gone far, but the ballroom had gotten fuller since he'd arrived, and he began to wonder if it was just a coincidence. Was he so obsessed with the fact Billy was in New York that he was conjuring others from the past? He paused and scanned the room in a complete circle.

Nothing.

Maybe all this Patrone business was finally taking a toll. Could he be trying to fabricate relationships where there were none? In his gut he knew there had to be a connection. He approached the bar, ordering another scotch and Sam's red wine when he heard a familiar voice behind him address the bartender.

"Excuse me, hon, when you get a minute, I'll take another double gin and tonic."

Dalton froze for a moment, taking in the tone, the hint of southern inflection. It had been years since he'd seen her. Could he be this lucky? Sliding his shoulder between two other patrons, he took his drinks from the bartender, who then reached past him with a rocks glass topped with lime.

"For the lady."

"Rebecca?" Dalton turned to gaze into brown eyes he'd known so long ago. She'd always been pretty, but the woman before him was a knockout. Her curly blonde hair was pulled up into some elegant style with twinkling gemstone clips and single curls framing her face. She appeared shocked to see him as well.

"D-Dalton?" she stuttered. "Oh my God, what are you doing here?" She leaned in as if she were going to give him a kiss, then pulled back abruptly and backed away. Her complexion had paled. "I thought you were dead."

"You're not the first person to tell me that over the years." He chuckled thinking of CeCe when she'd seen him for the first time, years after the accident. "I'm here with my date." He held up both drinks. "And you?" He asked, feeling validated that he hadn't imagined her.

"I'm with my husband." Her eyes darted about the room. "He's here somewhere…I think."

"How have you been? You look fantastic." Dalton rushed to get the small talk out of the way. "The last time I saw you was right before we shoved off. I think you'd just told Billy you were pregnant."

"Thanks, I've been good," she responded, continuing to scan the crowd around them. "Yeah, I think you're right." Becca didn't make eye contact for more than a second before she continued her search, probably for her husband. She stepped back a little and Dalton moved with her. He had to get to the point before her husband showed up and he lost what could be his only chance.

"Hey, I gotta ask…do you know where I can find Billy?" They'd been a tight group all those years ago. Billy didn't believe her about the baby, and they'd gotten in a huge fight. She'd left in tears, and Billy fired up the boat Louie loaned him to sail with the group of rich kids. Dalton could never forget that day.

That was where it all started.

"I don't run in those circles anymore, Dalton." She kept her voice quiet as if not to let anyone know the kind of background she came from, the kind they all had come from.

"I thought maybe, over the years, he might have reached out to you. If he did, or if you know of his last known address, I need to contact him. It's kind of important." Dalton could tell by the way she continually avoided his eyes and fidgeted with her drink she was very uncomfortable around him. But he had to probe one step further. "You had the baby, right? Billy's baby."

"I did. A daughter." She sipped her drink, and he noticed how the ice in the glass clinked as she tipped it and continued to scan the crowd. "I also have three sons. My life is different now." He caught sight of the large, brilliant diamond on her left hand.

"I can see that." He felt deflated thinking for a moment Rebecca would be the key to finding Billy. But just like Dalton, she'd found a better life for herself and fortunately, from the sound of it, had been able to put the past behind her. That was where they differed.

He didn't know if he ever could.

"If you don't mind me asking, when was the last time you spoke to Billy? I mean, you were upset, but I think at some point you'd want to prove to him the baby was his. Did you ever reach out? Or did he ever contact you?"

"Dalton, I don't know what you want me to say." She took a long drink from her glass this time, almost draining it, and the cop in him wondered if she was drawing on liquid courage to give him the information he needed. He tried to disguise his excitement by taking a drink of his scotch while Becca took a deep breath and exhaled as if resigning herself to speak the truth. "We—"

"Excuse me, Mrs. Maddox, you're needed for pictures." Two men in suits, wearing security earpieces stepped in and whisked Rebecca away before she could answer. In the second it took Dalton to decide to follow, she had disappeared once again.

"Damn it." He muttered. Then he emptied his glass and Sam's wine before deciding he wasn't ready for her to disappear. He found it too much of a coincidence Rebecca would be in New York the same time Billy was supposed to be here. Rebecca knew something, and he was going to find out what that was.

Tonight.

———

GREG GLANCED AROUND THE LOUD, CROWDED BALLROOM wondering what happened to Becca. She'd gone to get another drink, which seemed like forever. He'd been talking with Bianca and her detective husband when the blonde in the silky red dress approached. She moved in graceful strides, exuding a confidence he found sexy as hell. When she reached the group, the smile she blessed them with was almost his undoing.

The resemblance was incredible.

"Oh, here she is." Bianca boasted. "The star of the night. Greg, I'd like to introduce you to Samantha Taylor."

Greg felt starstruck. She was more beautiful in person. An anxious sweat crept across his skin under his tuxedo. It was like he'd stepped back in time.

"Mr. Maddox, it's a pleasure to meet you." Samantha extended her hand, and when he placed it in his own and kissed the back of it, he couldn't help but inhale the intoxicating scent of her. God yes, the taste of her skin on his lips was as delicious as he'd imagined her mother's golden skin would have been. He straightened up and smiled.

"The pleasure is all mine, Ms. Taylor. And please, call me Greg."

"Then you must call me Sam."

"Ah, the amazing Sam." He squeezed her hand before letting go, casting a wink toward Bianca. He had to pull himself together, yet he couldn't stop taking her all in. The way her dress caressed every inch of her skin as if wrapping a glorious present for him alone. Her mother had denied him, and rightfully so, he'd been a little rough around the edges back then.

But now…oh, how he wanted her daughter.

If he played his cards right, he might have the chance of a lifetime. But not if he spooked this beautiful fawn. If he didn't keep his shit together, Sam and her hot box of a boss would get suspicious. He could almost see the wheels turning behind Bianca's detective husband's judging eyes.

Fuck him.

That man had no idea what Greg had gone through to get to this moment. It wasn't how he'd planned, but it was a miraculous start. And there was something endearing about seeing the girl after all this time. Greg always knew he wasn't the monster her mother thought him to be, and her success here tonight proved it. He felt all eyes on him as he tried to think of something to say when he caught a glimpse of Becca.

"Here comes my lovely wife now." He raised a hand to motion them over, faster. "Becca, I'd like to introduce you to Sam. She's the superstar at BC Acquisitions Bianca told us about. Sam, my wife, Rebecca Maddox."

"Pleased to meet you," Becca said on a shaky breath as she extended her hand. Greg cast a curious glance at her. Something was wrong with his beautiful, usually put-together wife. When it came to entertaining, or being the prize on his arm, she was always on her game.

What the hell had happened at the bar?

Greg scanned the direction from which she'd come and didn't see anything out of the ordinary. He'd sent her with their security detail. Hey, when your worth millions you can never be too careful. He didn't know who might be around to recognize him while they were in the city. Thank God he'd taken care of a couple problems before they arrived.

"Everything okay, sweetheart? Did you get a call from home?" He placed an arm around her shoulders. "First time leaving all four kids with the nanny. She's been a wreck."

"No." Her eyes gazed at him wildly. She was lying, he could tell. "Home, home is fine."

"Then do I need to have words with someone at the bar?" He tweaked his wife's perfect nose, glancing from Sam and Bianca, back to Becca. He chuckled, trying to make light of a situation which now began to sour in his gut. This was not like Becca. One of the security team stepped toward them.

"Sir, the Gala committee would like to take some group pictures over by their sign. Everyone is waiting."

"Oh, yes," Sam chimed in with a slight bounce of excitement as if just now remembering. Her perky breasts shifted freely beneath the shimmering material of her gown, and Greg felt the stirring of lust return. "Bianca said she wanted to make sure to get pictures of all of us." Sam displayed a genuine concern as she asked his wife, "Do you have a few minutes?"

The slim fitting tux didn't give Greg much room as his body reacted. He attempted to adjust his stance, grateful when they all started moving. He kept his arm around Becca and slowed their pace.

"What's going on?" he said softly against her ear.

"I can't." She shook her head. "Not here."

"Do we need to step outside?" he asked as they approached the group, not expecting to have been heard.

"Is everything okay?" Bianca asked. "Becca, you don't look well."

"I'm afraid my stomach is a little off tonight. Must be from the travel." Becca placed a hand on her stomach. "I'm sorry." She glanced up at Greg and he realized drawing attention to his wife was the perfect distraction to any odd behavior he might have exhibited.

"Sweetheart, do you think you're pregnant already?" He placed his hand over hers with all the excitement and sincerity he'd feel when she actually did conceive again. He loved being a father, a provider, a wealthy man who others practically begged for money. "Maybe you shouldn't be drinking."

"Oh, my goodness!" Bianca cried out. "Congratulations, that's exciting news." Her eyes met Greg's, and he could see her counting dollar signs. More kids meant more income to support them, and she already mentioned the enchanting Samantha would be handling all his future business, which made him very happy…for many reasons.

"Heavens no," Becca answered and laughed. "I know I'm fertile, but we literally just decided to try again, and let's just say my husband's schedule hasn't been very open lately."

"Well…there was that time—"

"Greg!" Her eyes grew wide, and he noticed the blush highlight her pale face. "You're terrible."

"But I got you to smile."

"Thanks. I don't mean to ruin everyone's evening. My gin

and tonics were very good, but I haven't really had much to eat tonight."

"My wife has a habit of not eating," he scolded, and Bianca turned to address her husband.

"Baby, why don't you take Mrs. Maddox back to the buffet and make sure she has something to eat. The pictures with Rebecca can wait, and we can get started with Greg."

"Of course," the detective dutifully responded.

"That's not necessary. I can take her." The last thing Greg wanted was his anxious wife alone with the police detective. Cavelli would ask all the right questions, and Becca would be none the wiser. Until he knew exactly what was going on, she wasn't leaving his sight.

"Tony can handle it." Bianca nudged her husband. "We really need you for pictures. I can tell you're worried, so we'll be conscious of your time."

Before Greg knew what was happening, Bianca hooked his elbow and escorted him to the giant banner for BC Acquisitions. Bile rose in his throat as he watched Becca leave with Detective Cavelli. Greg couldn't overlook the curious stare from the detective. If he suspected anything, he was going to subtly question Becca until he got the information he needed. Greg trusted his wife explicitly, but he never trusted the law, and he still had no idea what had made her so spooked.

"Greg, why don't you stand in the middle?" Bianca said, taking charge and distracting him from his worries. And oh, how he loved a powerful woman.

"Of course." He smiled and positioned himself between the women, placing his hands at their waists and loving every second of it. His thumb grazed Samantha's skin through a side cut-out of her dress. He moved it and smiled apologetically. He couldn't love this as much as he wanted. Damn it, he had to get to Becca. He kept an eye on the clock as the photographer positioned them and moved them to a couple other locations.

This was the kind of shit the elite ate up, and now he understood why. Everyone doted on him. Servers begged to serve, the photographer apologized a million times for having to adjust his tuxedo, or physically move him into position. And the women…they giggled and fawned all over him. As they should. He'd put a lot of money through them to retain Penny Point, and he wasn't kidding when he said there would be more. He glanced at the striking young Samantha.

Especially now.

He had another reason to come to the city. *Well, two,* he thought as his gaze roamed over both sexy women, but he'd only be able to get away with that once. Seeing Samantha now, all grown up and so much like her mother, made him want even more what he had been deprived of. Knowing where she was and keeping tabs on her was one thing, but finding out she worked at BCA and was the key associate to his accounts? That was a sheer twist of fate.

The game changer had been being able to meet her face to face.

He hadn't been too concerned with recognition. His hair had been long back then and bleached by the sun and salt. He'd had an unkempt beard and was way too scrawny thanks to all the drug use. He didn't resemble his former self at all. Over the years, there was never any mention of her memory returning. That day had been so traumatic he felt confident if she were going to remember anything it would have happened by now. Instead, she'd just faded away like her unsolved case. He'd put most of that life behind him, until now.

Tonight, being this close, it was apparent she had no recollection of him, which worked totally in his favor. She approached him, radiant, and extended her dainty hand. He clasped it between both of his own, not wanting to release it but knowing he should. Before doing so, he breathed in the fragrance of her, committing it to memory until the next time.

"I want to thank you again for indulging us," she said, sliding her hand away. "I'm sure you want to check in on your wife."

"You read my mind. If you don't need me for anything else, then that is where I'm headed."

"Bianca wanted me to thank you. Please let me know when you're back in the city. I'd love to have lunch and discuss any other investments or opportunities—even if they're only thoughts. Let me make all your dreams come true."

"You have no idea how much I'm looking forward to that." His dick throbbed in agreement, and he smiled.

"Safe travels back to Florida and tell your wife I hope she's feeling better." Samantha placed a hand on his bicep before she walked away. "Right now, I need to go find my date before the awards start."

"I thought you were here alone." Greg captured her wrist before she could get too far. He'd gotten so caught up with the women, it never occurred to him she could be with someone. Then again, no one had been hanging around with Detective Cavelli. He found this very interesting, considering she was such a knockout. The man must be a complete idiot to leave this beauty unattended.

"I arrived with a very good-looking date who I've ignored for far too long," she replied, sliding her wrist free and scanning the room before turning back to him with a shrug. "I might have to send Tony to find him. He and Dalton have been best friends and partners for years. He'll know just where to look. I need to make sure I'm at the table with Bianca."

"How…long have you and this…*Dalton,* been together?"

He tried to sound interested but inside a possessiveness bubbled and boiled. *Fucking Dalton. What were the odds it could be a different Dalton?*

"We're not official, not yet anyway." Her sparkling smile reached her eyes, and a twinge of envy rose in his gut when she added, "I'm hoping soon, though…like tonight."

"I certainly hope he's worthy of a prize such as yourself." Truth was, she was *his* prize, only she didn't know it. One day she would, and this Dalton fellow would be a faded memory. And if it was indeed Dalton Riley, Greg was going to fuck him right out of her system.

"He's more than worthy, Greg." She interrupted his fantasy by giving him an odd look, but then she paused to bite her plump bottom lip for a moment, and he felt himself on the verge of slipping when she added, "I think he could be *the one.*"

"I wish you the best. We'll talk soon." Greg turned and walked away, uncomfortable with the jealousy brewing inside him. He had to get himself under control. He couldn't risk suspicion and ruin everything, not when he was so close.

Where the hell is my wife….

CHAPTER 16

ater that evening, Samantha was hoping to catch up with Dalton once again. She hadn't seen much of him the entire night. He'd made it back to their table in time for the awards but had seemed nervous and preoccupied. Once the formalities concluded and everyone was dancing or socializing, he excused himself again, claiming he'd missed an urgent call. That was at least an hour ago. Luckily, she'd been busy networking so his absence didn't bother her too much, but she couldn't deny the disappointment which weighed on her now.

"Samantha! I've been looking all over for you," Bianca said as she approached with a very distinguished looking gentleman on her arm. "I have another client I want to introduce you to."

"Hi Bianca!" Sam gave her a quick hug. "So sorry. I've been so busy networking, I've been trying to make my way to you, I promise." Sam smiled at the duo, but her gaze was immediately drawn to the most striking eyes she'd ever seen. They were almost as silver as the man's hair.

"Well, *this* is Victor Perez." Bianca all but busted at the seams. "I had extended the invitation, never expecting him to be here on such short notice." Bianca squeezed the man's muscular arm. "But I'm so glad he could fit us in between flights."

"Bianca, your company has been very gracious to me these last few days, and you come so highly recommended, how could I stay away?" He laughed and his deep tone was hypnotic.

Sam couldn't pinpoint his age because he had such a glow about him, as if he'd found the fountain of youth. His bronze skin seemed flawless except for what she thought was a scar line under his left cheek bone, but she didn't want to stare.

"Perez? You were referred by Greg Maddox, right? Goodness, you two must be missing each other all night. We'd all taken pictures together earlier this evening. When I'd said goodbye to him, he was going to find his wife, concerned because she wasn't feeling well. I'm sure he'll be sorry he missed catching up with you."

"His wife is such a sweet woman. I've spoken with her on the phone but unfortunately haven't had the pleasure of meeting her in person, yet."

"You will love her," Bianca added. "They are quite the power couple."

"Maybe he hasn't left yet? Bianca, do you remember what table they were seated at? I'm sure we can locate him for you."

"That won't be necessary. I actually have a meeting coming up with him very soon. We travel in similar business circles, and I want to make sure he's aware of a certain shipping issue which has caused a cascade of problems."

"I hope it's nothing serious." Samantha glanced at her watch and did a quick scan around the ballroom, still no sign of Dalton. "Is Dalton with Tony by any chance?"

"I haven't seen Tony since the awards ended. He's great

about letting me work the room." Bianca smiled. "Knowing them, they are probably together."

"True," Sam agreed. Since Dalton had missed a call earlier, maybe he was filling Tony in on whatever was going on with one of his cases.

"This evening has flown by," Bianca said after glancing at her watch. "I believe Tony and I are taking Greg and Rebecca to the airport. I should excuse myself and gather everyone up. You two continue the conversation, and Sam, I'll talk with you after the weekend."

"It's been a pleasure, Bianca. My regards to your husband." Victor kissed Bianca on each cheek before she walked away.

"I'm so thrilled to be meeting you in person," Sam said, slowly sipping what was left of whatever number glass of wine she was on. Thank goodness the event staff continued to check on their table, because she hadn't seen Dalton since he'd left to check on the missed call. She prayed everything was okay and he didn't have to leave. She'd been glancing at her own phone every couple of minutes to see if he'd sent a text update. "I must say," she said, focusing on her newest client, "at first glance, your resort idea is amazing. I can clearly see your vision, and our team will make sure you have the exact deal you're looking for."

"I appreciate that, Samantha. My team as well as myself have been impressed with your work. I can tell you are very talented and very driven. You will make an excellent partner someday."

"Thank you, I am honored you would say that." It was clear he was talking about business, and she enjoyed the compliment, but there was an odd tone to his voice that gave her the impression he was referring to her being a partner in life. She shook off the crazy notion, chalking it up to her obsession with Dalton. She wished he would see her as his life partner.

"Sam!" Dalton rushed over, as if summoned on cue, slightly out of breath. "Hey, oh sorry to intrude." Dalton nodded to acknowledge Victor. "The DJ is about to play the last dance of the evening. I didn't want us to miss it. Like I said, it's not my thing, but I figure I owe you at least one dance." Dalton glanced from Victor to Sam.

"It's been a pleasure meeting you, and I look forward to experiencing the wonderful work I've heard so much about." He shook her hand. "I'll be in touch."

"Of course, thank you Victor, please excuse me," she said as he waved his hand and walked away. Dalton took her hand and pulled her back toward the ballroom dance floor. "Where have you been all night? You pop in then pop out. I've been worried that something else has been going on. You know…with one of your secret things you don't want Tony to know about. Have you been talking to Tony?"

"No." He pulled her into his arms and the moment their bodies touched, nothing else mattered except he was holding her. "I'm sorry I was M.I.A. I didn't mean to take so much time away from you. I ran into a couple of old friends and the night got away from me. Unfortunately, I can't discuss the call, but I've been putting out some fires. I hope you can forgive me for not being much of an escort."

"I don't think there's anything to forgive. If it's work again, you can't really help it." Her head rested against his shoulder. She could smell soap with a hint of spice and pine. An almost familiar feeling socked her square in the gut, and for a moment, she was afraid to breathe. It surprised her at first, then she relaxed, letting it envelop her in comfort and peace. The music ended, and they slowly swayed to a stop. If she never left his arms, she'd be the happiest woman in the world.

"You ready to go home?" he asked, keeping his arms around her for once, almost in a protective way, and looking down at her with an odd smile.

He was holding her, and it meant everything. Every time he glanced at her she saw *home* in his green eyes. That constant feeling of something familiar between them. Tonight, was no exception.

"Yes, I couldn't be more ready," she said, and meant every word.

———

GREG MARCHED BECCA UP THE STEPS TO THEIR PRIVATE PLANE, still seething after his conversation with Samantha and the fact that Tony insisted on escorting them to the airport. It didn't matter how many times he told the nosey detective his security team would handle it, the man claimed it was the least he could do. In the end, his nervous wife sat in the back seat with Bianca, talking about babies and morning sickness. Right now, Greg couldn't wait to get to the heart of the problem.

"What the actual *fuck*, Becs!" he yelled and shoved her onto the leather sofa inside the cabin.

"Greg!" she screamed in surprise. He left her crying while he went into their private bath.

There were certain things he hadn't been able to come clean with. She had no idea about the business trips he'd taken on this plane or the things he did in the background to give them this life they wanted. The life she loved. Reaching behind the vanity mirror, he pulled down a small tin containing the special cocaine he'd received as a thank you from Manuel for investing in the man's business opportunity, and for giving him names of other potential investors.

"Just to take the edge off," he said to his reflection as if he needed validation to do whatever the hell he wanted.

Taking the small silver spoon, he placed the powder under his nostrils and sniffed the purest damn coke he'd had in a long time. After replacing the tin, he wet his hands at the sink and wiped them down his face and through his hair. He didn't do this all the time, only when he was entertaining important people, or feeling the stress of a hard negotiation. He didn't keep things from Becca, except when it came to his entertainment habits. She never had to worry.

He valued his new life over all the mistakes he'd made. He wasn't about to screw this up. He had way too much to lose and even more to gain by partnering with the right people. There were scores to settle, and he'd do it on his own terms. His wife would have to understand. Hearing her cry through the bathroom door broke his heart. He didn't want to be so angry, but the evening's circumstances brought to life the monster below the surface. Taking a deep breath, he exhaled and pushed through the door.

"Greg, I'm so sorry." She was up and in his arms. "Please don't be angry with me."

"What did you say to Tony?" He pulled her away and stared into her eyes. "What did you do?"

"I didn't do anything. I didn't say anything, I promise." Her eyes pleaded with him to believe her, and then she added, "to either of them."

"Becca, what are you fucking talking about?" He followed her back to the sofa, sitting next to her as dread gnawed at his insides. "Who else was with Tony?"

"Not with him." She shook her head, her eyes a mix of fear and confusion. "Before him."

"You're not making any sense, babe." He wiped her tears. "I'm not mad at you. It's been a long night and I'm worried because I don't know what's made you so upset."

"When I went to the bar...." Becca sniffed and everything came out in a rush of crying and tears. "Dalton is alive! He was talking to me. How could he be? You said he died when that boat sank, I-I-I didn't know what to do. You weren't around, and he was there right in front of me."

"Whoa, whoa, whoa...Dalton Riley talked to you?" Greg's head was about to explode. This confirmed without a shadow of a doubt—and he'd tried like hell to doubt—that Samantha's date was indeed Dalton Riley, Detective Dalton Riley to be exact.

"He recognized me. Asked about you and if I'd been in contact with you."

"What did you tell him?"

"Nothing. I remembered what you said about how important witness protection was for us. If Dalton isn't dead, then what if he's bringing the bad people to you...to us. I told him I didn't lead that life anymore, and that I had four children."

"That's my girl." His body relaxed a little. "Did he seem okay with your answers, when you didn't confirm or deny me?"

"I guess? The security team came and told me it was time for pictures. I never saw Dalton again. But I was so scared. Why would he want to see you after all this time?" She sniffed again and more tears fell. "I had to protect my family."

Greg cradled her in his arms, believing it wasn't possible to love her more than he did at this exact moment. "You did everything right, baby, *everything*."

Dalton Riley should have died all those years ago, he hadn't.

But, he was as good as dead now. Greg would make sure of it. No one knew his alias. He'd paid good money for all his documents. He and Rebecca were nobodies from small-town North Carolina. Neither one of their families cared if they lived or died. Miami was their fresh start in every single way. He didn't think anyone back home would recognize them anyway if they showed up. He'd dreamed of it, but the reality was he just didn't give a fuck. He ran in different circles in the south, and there were only a few old friends who knew who he really was, and they knew the cost if they ever crossed him.

Dalton was about to pay the ultimate price.

CHAPTER 17

Dalton walked out of the hotel into the balmy evening air, keeping a close eye on Sam. Since running into Rebecca, he'd been on high alert. He hoped like hell he was overreacting and being at the gala with her husband was the real reason she was in town. Dalton felt bad for leaving Samantha unattended for most of the night, but he couldn't sit still and spent most of the evening looking for Rebecca and patrolling for anything suspicious in the process. Neither of which he'd found.

"What an amazing night!" Sam rejoiced. "I just feel so alive." She breathed deep, turning in a circle and gazing up at the twinkling stars.

"Easy, there." Dalton steadied her on the uneven side-walk. "I don't need you spraining an ankle." He had to admit, the drinks from earlier still lingered. Not enough to slow him down, just enough to remind him he'd indulged more than usual. Given the circumstances, it was a wonder he felt as steady as he did.

After what happened to CeCe and Louie, he had to stay

alert and make sure nothing happened to Sam. She wouldn't be safe until the threat of Billy Benning was erased, for good.

"You missed all the action." She pressed her purse to her chest and beamed. Her blue eyes appeared a little bloodshot and their lids heavy, letting him know she'd had more than enough wine as well.

"What did I miss?" He pushed buttons on his phone, saying, "Hold that thought, let me order an Uber."

"Bianca introduced me to my clients, Victor Perez, who you sort of met, and Greg Maddox."

"Maddox? That's interesting, I met his wife at the bar." Dalton had wanted to talk to Rebecca further, but he never saw her again. He couldn't tell Sam she was the real reason he wasn't with her for most of the night.

"What a coincidence. She came back to our group and wasn't feeling well." Sam paused, disappointment evident in her voice. "Which was a shame because Bianca had said such wonderful things, I was looking forward to spending more of the evening with the two of them."

"She seemed a little off to me, too."

"Oh, you actually spoke with her?" Sam cocked her head.

Dalton hadn't realized he'd said that out loud. Running into Rebecca at the hotel had really messed with him. Now, to learn she was married to Sam's client? His instincts were telling him there was more than just chance at play here. Or maybe it was all the booze turning everything into a coincidence.

"Only small talk at the *very* busy bar. It took forever to get drinks. She seemed nice enough, but definitely preoccupied by more than the crowd waiting for their drinks."

"I could tell she felt bad for missing the photo shoot."

"The most important thing is you had a good time tonight." Dalton reassured her.

She blinked a couple times and her brilliant smile returned.

"I did. And you even danced with me." She twirled in front of him, stopped, and placed her fingers to her temples. "Oof, okay, that wasn't a good idea. Now I'm most definitely seeing double. Why is it I always drink too much when I'm around you, and you end up having to rescue me?"

"Take it easy," he chuckled and steadied her once more. "Protect and serve. It's what I do." He smiled. "Hey, the night wasn't a total bust. I told you I would dance with you." He took her hands to steady her before leading her slowly so she could get her bearings.

An eerie feeling settled over him as if they were being followed. He trained his ears to the air around them, picking up on another set of footsteps behind. When he turned to look over his shoulder, he thought he saw a shadow duck into an alley. "Let's keep you moving a little. How about we get a cup of coffee while we wait for our ride."

"That sounds like a wonderful idea."

As they walked the short block, he updated their pickup location with the driver and noticed that normally chatty Sam had gotten quiet, almost too quiet. He didn't hear footsteps again and had checked over his shoulder several times, never seeing anyone. They approached a small table outside the twenty-four-hour café, and he pulled out a chair.

"You doing okay?"

She nodded in response as she sat.

"Stay here in the fresh air. Keep breathing deep, and I'll grab our coffees." He hated to leave her alone outside, but at this hour the café was empty. He scanned the immediate area, and it remained clear. "Be right back."

"Okay," she replied, and he couldn't tell if that was a yawn, if she was deep in thought, or ready to pass out. Regardless, he had to get her home. Without the excitement of the music and lights of the hotel, the events of the evening were catching up with him, too.

He kept watch on her while he placed their orders and quickly returned to her side. "Uh-oh, you've still got that look in your eyes." Dalton handed her the Styrofoam cup containing her cappuccino. "Are you sure you're okay?"

"I've been reflecting on this entire evening and how magical it was."

"Magical? Boy, you must have some special powers because all I saw was a room full of wealthy business owners, acquisitions professionals, and of course my beautiful company."

"It's the company that made it magical."

He noticed life returning to her features and her doe-eyed expression warned him to tread lightly. Tonight, was not the night to give her the wrong impression. He pulled the lid off his cup, letting the steam escape, and took a welcome sip of his black coffee.

"I haven't had such an exhilarating night out in a very long time."

"Not even with Matt the auditor?" he teased, needing to change the mood steadily humming in the air between them. She stopped mid-sip, her expressive eyes conveying what she couldn't say with a mouthful of hot coffee. She forced the swallow, and he cut in before she could respond, "I know, you're just friends, don't get all excited."

"You just won't let that go, will you?" She laughed.

"Not when it gets a rise out of you every time. It's not my fault you're an easy target." He pointed to a white sedan parked at the corner. "There's our ride."

The ride to her condo on Chambers Street was short and silent. When they exited the car, she surprised him by boldly taking his hand and leading him up the steps to where the doorman waited. When the man started to open the door, Dalton put on the brakes, slipping his hand from hers.

"Thanks for inviting me tonight. I had a great time."

"Oh, it's not over yet, detective. You've declined every invitation, and this time I'm not letting you off the hook." Her blue eyes sparkled, and she laughed when his brows shot up. "That's right. I make a killer espresso martini, and you are going to have one with me to celebrate."

"Sam, it's been a long night, and I think we've had enough to drink." Experience warned he was venturing close to his tipping point, and he felt confident she was past hers.

"Maybe. But when I said tonight was magical for me, I meant it. I'm not done celebrating and if you don't come upstairs, I will be forced to go out alone."

"That's not a good idea." He squinted, trying to decide if she was serious or not.

"Exactly. So, humor me and come up."

Words failed him, and she jumped at the opportunity to call his bluff if he were indeed bluffing.

"Well, that's settled." She turned away. "I guess I'm off to the pub to celebrate with a bunch of strangers."

Dalton realized Sam wasn't bluffing.

She had no idea of the danger which lurked out there now —especially in that red dress. He'd always watched out for her, from a distance. Tonight, distance wasn't an option.

The urge to protect her surged, sharp and immediate. He spoke before he could stop himself.

"Don't."

They stared at each other until Dalton realized neither of them had taken a breath. His mind fired off warning after warning, but one truth overrode them all—Sam needed to be safe.

"Let's go upstairs," he said and held out his hand.

She took it without hesitation.

With every step toward the building, he reminded himself: a drink or two, then leave. He'd make things clear.

"Good evening, Erik," Sam said as the burly doorman pulled the door open.

"Miss Taylor," the man nodded.

Dalton felt his gaze linger as they passed. Not hostile. Appraising.

Until they stepped inside the awaiting elevator and the doors closed.

"He's protective of the residents here," Sam said lightly, pressing the button for her floor. "I don't usually bring men home."

Dalton said nothing.

Inside her apartment, resolve slipped the moment the door shut behind them. When she reached past him to close it, her arm brushed his side and something sparked, sharp and unmistakable.

All the more reason to leave sooner than planned.

———

Sam's heart soared the moment Dalton agreed to come upstairs.

She'd assumed he would be the ultimate gentleman just like every other time they were together. Sure, it had taken an ultimatum, but it worked. Between that familiar expression in his sexy green eyes outside, and just moments ago when they'd touched, she knew he felt the same pull she'd been feeling since the night they met at the Cavellis. Knowing Dalton, if she didn't play it cool he'd retreat at the first sign of any personal feelings being expressed.

She wasn't ready for the night to be over.

She'd taken a moment to remind herself she and Dalton were not an official couple…yet.

Now, with him in her home, she let herself believe this was heading toward something real.

"Your martini, sir." Sam handed him a very decadent drink.

"This looks…sweet? I've never been a martini guy, so this stays between you and me."

"Don't worry, I'll keep all the secrets you want to tell me." Fear kept her voice in check, but she continued to feel connected to him all night and planned to do whatever she had to for them to take the next step.

She sipped her drink and kept her eyes on him across the rim of the elegant, stemmed glass. She held his gaze, mentally transferring everything she was feeling, and hoped like hell he was receiving.

He mimicked her action, only making a face over the combination of vodka, coffee, and chocolate. In one movement he drained the entire contents.

She eyed him curiously. "You're supposed to sip it."

"Not my style."

"I could have made you something else."

"I didn't want to be rude. What else do you have?" He spoke so fast she couldn't hide her amusement.

She motioned toward the balcony doors. "The bar cart is over there."

She watched him pour three fingers of scotch, neat, ready and waiting when he turned around. She wasn't about to lose her nerve.

Tonight was too important.

"Great view." He broke the silence and opened the French doors. Stepping into the night air, he took a large breath.

Sam followed, hooking her arm through his and leaning

her head against his bicep. She dared think of waking up with Dalton in the morning, viewing the skyline together and breakfast on the balcony.

"I love this place." She allowed herself to return to reality. "Before Bianca signed me, she gave me three listings to look at and said the company would pay for the first year's rent. Who does that?"

"Yeah, that's a hell of a deal," he replied.

"This was the last one I toured, and it was love at first sight. Once the year is up, thanks to a generous bonus from BCA, I will definitely be able to afford it on my own. They just replaced the security system here, too. Erik was telling me the building owner wanted it upgraded to the finest around."

"Good. By the way, did you notice the light on your smoke detector is blinking? You may want to change the battery, or is it hard wired?"

"Boy, detective, you don't miss a thing, do you? I noticed that too, and I'm not sure. I guess they replaced them in all the units in the building. This is the only one in my place that's blinking, and I've been too busy to let Erik know."

"You should make that a priority."

"Are you worried about me?" She stepped close enough to touch him but held back. The attraction she felt for him was palpable. He had to feel it, too. She wanted nothing more than for him to react, to give her a sign.

"As a friend, and a detective," he clarified, using his drink for emphasis when he spoke. "I'm glad that as a single young woman you have such a secure building."

"Right." Sam slipped the glass from his hand and set it on a small table on the balcony. "What if you were more than a friend?" She placed her now empty martini glass next to his.

"Sam…." He took a step back, but she wrapped her arms around his neck, loving how his arms instinctively found their home around her waist, natural and unguarded. The last of her doubt fell away.

This wasn't imagined. This wasn't one-sided. With him holding her like this, she knew—beyond any doubt—that this man belonged in her life.

"Shh...." She placed a soft kiss on his neck, and she felt him stiffen. She couldn't lose this opportunity. It was now or never. She clung to him in the moonlight, pulling herself closer until she could rise on her toes and kiss his jaw. "Ever since I met you, you've felt like home to me."

"I'm not home, Sam," Dalton said on a husky breath that almost sounded defeated. He shifted within her arms, but she wasn't about to let him go. She wouldn't let him shut down again.

"I know you feel it." Her voice, a seductive whisper as she leaned back enough to look into his eyes. "I see it, right now, just like I've seen it every other time."

"Don't mistake my friendship for something else."

"I believe it's more than friendship."

"This is not what you think, and a very bad idea." He stepped away, and she followed him inside.

"Tell me why, Dalton?" Her pulse raced. After everything tonight, she couldn't let him dismiss their connection. "Stop fighting and start feeling."

He stopped halfway across the room.

Sam didn't give him time to respond or time for her to chicken out. She launched herself against him and kissed him. The jolt to her system buckled her knees and dropped them both onto the sofa, where they lost themselves in that one kiss.

Fueled by the reality of a kiss she'd only allowed herself to dream, Sam kissed him deeper. The instant their tongues met, he kissed her back. A soft moan vibrated within her throat, urging him to continue.

She shifted in his lap, and he slid his hands to hike her dress to her hips, giving her better access to straddle him. Her fingers hurriedly unbuttoned his shirt, all while she fed him kisses full of a desire she never knew she was capable of.

"Sam," he breathed before she kissed him again, and he pulled his mouth away. "We have to stop."

"No," she answered as their mouths met again. She slid his shirt over his shoulders until he shook his arms loose. When he tried to touch her, she pushed his hands against the back of the sofa, kissing his neck, pausing at the scar from the bullet wound and recent surgery.

"Sam." He gasped sharply when her tongue grazed each ridge of his scar before she kissed it.

She inhaled his scent, the taste of him on her tongue and lips as she explored with her mouth. With every kiss she could feel his muscles relaxing. Still holding his hands at bay, she sat up and met his gaze.

"I want you, Dalton Riley."

Daltons eyes grew wide as she reached back to unzip her dress, until the top slipped from her shoulders to reveal her full breasts. She placed his palms against each soft mound. He tried to remove them, and she struggled to keep them there. She didn't want to lose this feeling, lose him. She leaned forward to kiss him again, and he turned his head away.

Sam leaned left so she was gazing into his eyes, hazed with desire. "Stay with me," she whispered. "Don't go."

No sooner had the words left her mouth than Dalton surged to his feet, tossing her to the nearest cushion.

"Fuck!" he yelled and began to pace, scrubbing both hands through his thick, dark hair. "Fuck, fuck, FUUUCK!" he bellowed.

"Dalton!" Sam jumped into action, holding the top to her dress as she ran to him until they were standing face-to-face, panting to catch their breath. She could see the pulse in his neck beating at a powerful rate. "What's wrong?" She stared into his wild eyes, a sense of doom weighing on her like a summer storm.

Eyes that had gone dark, as if he didn't see her at all.

CHAPTER 18

"We can't be doing this." Dalton moved, gulping to take in air, not allowing her to get too close. Unable to control the surge of anger at himself, he moved again, needing distance.

Her simple, innocent plea had taken him back to a day he'd never been able to forget. A day when tear-filled blue eyes begged him not to leave her.

Only he'd had no choice. He'd never even expected to live.

"Do what, be adults?" Sam's voice crashed through the memory, and she was once again standing before him, crossing all personal boundaries. "We were doing a fine job a few minutes ago, all night for that matter. You came upstairs—."

"Because you asked me to." He cut her off, his voice firm. "I didn't want you going out alone."

"Liar. I saw it in your eyes. You wanted to be here as much as I wanted you here. I've seen this since the day we met. You come alive and then shut down."

"You don't understand."

"Then make me understand. Tell me what's going on in your head."

"This can never work between us. I'm—"

"Yes, you're older than me. I don't care about age. I want to explore what's happening here, now." She touched his arm and said, "We have a connection."

Only she would never understand how wrong it was, because of who he was.

Dalton jerked his arm free. "This. Us. It can't happen."

"Why not?"

"There are things I can't get into." He bent to pick up his shirt, and she was right beside him again, unwilling to let things drop.

"I can handle complicated, Dalton, I'm a big girl."

"It's not that."

"Then what is it. Tell me!" she shouted.

Only he knew she wouldn't be ready for the answers

Maybe someday. But not today.

"I don't want to hurt you." The words came out soft, sincere, and unavoidable.

"Keeping me in the dark is hurting me." She gazed at him, and he saw the tears she fought to hold back. "Dalton, I can't explain this. You're like no man I've ever met." She latched onto his arm, and he removed it once more, holding his palm in the air between them.

"Sam, stop."

"No, you need to listen." She shook her head and closed the gap. "When we're together, this *thing* happens inside me, and everything seems right in ways I never knew were *wrong*. I feel…safe."

Their eyes met and in an instant, he knew what was coming.

"Dalton, I'm falling in—"

"Don't say it," he warned in a low rumble, "don't."

He couldn't let it happen because he never wanted to be her reason for giving up on happiness…. Staying would only make the hurt worse for her. He turned to leave, shirt unbuttoned and jacket in hand. He should have been stronger.

"Believe me, I never wanted it to get this far."

She chased after him.

"What is so complicated in your life that you can't let me in and won't let me love you."

He spun around, unleashing years of anger and frustration she had no idea of and didn't deserve.

"Do you really want to know what's so complicated in *my* life? *You* are what's complicated, Samantha!"

"You won't even let me *in* your life. How am I complicating it?" her voice quivered, "You came upstairs, I thought—"

"*You* asked for this, *you* wanted this!" Dalton paced like a caged tiger, jabbing a finger in her direction. "I never wanted *any* of it! But you know what?" He stopped dangerously close in front of her, the tears trailing down her pale cheeks.

"I don't understand."

"I did it for *you*, Samantha. And I hope to God, someday you understand."

She'd forced his hand.

There was no turning back.

There was only his truth.

"From the moment I heard you had survived, I knew my life wasn't mine anymore. I put myself in a position where I could protect you."

"From *what*?"

"From an evil you don't remember."

"You're not making any sense."

"The same evil which took the lives of those we loved. You asked me to start feeling." He swallowed hard. "Protection means I don't get to feel, Sam. *That's* why I'll never be home to you…or anyone else."

"You're a detective, not a killer."

"I became a detective so I could have the resources to destroy a killer."

"The boat…My parents…." She locked eyes with him as if something from the depths of her past clicked together. Sam placed a trembling hand to her lips. "It wasn't a boating accident, was it?"

Suddenly Dalton saw that innocent little girl fourteen years ago who never asked for any of this. But through some sick twist of fate, she'd inadvertently asked for it tonight.

Sam walked to the door and pulled it open as if she somehow knew what he was about to say.

"I think you need to leave."

Dalton approached, but he couldn't cross the threshold, not until he aired what remained unsaid. All this pain she felt was his doing. He never meant for any of this, only to watch over her like he'd promised.

"Of course, we have a connection, Samantha. I knew your parents. I watched you grow up with your Aunt Helen and Uncle Frank. I saw you graduate high school and college. I know what happened that horrible day, and I've relived it every day since."

He met her eyes and worked moisture into his mouth to voice the last words she'd ever hear from him before he walked out the door.

"I know you're Little Girl X."

CHAPTER 19

Fourteen Years Earlier
Billy — The Con

I sat with my feet hanging off the dock, my anger like the ripples of the incoming tide. The nerve of Louie Patrone sending some flunkies to the marina to threaten me. If I don't pay for all the coke we used on the way to New York, the sonofabitch will take a hit out on me! After all the risks I took to run his shit, the guy can't take the damn loss.

Well, I've got news for him. I've got a doctor interested in his boat. If I play my cards right, this man is going to solve all my problems, and in the process, I'm going to pull a fast one on Louie. One day, I'll make my own damn millions and take care of him once and for all. He's not the only important guy around.

Right now, I'm waiting for the good doctor and his family to show up. We're taking the boat on a vacation test run for the man. I made it sound like I've got another buyer on hold, making him feel the urgency.

I heard some chatter, looked up to see this picture-perfect family pulling their suitcases toward me. I could smell the money now. "Hey, doc." I stood and greeted the man with a firm handshake.

"Ahoy, Captain!" he said with a huge, corny grin. "Let me introduce you to my wife, Nina, and my daughter, Sam."

Ignoring the girl, I glanced to his left at the tall, leggy blonde in a blue figure-hugging dress who looked like she should be sitting on someone's lap at the Playboy Mansion. Doc had some muscle, but that Nina...my balls ached just looking at her.

"Welcome aboard, ladies!" I swept my hand toward the catamaran and motioned for my first mate to take their bags. He and I had already discussed room assignments, in order to avoid an unexpected situation I wasn't happy about and didn't have time to take care of.

Two days into our journey I had the Doc at the wheel and he was loving life.

"You got a great looking family, Doc," I told him as I took a quick glance at the mother-daughter combo in matching little white bikinis. They'd been enjoying the sun on the trampoline at the bow most of the day.

"Thanks, Captain. Do you have anyone special back home?"

"There's this chick I've been on and off with for a few years. She just told me she's having my kid, but I'm not sure I believe her. Besides, I'm not really father material and being a boat captain doesn't pay much." He gave me a judgmental look, but must have caught himself because he pointed to a pod of dolphins leaping out of the water ahead.

"Girls! Look! Dolphins ahead!"

The girls squealed and something changed inside of me. Their skin was already so tan. Nina's hair was dancing in the breeze and when she cast a big smile toward her husband, I pretended it was all for me. She was rubbing more lotion across her chest and down her arms, almost like she was teasing me on purpose. She knew she was hot and when we made eye contact, I licked my lips in anticipation of licking every inch of her.

But the Doc was going on and on, breaking my focus.

"Don't be so hard on yourself. If you've been seeing her for this long, I bet she's telling you the truth. Have you done the math? Does the timing make sense?" He took his eyes off the water as I shrugged. "You're making an honest living," he continued, "that's all she can ask for. Looks to me like you're doing everything right. Little changes turn into big wins. Keep staying the course, you'll get there."

I glanced back at the bikini duo, laughing and enjoying the sun. I know the Doc was being nice, but I didn't want him filling my head with his righteous bullshit. I didn't have the smarts to be like him, yet the man had me almost believing I could have everything I wanted.

And I wanted Nina.

"Hey, if you don't mind taking over, your first mate says he'd set me up for some fishing." Doc pointed toward the stern and I gave him a nod.

"Go for it, man. Hope you hook a big one."

He left and my attention was drawn to the bikini duo like a magnet. If he wasn't around, I'd be popping that shit, making her beg me not to stop. Then the daughter stood up. She had a tight little body too. I knew she was jailbait, and I wasn't into that kiddie-porn shit, but give it another couple years and she would be a looker like her mama. I absently stroked the wheel, pretending I was stroking the mother. I was rock hard inside my shorts when Nina caught me touching myself and licking my lips. She must have thought it was directed toward her daughter. I couldn't hear what she was saying, but they both looked at me and then the girl put on a t-shirt. About that time, she saw some dolphins and ran toward the stern where Doc was doing some fishing. Good, now I had hot-mama all to myself.

Nina stayed and I had all I could do not to make a fool out of myself and offer to put more lotion on her or something. I would do whatever she asked if I could get a taste of her. Then I realized that was what I needed to get me through this, a hit from the shit I stored in the bunk room. My plan was for me and my first mate to relax and shoot up during the trip at night when the family was asleep and out of our hair.

Only I needed something now to calm me down.

But with this bitch, the coke had me more wound up. All I wanted her to do was suck my dick. She had the finest looking mouth to match those tits and ass. She had to be a fantastic lay. Doc was a lucky guy. I wondered if I could entice him with a little powder, get him to loosen up. He might think about loosening up, but he'd never. He's a fucking doctor. I was sure there was some sort of medical code of honor or some such bullshit. Now I had to suffer for the rest of the day, thinking of them living their spectacular lives.

I couldn't handle it. I wanted what the good doctor had, starting with his wife. I went below for a quick generous bump while Doc and his daughter got ready for some evening fishing. In my absence, Nina slipped into a pair of sheer pants and tunic over her bikini. What a shame to cover that magnificent body, but the sheerness of the outfit made her even more sexy. The extra hit of coke kicked in and I grabbed her wrist as she walked by.

"You are so fucking hot," I said close to her ear, flicking

her lobe with my tongue. She gasped and pulled back, but I couldn't break my hold and I tugged her closer. "You've been teasing me all day, making me crave you."

"Let go of me," she said in shock.

"Ah, Ah, Ah…Don't fight what you know you want." She pulled but I had an iron grip, and she was making zero ground in her attempt to break free. "You and I are going to take a little trip below deck so I can sample that sexy body of yours, and the Doc will be none the wiser."

"Stop it. Let go."

She resisted even more, so I yanked her to me with my arm around her tiny waist and my hand over her mouth. The more she moved against me, the more aroused I got. There was no way I was getting that hell cat below deck. No one was within eyeshot. All I had to do was slip her bottoms down. I started moving the feather light fabric, my finger skimming the curve of her ass, and I couldn't help but force it between her legs. She was whimpering and I felt tears drip onto my hand. I clamped it tighter because I was turned on as hell.

"I'm going to give you a ride like you've never had with the good doctor." She was panting and I almost lost it in my shorts. I was breathing as hard as she was, and we hadn't even screwed yet. I hated to remove my hand, but I couldn't trust her not to scream, and I need to release my throbbing dick from my shorts. Of course, the minute I created a little distance to adjust, she spun around and pushed me back.

"Ben! Ben, help me!"

"Don't you say a word," I whispered in her ear as the Doc came running from the stern.

"What's going on?" he demanded.

"Everything's fine," I started to explain. "Nina got a little too close to the edge, and with the chop, she started to slip, so

I caught her. She's a little startled." I gave Nina the look, but she was about to make my life hell for sure. She rushed to her husband crying.

"That's not true." She buried her head in his chest, and he wrapped his arm around her securely. "He touched me, he was trying to rape me. He said you'd never have to find out."

The Doc's eyes grew dark as he glared at me. This was my boat. If he wanted a fight, I would bring it. I was not afraid. He assessed Nina quickly and set her down on one of the storage benches.

"Is this true?" He approached me and I didn't back down. I had scrapped with worse than him. "I can tell you're high."

"That's right, I am. It's the only way I could get the nerve to approach your hot ass wife."

"Turn this boat around and toss the drugs overboard."

"I'm not doing it." Doc had no idea about the money sitting in the bunkroom. "You need to loosen up. Once your little girl is asleep, we can all have some fun." I shot a side-eye toward Nina which didn't go unnoticed by the Doc. That bitch and her box was all the fun I was going to want for the rest of the trip. "What do you think about having a little party later?" I watched the Doc's face morph into sheer anger.

"The deal's off. I'm ordering you to either turn the boat around or take us to the closest piece of land. If you don't, I will contact the authorities."

"I don't take orders from anyone, so why don't you calm down."

The heat of the moment weighed heavy on me. If he didn't buy the boat, I'd have to answer big time to Louie, and I already had plans for that sonofabitch. He returned to Nina's side with me on his heels.

"Listen, Doc, I'm sorry for any misunderstanding. Let me go below and make you two a nice drink." I had plans for both of them now. I still ached for Nina and at this point I'd take it any way I could get it. A little special cocktail might make her more complacent, and I'd make sure he was out cold.

Only the Doc made his first big mistake.

"I don't want anything from you," he said seething only inches from my face. "Turn this damn boat around and give me my deposit back."

"I don't like your tone," I growled right before I shoved him. I wasn't prepared for him to shove me back. When he came toward me again, I drew the fish knife from its sheath on my belt and I cut him.

"Ben! Oh my God!" Nina screamed, rushing toward her husband just as he was about to strike me. This time the knife plunged into her. It was almost as if she sacrificed herself as she turned toward me, causing the knife to twist and go deeper into her. I pulled the knife free. Nina went down. The deck went quiet.

I didn't step back.

"What have you done!" Doc grabbed me by the throat and shoved me hard against the wall. I worked like hell to reach the pistol I kept at the small of my back.

All of a sudden, our unexpected guest who I'd drugged below deck, stumbled into view. My first mate's pain in the ass brother. He was supposed to stay out of sight. We are a two-man crew, and I didn't need this idiot swaying the Doc not to buy the boat all because he didn't agree with our business plans.

"What the hell is going on?" he said, his voice still groggy from the dope I'd shot into his arm, but his eyes bugged out at the sight of the bloody Nina, the Doc and me. I guess we were so busy making nice with the family, we forgot to give him his evening dose.

"Like you can do anything about it, you prick," I stated. Doc's grip slipped enough for me to shove the knife deep in his gut. I pushed him off and drew my gun to shoot the intruder in the head.

I'm a fucking great shot.

Now all hell broke loose. The gunshot brought along the little girl Samantha followed closely by my first mate. He left the girl shrieking and crying, to rush to his brother. I stopped him because I was sure he was dead. Nina and the good doctor were still breathing, but they were bleeding out and didn't have much time. All the chaos turned into nothingness in my ears. I couldn't think straight.

"What the fuck are you doing?" My first mate yelled at me.

"Here's what we're going to do," I said while pointing my gun at him. "We get rid of all the extra dead or soon to be dead, weight. We continue down the coast until we figure out what to do with the girl."

"I won't let you kill her."

"I'm no kid killer, give me a break. I think we can make big money if we sell her, though. There's a market for this sort of thing. People are always wanting black market children." I left him to grab the bawling girl. She tried to stop as we passed her old man. He said something to her about being strong then something I couldn't make out, to my first mate. By this time, I'd had enough and dragged the kid kicking and screaming below deck where I locked her in her cabin.

"This would never have happened if you'd let me fuck your wife," I said moments later, when I came back and stood over the good doctor. Then the bastard spit blood at me! And here I thought he was such a great guy. I shut him up by kicking him in the ribs.

"Ben?" Nina's voice sounded so weak as she attempted to drag herself closer to her husband. I walked over and kicked her away.

"Not so fast, gorgeous. I want the last face you see to be

mine." I crouched next to her, wiping a stray tear trailing down her face. "This is your fault, too. I told you no-one had to know. Now, no-one will." I reached down and rested my hands on her heaving breasts. "Damn, these tits are real. It's a shame we're not going to get to play." I stood and hoisted her over my shoulder. She didn't have the strength to fight me now. I thought she knew what was going to happen. "Hey Doc, say goodbye to your beautiful wife!" I yelled toward the half-conscious man right before I tossed her overboard.

"Stop right there!" My first mate screamed from where he was trying to tend to the doctor's wounds.

"This would never have happened if you'd had the balls to stand up to your brother." I wiped my bloody hands on my shorts and stood over him. "Now we're fucked."

"I'm not fucked. You're the one who's murdered these people." He stood up and marched toward me as if he was going to take me down or something. "What did you do with Samantha? We need to take her back, call the authorities, tell them there's been an accident or something."

"Oh, there's been an accident all right." I fired my gun, shooting him in the shoulder and in the side. He tumbled below deck, and I followed. He was pretty much uncon-scious, so I shot him again for good measure. Someone needed to go down with the ship. While I was there, I went to my cabin and snatched the rest of the drugs, taking one more hit before getting to work.

I tossed the doctor's body overboard as well. He and Nina would be shark food before long. I left my no good first mate to die from his bullet wounds. He had already lost a decent amount of blood, no need to kill him. I decided to sink the boat. It was the only way. Before getting too crazy, I tossed my gear into the small motorboat.

Then, I proceeded to toss the transom drain plug, dismantle the intake hose and the joker valve. On my way back to the deck, I made sure all port holes were wide open. If anyone came upon the boat before it sank, they would think there was trouble, and it was a daddy-daughter sailing expedition gone wrong. With a little luck, they would all be dead and unidentifiable.

It was the only way.

CHAPTER 20

"Thanks for meeting me for lunch," Dalton said to Tony, grabbing their burritos from the food truck in the park. Tony pulled napkins from the dispenser and followed him with their drinks.

"Glad you asked." Tony sat across from him in the shade of the brightly colored umbrella table. "Haven't seen you around much since the gala. Matter of fact, I didn't see you much at the event either." He eyed him as if trying to put clues of some unknown plan in place. "Everything all right?"

"Yeah, just busy." Dalton took a huge bite from the soft shell not wanting to discuss what was obviously on his partner's mind. It had been three days since the blow-up with Sam. He felt confident neither one of them had recovered yet. Several unanswered calls told him she'd meant what she said, and while he expected that, it still hurt like hell. He'd invested so much of his life watching out for her, waiting for the moment when it would all come together, and justice would be done.

"Busy with Sam, I take it?" Tony appeared hopeful and Dalton shook his head.

"No."

Since she'd forced his hand, Billy would remain on the loose which would mean Sam could never totally be safe. Being close to her had been an ill-fated gift. Once Dalton had his head on straight again, he'd go back to his covert surveillance methods like he used to do. She'd probably never forgive him anyway. The best he could hope would be for Sam to forget him.

"Serious? You two made quite the couple on the dance floor."

"How about we talk shop, and not my personal life." Dalton reached for his drink.

"Ouch." Tony sat back in the chair. "Are you saying there's something going on?"

"I'm saying I'm not talking about what is or isn't happening with Sam." Dalton saw the wheels spinning in Tony's eyes. "Or Nicole, for that matter so don't even try."

After everything with Sam, Dalton had wandered the streets to clear his head, never once checking in with Nicki, or answering her messages. He'd finally made it home around four in the morning with a bag of bagels and coffee, but Nicki wasn't there. He couldn't blame her, and he hadn't been in the right headspace to get into it with her and call.

"Hey, I was ordered to get intel," Tony interrupted his thoughts. "You know how my wife can be." Tony swallowed some of his drink and then asked, "How were things with your friend, you know, the one you ditched us for?"

"First of all, you know I love Bianca, but she needs to back off." He pointed the burrito at Tony for emphasis and then took another large bite, giving himself time to carefully weigh how he should answer Tony's question. "I didn't intention-ally ditch you guys. I wasn't expecting to know anyone there and it just happened to be someone from my hometown." He shrugged. "We got lost in conversation and catching up."

"Understood." Tony nodded, but still didn't look confident in Dalton's explanation. "You know Bianca only wants you to be happy, whatever happiness for Dalton Riley looks like."

"There's no time for that right now. Listen, Louie's death is really eating at me. I worry CeCe's life could still be in danger."

"We can always keep a detail on watch."

"Too risky right now. I still believe there's an outside player bringing in the fentanyl. You know Louie ran a clean ship. Without Louie, Rocco's not that smart. He'd never think of this on his own."

"Enso? Maybe baby brother met a shady friend?"

"No. Nicki and I ruled him out. Louie was very protective of him, and Enso plays by the rules even more than Louie."

"Do you think Rocco tried to flip Enso?" Tony asked, having all the same thoughts he'd had with Nicki which was why their friendship clicked when they were all in the academy together.

"He'd have to know Enso would never go for it and might even rat him out to Louie."

"What if he did? Maybe Louie died because things went too far."

"I don't buy it. CeCe said Rocco was there with some other men. I'm telling you, Tony, someone else is pulling the strings. The fact that CeCe is severely injured tells me someone else called the shots, someone who really wanted to make Louie suffer."

"Like some kind of hit?"

"I have no doubt Rocco is behind it, he probably organized it. But someone else put the idea in his head."

"Who?" Tony sat in quiet thought for a moment and then said, "Do you think he's made connections with Manuel Salazar? He's tops on our fentanyl list right now."

"I think Salazar is way over Rocco's head. I'm thinking there's got to be someone from Louie's past."

"Why don't you see if CeCe can remember anything more?"

Dalton wanted more than anything to run through his theories about Billy Benning, but he knew his dedicated partner would have questions Dalton wasn't prepared to answer. Dalton also knew how guilty he would still appear, especially through Tony's by-the-book mentality, and Dalton couldn't protect Sam if he was behind bars. "I'll see what I can do."

On his way to PT, he mulled over all the information he had. The connection between Rebecca and Billy being in New York at the same time still troubled him. Sure, she could have cut ties with him and moved on with her new life and husband. But they shared a child, which he'd think would have to bind them somehow. He only hoped he could find what he needed in order to locate Billy before it was too late.

He stopped walking and pulled out his cell phone, noticing a couple guys across the street had stopped as well. He couldn't see their faces under the brims of their ball caps and when he stared in their direction, they ducked into the nearest alley.

He was being followed.

They'd pretty much kept pace with him since he left Tony at the park. He had half a mind to follow them, but he was due for his appointment in ten minutes and needed to call Nicki. He dialed her number, not surprised when her voice-mail spoke in his ear. He thought, *yup, I deserve that*. But he also needed her help.

"Nicki, I owe you an apology and I'll make it up to you I promise. Things have been…crazy…damnit, that's not even the right word and I don't know how to explain it right now. I need your help on something. I need you to look into Rebecca Maddox for me. I ran into her at the gala the other night and I have reason to believe she might be connected to Billy Benning."

———

SAM SAT IN BED, STILL IN HER PAJAMAS, STARING AT HER PHONE. Six ignored calls from Dalton and six voicemails in the last three days. She hadn't listened to them and didn't know if she could handle hearing his voice. She never wanted to see him again. Not now, not ever.

"Damn it," she muttered and reached for the tissue box as more tears fell. How did she still have tears after crying all weekend? There was no way she'd be able to make it through a day of work without bawling her eyes out at least once in the lady's room. Letting loose a heavy sigh, she ignored the pull of her voicemail and dialed Bianca.

"Good morning!" Her friend's voice chimed, and Sam wished she felt as happy and ready for the day as Bianca.

"Hi," she responded, not even trying to fake it.

"What's wrong? Are you sick? You sound all stuffed up." Bianca sighed. "Well, that's a shame, I was hoping for all the juicy details of your weekend with Dalton. I mean, I'm assuming you two spent it together?"

"No," Sam squeaked then pulled the phone away from her face as she fought to gain control.

"Samantha?"

"I," she released a breath into the phone, "I wasn't with him." She shook her head for her own benefit, not wanting to have this conversation so soon.

"Did he get pulled into a work thing? I didn't think he was cleared from leave yet. Doesn't surprise me, though, it's happened with Tony before."

"No. It just didn't work out, Bianca. I should have listened to you."

"Oh, no."

"Everything was so perfect. We came back here, and he kissed me." If she were being honest with herself, she kissed him, but he did respond.

"Then what happened? But listen, if you don't want to talk about it, I understand."

"Everything was great, and then it...wasn't." Her voice trailed off, ending with a sob. She pinched her eyes shut as she remembered his anger and felt the sting of his words as though he were saying them again.

"Oh sweetie, I'm so sorry."

"I just wanted to let you know I can't come in today. I'll work remotely for the next couple days if that's okay."

"Of course. I'll check in with you tomorrow."

"I need a little time, that's all. I have so many unanswered questions." She plucked a few more tissues from the box, dabbing at her eyes and nose.

"You may not be able to get the answers you need. Dalton is—"

"Complicated. I know. I thought we were moving in the right direction and that I could handle the complicated." Sam choked back another sob. "I was so wrong."

"Don't beat yourself up. Just because it didn't work out between you, Dalton Riley is still a good man. I'd stake my reputation on it."

"You've known him longer. I'll need to make my own judgements. Right now, I feel like there's something very, very, bad about him."

"I know you're hurting, and it's going to take time. Yes, I've known him for a long time, and I know he has dark parts from his past he doesn't ever talk about. I asked you to respect that and not push him."

"He was pushing me away again and I called him out."

"Take the time that you need this week, Sam." Bianca switched back to an executive tone, making Sam keenly aware any discussion about Dalton was over. "I need you back in performance mode. We've got all eyes on us to finish Q4 strong and that means all hands on deck, especially my super star. Got it?"

"Sure."

"Don't lose sight of the prize, Sam. You're too good at what you do to lose it all because of a man. I spoke as a friend and now I'm speaking as your boss. Your broken heart will heal, but your new reputation in this industry might not take the hit well."

"I understand."

"I'm not sure you do," Bianca continued, "I've received emails from Victor Perez saying how much he enjoyed meeting you and is looking forward to continued discussion on his projects. He's going to reach out to you soon to schedule an on-site meeting so you can truly see his vision. He's going to be as big of an influence on your career and numbers as Greg Maddox. Shake this off and get your ass back to work."

"Of course. Thanks, Bianca."

Sam hung up the phone feeling the bite in Bianca's words. She needed to snap out of this for the benefit of her career as much as her mental health. She had been handed two exceptional and influential accounts. Greg Maddox was a charismatic man. A little preoccupied, it seemed, but it had been exciting interacting with him in person at the gala. He'd been gracious enough for pictures and agreed to work with her on some advertising text she could give the marketing team for promotion of his business.

Meeting Victor Perez was a bonus. The slightly older man was equally as charming. She'd read their biographies. Both men were multi-billionaires, and she planned on servicing their accounts above and beyond the best of her ability. Her career was on an uphill trend, and she was eager for what was to come in her professional life.

Meanwhile, her personal life was a train wreck.

Dalton's confrontation still smoldered within her. She couldn't decern what was true or a lie. Nothing made any sense. When she'd mentioned her parents' boating accident, he never said a word. But he was there. He'd witnessed everything, so why wouldn't he admit that to her?

He'd spoken about protecting her. What if he was stalking her to protect himself in the event she suddenly remembered everything?

"What if you're the killer, Dalton Riley?"

The only problem was, after all this time she still had no recollection of what happened. She couldn't prove Dalton did anything. If what he said was true, then his presence there would explain why she felt so comfortable with him. Some part of her was linked to him in the past. She inhaled deep, then exhaled long and low to try to clear her head.

"I don't care what Bianca says. You're not a good man at all." Sam fell back on her bed and let the next round of sobs wrack her body.

CHAPTER 21

"Hey, Manuel, how's everything going?" Greg asked when he answered the ringing cell phone.

"I'd be doing a lot better if you were ready to settle up," Manuel replied, and Greg felt his body tense even though Manuel didn't seem as agitated this time.

"I know, I know. I've had some things come up needing my immediate attention."

"Don't I deserve your attention? You agreed to invest in this business. I hope this is still the case because our agreement has not been satisfied. I accepted your payment after your man screwed up with my product."

Greg closed the office door and took a seat behind his large teakwood desk. He should never have let Rocco take the ladies to Victor's estate on Margarita Island. Greg knew from past dealings Rocco Patrone was a wild card. Then again, they'd all been at one time or another, including Manuel. Greg agreed to give Rocco a chance, sending him with enough rope to hang himself and the dumb ass didn't disappoint.

"Of course, you have my attention. What do I need to do

to make things right." Greg tried not to sound frustrated, but he didn't have time to cater to Manuel. There was too much going on, too much at stake. More important business he had to take care of instead of shuffling a half dozen young women to Venezuela, along with ten kilos of Manuel's special blend.

"Your payment will handle the product that was, let's just say…stolen. But unfortunately, I need a replacement for the girl who over-dosed, thanks to your man Rocco."

Shit.

"I thought the girl was okay?"

"When we first spoke, we thought she was going to recover. Unfortunately, that is not the case."

"Do you know who it was?" Greg began to panic. One of those girls belonged to Victor, and that idiot, Rocco, should have listened to his advice.

"She was Victor's."

I'll fucking kill him.

"Sorry to hear that." Greg's pulse pounded in his head, and he paced in front of the window. "I'll get working on this right away. Better yet, I'll have Rocco handle it."

"You still trust him after this?"

Greg understood Manuel's disdain. Rocco was about to learn shit like this was not acceptable. Greg was going to have to go out on a limb with Manuel, and kiss Victor's ass. In his current position he shouldn't have to do either. They should be kissing his ass and so should Rocco after this.

"If he wants to continue to do business with us, he's going to have to prove himself. If he screws up this time—"

"*I* will kill him," Manuel's tone sounded deadly. "It is my reputation in this partnership as much as it is yours."

"I would expect nothing less," Greg said and swiped a hand down his face. Not what he wanted for Rocco, but it was better than Manuel coming for Greg or his family. Hell, or Victor, too. Rocco had caused more trouble than he was worth. "Give me a description. You'll get your replacement."

"Her name was Angela on your roster. The blonde angel. I'll send a picture. Victor put down an extensive deposit, after meeting her in person, to ensure her safe arrival. I've already had to break the news of her passing."

Greg scribbled on a notebook, becoming more furious with Rocco with each stroke of his pen. He didn't need this shitshow, not now, not ever. He'd become successful on his own and he'd kill Rocco himself if he caused problems for his family. He knew he should be thankful Victor wasn't pounding down his front door right now. What Manuel had offered was a risk, and he'd signed up willingly as a silent partner. It was a win-win of moving cocaine with the bonus of transporting the women.

Nothing should have gone wrong.

"I'll take care of it." Greg paused when there was a light tap on his door.

"Greg, honey, do you want breakfast?"

"Not right now. I'm on a business call. You guys can start without me." He hoped like hell he kept his voice as normal as possible. He didn't need Becca to become suspicious.

"Ah, your lovely wife," Manuel crooned from the phone, making Greg's skin crawl. "I look forward to meeting her and your family someday."

"And I look forward to meeting yours as well." Bile rose in Greg's throat. That was one request from Manuel he'd make sure never happened. He didn't trust this man any more than he could apparently trust Rocco. "I'll get to work on your request." He no sooner hung up the phone than the picture of Angela's lifeless body appeared on his screen. The poor girl, she could have had a fantastic life living with Victor. He stared at the image, wondering if he replaced her with someone even more exquisite maybe he would keep

Manuel at bay and not thinking about crossing the boundary line of a silent partner.

For as much as Greg wanted to be selfish, he needed to protect his family. He swore years ago, Becca and the kids would always come first. Right now, he needed to have a come-to-Jesus moment with Rocco. And while he was in New York, he'd be able to pay a visit to Samantha.

"Now that will make me feel better." he said out loud, excitement replacing his irritation. Scanning his contact list, he pushed a button, trying not to sound too eager when she answered. "Samantha, hi, it's Greg Maddox. I wanted to let you know I will be flying to New York tomorrow on business. How about we get together for a late lunch? Perfect. I'll be in touch."

———

"Are you okay?" Becca asked as she cleaned up the breakfast dishes.

"I'm fine, babe, just business." He handed her his untouched plate and kissed her cheek.

"Greg, you know you can talk to me." She wiped her hands on the nearest towel and poured him another cup of coffee. "You've been acting strange since we came back from New York. I don't want Dalton Riley to come between us like this. I told you I didn't tell him anything. He has no reason to suspect who you are, and we don't even live in New York."

"I'm over that, Becs. But the man is a damn detective. It's not going to take him long to figure out that you, specifically, live in Florida now. He'll come sniffing down here, I know it."

"Maybe he'll let it drop." She stood next to him, cradling her own cup. "We didn't hang around the city so no reason for him to keep thinking of us, right?"

"One can only hope." He sipped his cup knowing if he was thinking of Dalton, then Dalton was one hundred percent thinking about him. The question was, who would get to who first?

"Was your call bad this morning?" Becca kissed his cheek. "I hated to interrupt, and you seem so distracted."

"There are a couple problems I need to take care of." He sighed. "The cost of hiring the wrong people."

"Well, I'm sure you'll handle it just fine, you always do."

"You're right, I always do." He stared through the window at their ocean front view. He had to get a jump on this Rocco situation for many reasons. The most important one being his family. "And I will again." He nodded in affirmation, set his cup down and kissed his wife fiercely. "Thank you, for continuing to believe in me."

"I love you." Becca wrapped her arms around him, and they stood in each other's arms, gazing at the view. "Are you going to have to travel?" she said, with a hint of disappointment in her voice.

"I'm afraid so." He squeezed her tight and kissed the top of her head. "I need to do some damage control for a customer and meet with BC Acquisitions about an expansion off Long Island Sound. And then there's Dalton."

"I think you should leave it alone, Greg."

"I just want to talk. He'll understand about the witness protection. I need to do this for your safety and the kids. That's all."

"I love you for taking such good care of us. How long will you be gone?"

"I love you too, babe. I'm not sure. It might take me a while to find Dalton." And find him he would, but talking was the last thing he wanted to do. Greg planned to clean house to protect his house. He'd taken care of Louie, and he wasn't sure yet what the hell he was going to do with Rocco. But Dalton? Oh, Dalton was going to die, and this time he'd make sure he stayed that way.

CHAPTER 22

The captain announced they would be starting their descent. Greg snorted a line of cocaine and slapped the bare ass of the flight attendant bent over his lap. Nothing like a high in the sky and a few useless fucks to ease the tension. He had a lot to deal with and apparently, he needed to handle things himself. Erik was no help, and Rocco wasn't returning his messages.

Greg was running out of time.

His ears popped with the altitude change as the scrawny woman slid down to give him a blow job. Sure, it felt good, but he needed more. He yanked her by the hair, pulling her off his stiff cock.

"Hey," he said, motioning to another naked woman. "Get over here and bring that dope with you." Greg licked around each of her breasts and dipped them onto the tray of cocaine. "Now I want you to suck that shit off," he commanded the woman whose ponytail he still held. Like a good girl, she did as she was told, and he loved every second of it. He took another hit, laying back on the sofa. "I want you right here." He positioned her over his cock. "And you." He gazed hungrily at the other's perfectly groomed pussy. "We're going to powder that kitty right up." Greg patted the white powder against her glistening skin. I'm about to make you purr." He grabbed her tiny waist and forced her down on his mouth.

Sweet Jesus he was in heaven.

While he licked and sucked Candy, Josie ground against his rock-hard cock. An actual first for him, and it was the supreme feeling of 'getting off". The groans from both women made him work harder. Candy let loose first, and he graciously lapped up every bit of her. His tongue encouraged her to go again, but she was beyond fucked up at this point. "Get off me," he said, pushing her to the floor the minute she appeared to be passing out. Josie continued to ride like a pro. He assisted with a pitch of his own hips. When she cried out, he slapped her firm ass, and she moved faster.

A bell sounded and the captain's voice came over the speaker, "Sir, you'll need to fasten your seatbelts."

"Perfect timing," he grunted. With one final thrust, he exploded into Josie. "Move." He discarded her as he'd done Candy. "I've got shit to do."

After a smooth landing, Greg tucked in his shirt and met the captain at the door.

"Your bags have been loaded in the car, sir."

"Thanks, Randy." He glanced over his shoulder at the remnants of their party. Candy still lay naked and passed out on the floor. Josie had passed out in her seat before she could buckle up. Greg snorted, *bitches*. "Sorry about the mess." He turned his attention back to the captain. "This is for you." He handed the man a vial of powder and a wad of hundred-dollar bills. "Get these whores off my plane and take some time for yourself. I'll see you in a few days."

———

SAMANTHA DECIDED TO TAKE BIANCA'S ADVICE TO HEART. HER professional career was taking off and she had so much to look forward to. The job was exciting, kept her learning and kept her busy. She truly believed the rest of her life would fall into place in divine time.

Her experience with Dalton had taught her to protect her heart a little more, and that was okay. She'd been so busy crying over her broken heart, she'd neglected her mental and physical health. And her condo was a disaster.

Today was a new day.

"You can do this," she said to her disheveled reflection in the bathroom mirror as she started the shower for the first time in days. She didn't even recognize herself, but that was about to change. She turned the temperature as hot as she could stand it, letting the steaming water beat against her skin and wash away the hurt caused by Dalton Riley. She was through allowing others to control her emotions. It was time she put herself first for a change.

By the time she was out and dressed, Sam felt ready to start the healing process and move forward. For the next couple of hours, she spent time deep cleaning and re-organizing, returning her home to the pristine condition she was accustomed to. She even lit her sage bundle to clear the negative energy.

Now that she'd tackled the exterior mess of her life, it was time to focus on the interior. With one giant sweep, she tossed out all her depression-snacks from the pantry.

"Online grocery shopping when you're upset is not a good thing." Sam shuddered over the things she'd filled her body with, vowing to do better.

With a renewed sense of purpose and more energy than she'd had in days, she decided the next thing to do would be to treat her body and mind to some exercise. Rockefeller Park was calling. Sam stayed in her flamingo pink sports bra and shorts, grabbed her water bottle, I.D. and laced up her running shoes. Pulling her hair into a ponytail, she headed out the door to clear her head.

Within moments she was reminded how Dalton had been running when she had called to ask him to accompany her to the award gala. She sighed and tightened her laces in determination. *Clear your head and put yourself first, Sam,* she reminded herself. All the more reason to leave her condo and go for a run.

She exited the front door to her building with a wave and smile to Erik as she adjusted her headphones over her ears. Halfway down the street she realized she'd forgotten to tell him about the blinking smoke detector. *If he's on duty when I get back, I'll tell him then.*

As she ran, she worked on pushing all thoughts of her Dalton drama aside and focused on her breathing and the beauty around her. Trees blocked her view, but she knew there were always kids playing basketball at Washington Market Park. The sign for the Tribeca Performing Arts Center reminded her to check their summer schedule and coordinate a night out with some friends from the office.

This is exactly what I needed.

She loved jogging along the Esplanade, the breeze refreshing against her face as the sun sparkled on the water. By the time she reached the Lily Pond, she was ready for a cool down. Ready to recharge, she walked from the pond to her favorite bench along the river. She liked to come here when she needed to clear her head, finding it relaxing to watch boats glide along the Hudson River and the ferries coming and going.

She sipped her water and closed her eyes against the sun, welcoming its warmth to cleanse her spirit. Filling her lungs with fresh air, she held it in until the count of four and then released the breath in a slow, controlled count of four. She repeated this four times, loving how the stress easily left her body. For the first time, she felt more like herself. She needed to be on her game and not distracted by her personal problems. Greg Maddox was coming to town. Although, she didn't remember ever giving him her personal cell phone, so he must have been in touch with Bianca. Regardless, she couldn't wait to see him again and hear about his upcoming plans. Leaning forward with her water bottle between her knees, she kept her eyes closed as she tuned back into the noises of her surroundings. She just needed to be in the right headspace, like she had been before Dalton Riley had appeared in her life.

Something bumped her sneaker from underneath the bench.

Samantha opened her eyes.

A soda can rolled to a stop near her foot. She frowned.

Curious, she nudged it with her toe and bent to pick it up. The brand name wrapped around the aluminum, familiar and bright. She turned it once.

Then again.

Her name stared back at her.

Samantha

Her pulse spiked. She jumped to her feet, scanning the immediate surroundings.

Joggers passed. A couple walked their dog. Two women pushed strollers. Nothing looked out of the ordinary. No one appeared suspicious.

Still, the sour knot in her stomach didn't ease.

She set the can back on the bench.

The air shifted.

The sky darkened as clouds quickly pushed in from the west, the sun slipping behind them like it had been switched off. The path cleared faster than it should have.

She felt it before she saw him.

A figure stepped out from the trees farther down the esplanade. Baggy shorts, sunglasses, and a ball cap pulled low.

He didn't move.

Samantha's mouth went dry.

She couldn't tell where he was looking — but she knew it was her.

She took one step back.

A light tap brushed her arm. She yelped and spun. A little girl stood beside her holding a bouquet of yellow roses.

"My goodness you startled me," she said, smiling down at the girl.

"Allison!" A brunette with a stroller appeared and put a protective hand on the little girl's shoulder. "I'm so sorry," she said to Sam. "I hope my daughter wasn't bothering you." The woman turned to the girl and asked, "Where did you get those flowers?"

"That man." Allison pointed down the esplanade. "He told me to give them to the pretty lady in pink." She pushed the flowers closer to Sam, who instinctively took them and glanced back at the figure in question, trying to keep her hand from shaking.

"Let's go. Your brother needs a nap." The woman grabbed her daughter's hand and pulled her away. Sam heard the woman reprimand Allison, "Don't you ever take something from a stranger again."

A stranger.

Samantha looked up from the flowers as the man took a deliberate step. The wide smile on his face sent a jolt of fear through her body. Thunder rumbled in the distance and Sam felt the vibration beneath her feet as the final ferry left the dock. The man started moving, his stride growing longer, faster, straight for her now. There was only one thing left to do.

Run.

Sam released the flowers as if they'd burned her palm, spun around, and took off like an Olympic sprinter with her heart slamming against her chest. She could hear the pounding of his feet somewhere behind her, being overtaken by the rush of blood thumping between her ears.

She reached for her phone in her back pocket, only it wasn't there. Her throat went dry as she exited the park. She increased her pace, hell bent on getting home in one piece. Her ears rang and her head throbbed with building pressure while her sneakers splashed through puddles.

I didn't imagine him. I'm not crazy. I still have pollen on my shorts from the flowers. Could it be possible he wasn't chasing me?

Not feeling confident that she still wasn't being followed, she ducked inside a storefront to wait.

"Waiting for someone?" a store clerk asked, startling Sam as she kept vigil by the door. "Sorry, I didn't mean to scare you. It's just that there's no loitering here."

"Yes. I-I'm waiting for someone. They're new to the city and should be here any moment." Luckily, the clerk nodded once and smiled as she went back to organizing displays.

Sam waited a few more minutes and then shrugged at the clerk, raising her hands as if she'd been stood up, before cautiously stepping outside. She held her breath and searched the area. Relief washed over her like the continuous rain when she saw no dark figure lurking about. She was only five blocks from home.

Having no choice, and still too spooked to walk, she started jogging again but kept herself alert the entire way home. With no distractions, she'd convinced herself that her fear and paranoia stemmed from everything Dalton had said about her parents' accident. That is, until she rounded the corner of her building and sucked in a sharp breath. The dark clothed man leaned against the building across the street. He straightened up at the sight of her, and she slowed her pace in disbelief.

He knows where I live.

With a burst of speed, she sprinted up the steps of her building and through the door before Erik could open it. She pointed toward the street, unable to form the words.

"I see you got caught in the rain too," Erik said with a curious glance in her direction before pointing to his wet uniform. "I should have remembered my umbrella."

"There's a man across the street. H-He followed me from the park," she panted, following him to the door.

"Stay here, Ms. Taylor." Erik pushed through the door and stood on the top step.

Sam saw him pointing at the man but couldn't hear what he was saying. The stranger made eye contact, pointed at her, and smiled. As Erik marched down the steps toward the street, the stranger backed up a couple steps, waved to her and took off running.

"I think I should call the police. Did you get a good look at him?" she exclaimed when Erik returned inside.

"You won't have to worry." He placed a large hand on her shoulder as if to console her. "I told him if he stepped foot on the property he would be arrested. We have the new security system, remember, with cameras around the entire building. He's not going to bother you again."

"How can you be so sure?"

"There's someone about his size who has hung around here before, but he never bothered the tenants. Haven't seen him in a while, though. He was harmless for the most part. Maybe he has friends or family in the area."

"He followed me home! I don't call that harmless." Fear crackled in her voice, and she wasn't sure if she could keep it together much longer. "What if he comes back, or is there when I leave for work in the morning?"

"I will be watching for him, Ms. Taylor." Erik stared beyond Samantha to the street, then back to her once more. "You have nothing to fear."

Her gaze returned to the empty street. She lived in a nice neighborhood. Erik's explanation seemed logical enough, yet she just couldn't shake the feeling things weren't over with this stranger. Sam took a calming breath and stretched the coiled, neon green plastic keychain from around her wrist. "Thanks, Erik."

"If you need anything, I'm just a phone call away." She heard him say as she pushed the button for the elevator. Then she remembered.

"Oh, I forgot to tell you to please send someone up to look at my smoke detector."

"Smoke detector? Is something wrong?" Erik reached for his phone.

"The light is blinking, and it never used to, but then sometimes it goes out and the next thing you know it's blinking again. I think there might be a short somewhere."

"Hmmm, that's strange. Maybe it's just the battery."

"Thanks. All the others are fine. It's only the one in the living area." The elevator opened and she stepped inside.

"I'll get someone up there to take a look," Erik stated, and she waved as the doors closed.

Sam stepped off the elevator , then slipped her key in the lock and opened the door. Once inside, she locked the door and kicked off her shoes, making her way to the kitchen where she replaced her water bottle for a glass of red wine. Not the best thing after a good, hard run, but her nerves were shot. All she wanted right now was another hot shower, comfortable clothes and to lose herself in Maddox Charters files.

She stayed in the shower longer than usual, letting the hot water and steam work their magic once more. After she towel-dried her hair, she put on her light blue bralette and matching bootcut yoga pants. Grabbing her wine, she started down the hall when she heard a loud thump as if someone had walked into the console table by the door.

She froze.

What if it was him? How did he get in?

She didn't breathe, couldn't breathe, with her heartbeat thundering in her ears. Her phone sat across the living room like a cherry on a cupcake, atop the neatly stacked Maddox files. Taking a soft, deliberate breath, she focused on slowing her racing heart. Maybe Erik had come to check the smoke detector himself or sent someone else.

"Hello?" she called out, taking a hesitant step closer and gently setting her glass on the edge of her breakfast bar. Sam rounded the corner just as her door was swinging closed. "Hey!" Without thinking, she rushed to the door, yanked it open and scanned the empty hall. "What the hell?"

Stepping back inside her place, she turned the deadbolt this time, double checking that it was secure. When she walked into the living room, she spied the solid red light of the smoke detector. Her muscles wilted with relief and a small hysterical laugh slipped out of her mouth.

Someone had been in to fix it.

"They should have at least left a note," she said to herself as she wandered back to straighten the console table which had been moved out of place. She'd have to let Erik know someone had entered her apartment unannounced. Sam stopped to top off her wine glass and returned to the living room more than ready to get lost in her work.

Only the image of the ominous figure across the street refused to fade.

CHAPTER 23

Greg stared hard at the man before him. Rocco reminded him of what he would have become had he stayed the course and never straightened out his life. The moron still didn't know how to dress the part. How he thought a baggy-ass pair of jeans and a Nets hoodie made him look like boss material remained lost on him. The thought of this piece of shit being so close to ruining everything he had worked for made him see red.

"Do you have any idea what you've done?" The question was more of a statement, spewing from his lips with deadly accuracy.

"Listen, man, I got a little carried away." Rocco's mouth quivered, revealing his fear. "I'm sorry about the bitch who died. She—"

"That bitch had a name. And *Angela* never reached her destination. She was a gift that now needs to be replaced."

"Okay, sure, I'll find another broad and take her back."

"You're not going to do anything. Manuel wants nothing more than to kill you for all the money you cost him. Money I so graciously paid on your behalf because scum like you blow through your money faster than you do your sluts."

"Listen, I can fix this. Give me another chance."

"Why should I? You couldn't even kill Louie. I had to do it for you. And then you had them beat down Cecelia, you couldn't even handle that on your own. You should have put a bullet in her head too. She will never let the death of her husband go unpunished. And she knows it was you!" Greg slapped his palm across Rocco's face. "What the hell is wrong with you?"

"I did what you wanted." Rocco grabbed his face and cowered as if he thought Greg would strike him again.

"Almost. And then you fucked me over, Rocco. I'm not someone you should be fucking over."

"I'm telling you I'll make this right. I'm making it right as we speak."

"Go on...." He crossed his arms, intrigued by the eager excitement displayed on Rocco's puffy face.

"I've got some guys watching that cop who you said is making trouble for you. I gave them the word this morning you wanted him taken out."

"Perfect." He clapped Rocco on the shoulder. "Make sure there's no trace of the sonofabitch, got it?"

"Yeah, yeah. Don't worry, it's all good. When are we moving on Enso? You promised me I'd be in charge...of things." Rocco was quick to add as if remembering who was really in charge and who would always remain in charge.

"What part of fucking me don't you understand?" Correcting this fuck-stick was exhausting. "You don't get to screw me and then receive some grand reward. You must earn it. Prove to me I can trust you."

"What more can I do?"

"Fix the problem, Rocco. I need a replacement for the lovely Angela. And I need Dalton Riley gone. You take care of those things, and you will be in better standing with me. Screw up again and you'll be dead. If it's not Manuel, then it will be me, you can be sure of it.

The sloppy man visibly shook in his shoes. Greg expected him to piss himself at any moment. Watching this weak follower sent a surge of dominance through Greg's body. This life he had was one gigantic power trip. Low-lifers like Rocco begged for a chance to be like him-knowing they never would —while middle and upper-class citizens begged him for his money and opportunities. They were all at his beck and call and he loved it.

One day, everyone would know who Greg Maddox was.

———

GREG RETURNED TO HIS HOTEL ROOM AFTER A STRESSFUL MEETING with Rocco. On the way to the hotel, he thought long and hard about his current predicament. He could sense things escalating, and he didn't have much confidence in Rocco's abilities to do anything right now. Raking a hand through his hair, Greg cracked open a bottle of vodka from the mini bar, tipped back the whole thing in one shot, and held the empty bottle toward the ceiling.

"I hate to admit it, Lou, but you were right. Your brother is a weak piece of shit. You should have rid yourself of him years ago and trusted me a hell of a lot more." He grabbed another bottle and repeated the action. "Fuck you, Louie." Greg tossed the empty and twisted the cap off a fresh one when his phone rang.

"Make it fast. You've interrupted my celebratory mourning." He tipped back the nip then chucked it in the direction of the trash can.

"Sorry, boss, but I think we have a problem."

"We've been over this." Greg sighed, rubbing his forehead

as he scanned the remaining mini bottles of booze. "I pay you good money to handle the problems, so I don't have to be bothered. I have enough shit to deal with."

"Check your feed, sir. I wouldn't bother you if it wasn't necessary. I think the system has gone offline."

Greg frowned when a nagging feeling settled over him. He wasn't going to be happy with this news, and just when he was starting to enjoy himself. "Why?" he answered carefully and scrambled to find his tablet, dreading what he was about to see. A hesitant silence filled the line. When he clicked on the app, all that came up was a giant red X. "Fuck!" He slammed his hand on the mini bar, causing all the lined-up nips to clink together. "Erik, what the hell happened?"

"I'm not sure. She went for a run and was apparently followed by someone. I had to scare them off. Before she went upstairs, she told me the smoke detector wasn't working, said the light was blinking. I haven't had a chance to check it out, so I tried bringing up the camera feed. There's nothing there. It's as if it doesn't exist."

Greg's anger dulled to a soft boil as lust stirred anew. "Looks like my little doe realized she was being hunted," he said as he paced around his room, enjoying the thought of a little cat and mouse game. Taking her would be all the sweeter if she played along. "Although." He stopped short with his finger in the air and a muscle pulsing in his jaw. "I think she had some help."

"Sir?"

"C'mon, she had to, right? An innocent little beauty like her wouldn't suspect...but a detective sure as hell would." Greg clenched his jaw until his teeth ached, reigniting his anger. *Damn you, Dalton Riley.*

"I'll make a service appointment right away and check it out. I just wanted you to be aware of the situation."

"Find out who the hell followed her. And when you do,

make them disappear." Greg hung up the phone and dropped it on the thick down comforter, pumping his fists as he returned to the mini bar. He didn't like the thought of someone new sniffing around.

The way he saw it, he had two major problems. Taking care of them both would secure the return of normalcy to his life. Dalton, of course, was too close to Samantha. Now that Greg would have more and more contact with her, the odds of running into Dalton were greater. Not to mention the likelihood of Dalton snooping around Rebecca. There was a trip to Florida in the detective's future, Greg was certain of it. All the more reason to have him eliminated, like he should have been fourteen years ago.

The lovely Samantha had become problem number two. All these years he'd watched her, setting himself up for success in the process. He'd established connections in New York, planning, leading to use of the bank she worked at. Then came the welcome bonus. She'd become more accessible when she started working for BC Acquisitions, and he didn't have anything to do with that. Only now, all this contact with her gave him an obsessive need to fulfill the fantasy.

He loved his wife deeply. Becca and the kids were his world. But Samantha, damn it, she was a reincarnation, if not better, of that bitch Nina. Samantha was strong and independent, and he knew he wouldn't be able to manipulate her for long. He'd have one shot at getting everything he wanted from her before she'd go to the police. He wasn't about to lose the life he created over his blood lust for this woman. He also knew he wouldn't be able to settle down until the urgent need was satisfied. He'd cracked open another bottle from the mini bar when it hit him.

The perfect solution.

"I'm a fucking genius!" he said to his reflection in the

mirror before tipping back a bottle of whiskey this time. "You *will* be mine, and then it's bye-bye Samantha."

As far as Victor's bride was concerned, Greg had discovered the answer, and he couldn't wait any longer to share it as he stretched to grasp his phone.

"Victor!" he yelled with excitement when the man answered his call.

"Ah, Greg, nice to hear from you. I thought maybe you'd gone into hiding." Victor chuckled, and Greg was thankful they were not on a video call so the man couldn't see his balled-up fist turn into a middle finger salute.

"Now Victor, I've got nothing to hide from. I would like to apologize for the extreme error of my associate, Rocco Patrone. He's been reprimanded and will be stripped of all senior duties until further notice."

"He killed my Angela."

"No, Angela killed herself by taking part in the drugs presented to her. She should have said no."

"You're defending your man? I was under the impression you were stronger than that."

"I'm not defending him. He had instructions to follow, and he did a pretty shitty job. But he did not commit murder."

"I see." Victor paused and Greg chalked up a soon to be victory. He just needed the right lead in, so he didn't sound too eager. "Manuel says you are personally looking for my wife's replacement."

Bingo.

"Funny you should mention it. I'm about to make things perfect in your world. All of your dreams and desires are about to come true." *And mine, too,* he thought, as he imagined touching every inch of her soft, sun-kissed skin.

"What exactly do you have in mind?"

"Correct me if I'm wrong, my friend, but from an earlier

conversation did I or did I not receive the impression that you have a particular, how should we say it, *interest* in Samantha Taylor?"

"You are very intuitive, my friend. Your impression would be correct. Since meeting her in person and talking, let's just say my interest has grown."

"I know exactly where you're coming from. She seems to have that effect on people."

"As I am also very intuitive, are you trying to tell me Samantha could be my future wife and partner?"

"Not could be, Victor, *will* be." Greg's entire body tingled at the thought of this wonderful plan working out for everyone involved. "I have some unfinished business I need to settle with Samantha. I want to make sure my accounts have her full attention. Once we are finished going over everything, I will personally deliver her to you."

"That won't be necessary. I have some business dealings in the Bahamas. Once I arrive, I will contact Manuel and he will meet you at a designated location."

"I get the feeling you don't trust me." Greg hoped once he had Samantha, Victor would be so busy he would stay the hell away from him and his charter business. And Rocco better finish off Dalton or there would be hell to pay.

"I don't," Victor said before the line went dead.

"Fuck you, asshole." Greg tossed the phone onto the king-sized bed. Opening his suitcase, he pulled out a small plastic bag. "Come to papa," he cooed, "It's time to party." He dipped his index finger into the powder and rubbed it inside his mouth. Crawling across the bed, he snagged his phone and made a call.

"Hey, Randy, I need you to do me a favor. I'm at the hotel, penthouse suite. Grab some drinks and bring Josie and Candy with you. Have them bring some friends, too, I've had a hell of a day."

CHAPTER 24

"Thanks for meeting me," Dalton said as he sat across from Nicki at their favorite table inside O'Grady's Pub. He'd been surprised she'd returned his call and agreed to meet for lunch. To be honest, he'd expected his stubborn Irish firecracker to make him suffer. He stared at her, waiting for her response, and his heart softened.

Her thick hair hung in loose waves of fire around her face, and Dalton took full responsibility for the lack of brightness he noticed in those golden eyes staring back at him. He figured she'd cooled off enough to not be horribly upset with him, since she sported his black NY Rocks hoodie from three years ago during Central Park's concert series.

And she looked damn good in it.

"Of course," she finally answered, as if she'd been contemplating how she wanted to handle the situation. She smiled, drawing his attention to her full lips, then quickly added in a tone which said she clearly had something on her mind, "You know me, any excuse to get you alone."

He pursed his lips into a tight smile of acknowledgment,

and regret filled him. "Yeah, about that. Sorry I've been out of pocket. I have a lot of explaining to do."

"You don't have to apologize or explain. I think this one's on me." She took a sip of her lager then fiddled with the cocktail napkin. "I shouldn't push you so hard to be in a relationship your heart's obviously not into."

"Nicole…." He'd been expecting some resistance, not all out surrender.

"No, let me say my peace." She held up her hand to stop him from going further. "You took Bianca's protégé to the ball, giving her a Cinderella moment, and then suddenly you go dark. You told me to be there when you got home, and I was Dalton." Her gaze met his, and the hurt was evident before she looked down. "I waited around until three a.m. That's when it hit me." She paused again and it took a moment before she glanced up from the pile of napkin scraps. "I'm not usually the paranoid type, but I can't help but think you've developed feelings for this girl."

"Not even close." He reached for her hands across the table, and she pulled them back.

"That's what it looks like. You have to admit it. What we have is amazing and you know I've been fine with our current arrangement. Do I want more? Of course, I do, but I'm smart enough to know there's something holding you back. I've been okay with it. I understand your past. Just be real with me, Dalton. That's all I ask. We can't move forward if there are secrets, especially if they could come back to hurt us later."

"You have no idea." He shook his head and took several gulps from his IPA.

"That's right, I don't. You need to let me in, Riley, it's either that or let me go." She stared at him with no walls up, and Dalton felt every bit of raw emotion he saw clouding her beautiful marigold eyes. "There's more going on than just vengeance for your brother's death. I don't know exactly how, but I somehow think it has to do with this girl."

"You're right," he said, grasping her hands before she could move them. "This hasn't been fair to you, and I'm sorry. Really, I am."

She hesitated a moment and studied him. "It's not about being fair, Dalton. It's about being all in. Our jobs, our relationship. If we're a team, then we're all in. I'm always going to have your back."

"No, I mean you're right." He signaled the server for two more beers. "About everything."

"Everything?" Her brows became lost behind waves of red hair. "Which part exactly. I kind of vomited all my feelings."

"This absolutely involves Justin's murder." The server brought their beers, and he took advantage to drain half his glass. He owed Nicki the truth. "Samantha was there."

Her jaw fell open and eyes widened. "Holy shit, she's a witness?" Nicki slammed the bottle on the table. "You've been protecting and watching her all this time?"

"Sort of." He paused, gathering all the information which had been locked in his head for fourteen years.

Nicki propped a fist against her cheek, as if she were about to hear some juicy gossip. Her eyes transformed into twinkling orbs of excitement as she leaned in. "Go on, love, I'm all ears."

"Remember how I've told you I made a promise to a dying man?"

"Yes, to Justin."

"No, it wasn't Justin." He watched her tilt her head and a confused scowl crossed her face.

"Go on."

"It was Samantha's father."

"Wow, okay." Nicki sat up straight, blinked rapidly and

took her hand off the beer bottle. "You need to keep explaining because I've suddenly got puzzle pieces that don't quite fit."

"The Taylors were the charter we were taking to the Bahamas and back, the goal being to sell Doctor Taylor the boat. Justin was hell bent on getting me off that boat and since I wouldn't leave, he decided to stay and 'save me from myself.' Billy wasn't happy with Justin on board, but there was no time to convince him to leave. So, Billy drugged him, keeping him down below, where he wouldn't screw up the deal with the doctor."

"What the hell? No wonder you feel the need for revenge." She shook her head. "This explains so much."

"That's not all." He held up his hand. "We had some fun days at sea, but Billy started fixating on the Doc's wife. She was a gorgeous woman."

"Oh, boy, I think I know where this is going."

"I was fishing with Samantha when all hell broke loose and Captain Billy killed her parents, then Justin, and tried to kill me."

"You lived." Her eyes softened and voice lowered tenderly. "How on earth did you get away?"

"I found some scuba gear on the boat and used it to make my escape that day. I remember panicking when the oxygen ran out and struggling to break the surface. I'd lost so much blood I honestly didn't expect to survive. I figured sharks would find me first. The next thing I knew, I was waking up on some Caribbean Island where a doctor did their best to remove the bullets and repair the damage." He paused long enough to take another drink and push aside his burger and fries. Nicki stayed glued to his every word.

"What the hell, Dalton."

"I was in so much pain. It was the doctor who told me the girl had been found. She thought the girl was mine. I told her no, and I never said a word about the Taylors or what happened that day. I stayed on the island until I was fully recovered and at the same time detoxed from all the drugs in my system. By the time I made my way back home, Samantha was a nation-wide story. They were calling her Little Girl X until a relative came forward to take guardianship of her."

"Right...I remember the story now that you say that. She was so young and so traumatized authorities could never figure out where she'd drifted from. I believe the case closed within a year."

"I was just relieved she was alive. But it meant I had more work to do."

"Jesus! Why have you kept this to yourself for so long? Why didn't you come forward?"

"In the back of my mind, I worried she'd remember what happened. That's why I never came forward. The authorities would either think I did it, or that I was an accessory to murder. Either way, I couldn't go to jail. Now that Justin was dead, I was all my parents had left, and that guilt ate at me, as did the lies I had to tell to make sure they never felt this pain."

"I'm so sorry. I wish you could have told me."

"I told you enough. I couldn't take the risk of you knowing any other details. I always knew the captain didn't go down with his ship, and now CeCe pretty much confirmed he's still alive. If I know my old friend, Billy Benning, he's somehow messed up in this fentanyl dealing."

"What does this have to do with Samantha? She's been fine for fourteen years, and she obviously hasn't remembered you."

"If Billy is back in New York, and he's into this drug market, my gut says he's not going to leave Samantha alone for long. I need to find him and stop him. I thought for sure when I ran into Becca at the hotel, she'd give me some kind of lead."

"Speaking of Rebecca Maddox, she had some prostitution pickups when she was in her late teens and some drug usage. She's been married to Greg Maddox for eleven years. She must have cleaned herself up when she met him. They have four children and live in coastal Florida."

"And what about Maddox?"

"The man is a multi-billionaire, upstanding citizen and doesn't have so much as a parking ticket. He's mister squeaky clean. Strange thing is...the man is a ghost prior to his marriage to Rebecca. It's like he never existed."

"WITSEC?"

"Maybe. I'd have to call in some favors and pay for some lunches to gain access to that information."

"Damn it! I feel like we're back to square one."

"Not so fast." Nicki pulled a document from her bag and unfolded it on the table. "I think you'll find this interesting."

"What is it?"

"A list of recent real estate transactions. It seems Greg Maddox owned a condo unit in Tribecca." She paused as Dalton shrugged. "The same unit being rented by Samantha Taylor."

"What?" Dalton snatched the paper to read for himself. "How coincidental is it to have the young woman managing your accounts also live in your personal condo?"

"Not only that, but this document shows he purchased the entire building five months ago."

"One month after Sam moved in." Dalton set the paper on the table. "Sam said Bianca gave her three to choose from. She chose freely, no one coerced her."

"I'm seriously feeling this was a stroke of unexpected dumb luck." The way she methodically shook her head told him she was connecting some very important dots. "He already knew she was the tenant."

"Right, we've established that."

"No…no…hold on!" She searched through her bag. "Oh my God, wait a minute."

She was like a bloodhound on the hunt, and he trusted her instincts.

"Holy shit." Nicki brought out what looked to be a legal document. "Before Maddox purchased the building…are you ready?" She paused until Dalton nodded. "It was previously owned by Primo, LLC which is owned by Louie and Cecelia Patrone." Dalton met Nicki's eyes from across the paper as she spoke, "You thought Billy had something to do with Louie's death. If he did, that means…."

"Greg Maddox is Billy Benning!" Dalton dropped the paper.

"What do we do now? Do you want to call Tony?"

"Not yet. I want to talk to that doorman."

"Why?"

"He hasn't liked me since the first time I showed up, and now I know why." He fiddled in the pocket of his hoodie and pulled out a tiny black square with a lens. "This."

"Is that a camera?" Nicki took it from his fingers and studied it. "Impressive. Very high tech." She handed it back and he deposited it into his pocket.

"It was hidden in Sam's smoke detector. I noticed it the last time I was there. I wasn't one hundred percent sure, but my gut told me something wasn't right. I'm pretty sure he put it there."

"Do I want to know how you gained possession of the device?" Nicki's arched brow told him she had some ideas.

"I snuck in through the loading dock while she was out. Problem was she came back before I had it disconnected. I had to sit tight in the closet until she went in the shower."

"The shower?" She tilted her head and pursed her lips.

"Don't even go there." He pointed a finger toward her nose. "I finished the job and left."

"You think Mr. Doorman is feeding information to Billy?"

"I'd bet money on it." Dalton stood, tossing a wad of bills on the table. "He's the eyes on Samantha that Billy needs, and by now he knows I'm in the picture. Well, was in the picture."

"You think he's going to make a move?" Nicki rose, snagging a fry from her plate of uneaten food, and followed him toward the door.

"Eventually, but I need to talk to Sam, make her aware of who she's dealing with. Considering how we left things, I don't think she'll believe anything I have to say and that's even if she agrees to talk."

"Speaking of talking, forget everything I said. Ugh…I hate when I turn into an emotional female." She rolled her eyes and flipped the hood of her sweatshirt up as sprinkles of rain tapped the sidewalk.

"Trust me, I don't mind. You keep me grounded, Nicole Morgan." He winked over saying her full name, feeling her relax when he took her hand. They walked in a comfortable silence for the next block toward the subway entrance, and then he stopped. "Look, I know we've never been conventional, but I want to do this right with you."

"Dalton, no, forget it." She tried to back away, but he wouldn't let her. This was important. He needed to say it, and she needed to hear it. "We're going to be soaked," she remarked as the rain fell harder. You can tell me later."

"No." He pulled her, walking backwards until they were both protected by the store awning. "I'm telling you now."

"It's okay, really. It's more important we reach Sam." She tried to tug him back to the sidewalk, but he held his ground.

"What I have to say is important." He stared into the beautiful face of the woman who meant everything to him.

He'd been so obsessed with finding Billy and now Samantha, he'd almost lost the one person who understood him and loved him despite what he'd done. He pushed the hood away from her face, her thick black eyelashes fluttering as she gazed up at him. Dalton felt as if his heart were going to burst if he didn't tell her right this minute. He skimmed her soft cheeks with his thumbs, saying, "Nicole, I—"

Dalton heard the 'thwack' of the bullet penetrate her clothing before her face registered the impact. They both gazed at the blood seeping to the surface in a growing red pool through the center of her shirt. Her face paled and she collapsed to the ground.

"Nicole!" He drew his weapon and scanned the surrounding area for any sign of movement or possibly another shot. "Baby, c'mon." He tapped her cheeks and rubbed her arms, trying to keep her conscious. After pulling off his own hoodie to prop under her head, he then made the frantic call to 911. "You're really going to make me work for this?" he said as he leaned over her. Through his worry, he grinned with relief when his teasing made her open her eyes.

"Of course, I am," she said then coughed up blood. Their eyes held mutual fear. "You have to go to her," she said before blood crept from the corner of her mouth. "Sam. Go save Sam."

"I'm not leaving you." He brushed the sopping red strands of hair away from her face and kissed her forehead.

"Not. Going. Any...where." Her weak smile melted his heart, and he prayed the ambulance would get there in time.

CHAPTER 25

"Shit!" Rocco said into his phone, drawing Greg's attention to the man's increasingly annoying face. "What do you mean he moved? Are you sure?" In a quick motion he shoved the phone into his pocket and swiped at the beads of sweat decorating his pudgy face.

"Trouble?" Greg arched a brow.

"No, no. I'm pretty sure we can fix this. Give—"

"Fix what, Rocco?" Greg lit the bowl and inhaled the weed smoke deeply. Once satisfied, he blew out a long cloud into the air. "What have you screwed up now?"

"My guys, you know the ones watching the cop?" Greg narrowed his eyes, not saying a word, dreading what was coming. "Yeah, well, they shot the wrong person. They had him in their sights and then he moved."

"Well, you moron, that's what living people usually do. They move!" Greg's voice boomed like thunder in the air. "After all this time, Rocco, you're still running an amateur operation. And yet, as clear as can be, you want me to give you more." He walked a circle around the quaking excuse of a man, his blood pressure increasing with every step. "Tell me why a piece of shit like you deserves chance after chance?"

"Because I've always been loyal to you. Always."

"You call using product that was not yours being loyal? Allowing a young woman to overdose on drugs you never should have had in your possession. You call that loyal? You put a huge dent in Manuel's trust in *me* and our partnership. How the hell do you see that as being loyal?"

"I, I know I messed up. And, and I appreciate all you did to pay back what I lost. I'll work it off, I promise. I'll pay you back."

"We both know you won't."

"That's not true," Rocco pleaded. "I really will."

"I believe I told you, personally, to keep an eye on Dalton, not hire others to do it for you."

"Something came up, so I had to ask a buddy to cover."

"Now that's just being selfish, Rocco." Greg pulled back and punched Rocco in the center of the gut. When he fell forward Greg landed an uppercut under his chin, sending him back several steps. "I think you can tell I don't like self-ishness. There's no place for it when I've given you a job to do with what I believe were precise instructions." He once more circled Rocco, who stood panting and trying to stay upright.

"I'll make it right. I'll handle Dalton myself this time. I will."

"You're not very convincing, Rocco. Dalton is the very least of my worries. While he's a concern, the most important thing is keeping Manuel happy and thereby keeping Victor happy."

"I found a replacement girl for Victor."

Greg hesitated a split second "Go on...." He tried to sound encouraging but didn't hold onto much hope. Then again, if it meant he could keep Samantha to himself for a while longer, he wouldn't mind stringing Victor along with an appropriate teaser. He'd show that pompous asshole who was really in charge and deliver Samantha when he was damn good and ready.

"I followed that Taylor girl."

"What?" He felt possessiveness boil within him as he glared at Rocco. "Why would you do that?"

"I wasn't planning to at first. I was out picking up some pastrami for my cousin when she jogged by, and I had an idea." Rocco paused until Greg made a move with his hand for the man to continue. "She can be the replacement girl for Victor!"

"Well done." Greg clapped.

"Right?" Rocco beamed with pride. "I followed her all the way to the river. And then I gave her a good scare. I kind of enjoyed it, like, I know why stalkers get off on this shit."

"What do you mean you scared her?" Greg narrowed his eyes. "What did you do, Rocco?"

"I found some kid to go give her flowers and then I stepped out from the trees and started to walk toward her."

"What is wrong with you?" Greg shook his head. "Obviously, you didn't learn your lesson with Cecelia. What are you going to do if she reports you to the police, or God forbid can pick you out from a picture."

"Nah, I didn't get that close." Rocco flicked his hand in Greg's direction. "Plus, I was dressed in sweats and a hoodie. She'd never know who I am anyway. Besides, she took off running. I followed her for a while, then decided to wait for her near her place."

"So, you're the one Erik told me about."

"Who?" Rocco puckered his brow then shrugged. "Anyway, while I was waiting, I thought that little bitch would be perfect for Victor. She'd be out of your hair and then you wouldn't have to worry about Dalton nosing around where he wasn't wanted."

"Dalton who should already be dead."

"Yeah, boss, but I'll go back and take care of him, don't you worry. Then we can work together on securing the package for Victor."

"You poor, rotten bastard. There is no *we* in this equation. This is just another failure on your part. You see, I'm one step ahead of you as far as Samantha Taylor is concerned." Greg continued to be annoyed with Rocco, but the dimwit may have done him a favor. With sweet Samantha on edge, and nervous, she would be more receptive to him comforting her. Staring into the confused brown eyes before him, Greg pulled out his phone and started to dial. "I'm taking care of things myself."

"Wh-What are you going to do?"

"This." Greg said. Whipping out a gun, he shot Rocco in the head with an immense amount of satisfaction. The man hit the ground seconds before Greg's call connected.

"Hi, Sam, it's Greg Maddox," he greeted in a calm, soothing tone as he rubbed the warm barrel of his gun against the bulge of his dick within his pants. "My current meeting has run late, and I'm just now cleaning up a couple of messes. I'm going to send a car for you since this is all my fault. I took the liberty to change our reservation to a location closer to where I am now. It will give me time to clean up. I hope you don't mind." He listened to her very gracious response, smiling at the eagerness in her voice. *This is too easy*, he thought before responding, "Wonderful, I'll see you soon. Looking forward to another amazing merger."

DALTON WAS PACING IN THE HOSPITAL WAITING ROOM WHEN Tony rushed in.

"Jesus, D, where's Nicki? Is she all right?"

"I, I don't know. Doctors are checking her out now." Dalton scrubbed his blood-stained hands through his wet hair and down his face as he sat on the very edge of a cushioned chair. "We were talking, I was going to tell her...I heard the shot go through her. Tony, if she dies—"

"She's not going to die, Dalton. Nicki is strong."

"You didn't see her. She lost so much blood." He cleared his throat and looked away, as he fought the tears building behind his eyes. "I think that bullet was meant for me."

"On my way here, I found out that Rocco Patrone is dead."

"What?" There went Dalton's theory that it was Rocco who had tried to kill him.

"Do you have something you want to tell me?" Tony's face held compassion, but his eyes were in detective mode as they watched Dalton's every move.

"About Rocco?" Dalton's brows knitted together. "No. I don't know anything about his death. I was thinking he might have been the one who shot Nicki."

"Not about Rocco." Tony paused. "Too many people are dying lately, and their common thread is you, my friend."

"Are you trying to say I had something to do with Louie and Rocco's deaths? Jesus, Tony, I would never hurt CeCe or Nicki." Dalton shook his head in disbelief.

"I know you didn't have anything to do with it. But I believe you do know something about it. Care to discuss?"

"No." Dalton couldn't give Tony the details he wanted, not now.

"Wrong answer."

Thankfully, Dalton didn't have to answer. Nicki was wheeled out of the room on a gurney, surrounded by a medical team. Her color was a little better since the last time he saw her, and she was semi-conscious.

"What's going on?" Dalton asked as he approached.

"We're taking her into surgery to get the bullet out and repair some tissue," the doctor replied.

"Is she going to be okay?" Dalton hadn't stopped worrying. He needed definitive answers.

"All scans look good. Unless there's something in there we don't know about, I can confidently say she can expect a full recovery."

"Did you hear that?" Dalton brushed her cheek and she fought to keep her eyes open. "You're going to be just fine."

"Excuse me, sir," a nurse said while navigating the gurney, "We'll let you know when she's in recovery."

"Okay." He leaned down and kissed her cheek. "I love you," he whispered near her ear. To his surprise, her hand reached up to touch his face.

"Did I hear you right?" Her voice sounded froggy. The corners of her mouth pulled up into a little grin. "Say it again."

"I will when you come back and make me." Her eyes lit up and Dalton watched his whole world enter the operating room. With Nicki out of danger, he was eager to warn Samantha. He started for the hospital door when Tony grabbed his arm.

"Where are you going now?"

"I'm asking you to trust me, Tony. I promise to fill you in when I can, but right now I've got to go." Dalton clapped his partner on the shoulder and ran out of the hospital. He needed to reach Sam before it was too late.

CHAPTER 26

Dalton exited the cab just as Sam walked out of her building toward an awaiting car. The summer rain shower had stopped, leaving in its wake heavy, humid air. She looked beautiful in a cropped white blouse and matching long, flowing skirt, with a jacket draped over her arm. He kept his pace steady, taking in the scene before him for anything out of the ordinary. And there it was.

No rear license plate on the blacked-out SUV.

"Samantha, wait!" he yelled as he broke into a run. She froze with her hand on the door.

"Dalton!" The shock in her voice was undeniable. "What are you doing here?" He watched as her surprise transitioned to what he recognized as fear, as she scanned the area beyond him as though expecting to see someone else.

"I need to talk to you." When he reached out to reassure her, she took a hesitant step closer to the vehicle. He'd been expecting residual anger, but not this. "Please, it's important."

"We have nothing left to say to each other." The quiver in her voice remained even though her tone held no emotion. "I won't make a fool out of myself again."

"You don't know how sorry I am about everything. But Captain Billy got away, Sam. I've been searching for him all these years."

She closed her eyes and sighed. "Dalton, you need to stop living in the past." When she opened them, he took full responsibility for the weariness he saw in those ocean blue depths. "Whatever it is you think you know, I don't want any part of it. I have a life. I've moved on."

"You could be in danger until we catch him."

"Is there a problem Ms. Taylor?" The hulk of a man said from behind Samantha, making her jump. His muscular build and tailored suit reminded Dalton more of a bodyguard than a driver, and he wondered why he was here for Sam.

"Why don't you just get back in the car, buddy, and let the lady and me finish our conversation. And you, too, doorman, get back inside and mind your own business. This doesn't concern you." Dalton pointed at where the doorman stood at the top of the steps.

"Everything's okay, Erik," Samantha said. Erik sent one more glare toward Dalton and a nod to the driver, before returning inside the building. "Dalton, I have to go." The driver opened the door, and she got inside.

"I know where he is and who he is." At those words, Sam kept her hand on the door and nodded to the driver who reluctantly returned to the front of the vehicle. She refused to look at him. Feeling as though she would bolt at any time, he tossed out his next words in a rush, "It's Greg Maddox." Sam removed her hand and Dalton was not prepared for her to go on the offensive when she swung her legs outside the door so she could face him.

"You didn't even meet the man so how can you make such accusations? As a matter of fact, I'm on my way to meet Greg now. But don't worry, I won't repeat any of the lies you just concocted."

"Don't go." Dalton's heart raced at the sudden thought of her being alone with him.

"He's my *client* and I won't risk losing his business because of your horrible insinuations."

"Think about it, Sam. Why would he want you to handle his business? The man is a multi-billionaire, and you have what…six months experience? Someone in his position with so much to lose would request a seasoned employee." *After everything he'd said, how could she not see it?*

"Stay out of my life, Dalton." She pulled her legs back into the vehicle. The door slammed shut and the SUV pulled away from the curb.

"He's been keeping tabs on you, too!" Dalton yelled knowing she couldn't hear him.

Dalton flagged the nearest cab, flashing his detective badge and hopping into the passenger seat. Wherever that driver was going, Dalton planned on being there, too. He wished he were wrong. He'd love to think Samantha was at a normal business meeting with a normal client. But knowing Greg Maddox was Billy Benning changed everything. No matter who he pretended to be, deep inside Greg would always be Billy Benning. It was only a matter of time before he'd do something to Sam.

"Don't lose that SUV," he ordered the driver.

If Billy took care of Sam like he'd tried to take care of Dalton, the man would be home free, and no one would ever know about the boat, the Taylors, or Justin. Dalton's mind wandered to Nicki, who'd taken a bullet meant for him. He didn't deserve her. Reaching in his pocket for his phone, he pressed his first contact. Dalton vowed in that moment he would finally get his revenge and Samantha would be safe to live her life the way she chose. Maybe one day, she'd be able to forgive him.

"Hey, Tony, I'm going to need your help."

———

Sam pinched the bridge of her nose, willing herself not to shed one more tear over Dalton Riley. She refused to put an ounce of faith into anything he'd said. She'd read business reports on Greg Maddox. She'd met him in person with his wife. Bianca had confirmed after returning from Florida what an amazing couple they were. She may not have years of experience, but with Bianca's guidance she'd obviously done things right. Greg had personally told her what a great job she'd been doing. There was no way he could have ever been involved with the disappearance of her parents. Why would Dalton want to hurt her this way?

"You okay back there, miss?" the driver asked as he maneuvered through the streets.

"Yes, I'm fine, thank you."

"Mr. Maddox has asked me to bring you to the North Cove Marina."

"Marina? I thought we were having dinner?"

"He's going to meet you on his yacht. He's been known to entertain there when he's in the area."

"Oh." Sam leaned back in the seat, breathing deep to calm her nerves. The harbor cruise from hell reared its ugly head and she couldn't let herself vomit all over her client or his million-dollar yacht. She closed her eyes as the vehicle sped up and entered the highway.

"We'll be there is about ten minutes."

Sam reflected on her time with Dalton. He'd always been her cheerleader, and the perfect gentleman, until she'd pushed him too far. He'd told her things she didn't want to hear, things she didn't remember, and they didn't make much sense to her now. He said it was the truth, and even though she didn't want to believe it, he had no reason to lie to her. Something deep inside hummed a warning.

Maybe she shouldn't be meeting Greg alone until she had proof of her own.

Don't let Dalton get into your head again, she ordered herself, then shook her head over her own foolishness.

Greg had to have staff on board so they wouldn't be totally alone. With a little luck, it would be a floating dinner, and he wouldn't take the boat out on the open water. Now that she could handle. Sam relaxed into the soft leather seat allowing the altercation with Dalton to leave her mind.

Yes, she would think positive until proven otherwise. While she told herself to be confident in her decision, the tingle up her spine reminded her to stay alert. Before she knew it the vehicle came to a stop.

"We're here," the driver said as he got out and opened her door. "I'll walk you down to Mr. Maddox. He's ready for you."

"Thank you," she said as he helped her and closed the door. "Do you know if he plans to take the boat on the water? I don't want to insult him, but I have a phobia with open water."

"I'm sure you'll have nothing to worry about. He's always very accommodating to his guests."

"I can only imagine." There, she pointed out to her stubborn imagination. Nothing to worry about. She's his guest, and a business partner of sorts. There was no way he could be as bad of a man as Dalton insinuated. And that was the last she was going to think about it.

They walked down the dock to the very end. The smell of fish and algae doing little to settle her nerves. Gulls circled and dove for fish. "Ride the tide," she said softly, remembering that connection between Dalton and her father. *How easily he pops into my thoughts.* Was there more Dalton didn't tell her? Should she have given him more of a chance to explain?

If Sam were honest with herself, she'd realize she couldn't hide behind the trauma of her past anymore. Maybe it was time for her to hear the truth, or at the very least, what Dalton claimed to know about what really happened to her parents.

"Here you go." The driver motioned toward a small walkway which would get her from the dock to the boat. "Mr. Maddox is waiting in the stern side lounge for you. Enjoy your evening." And just like that, the man left her.

Sam watched him walk away, suddenly feeling awkward and alone. She looked at the bright red letters on the side of the boat *'Livin' the High Life'*. The prickle up her spine returned. "Samantha, you're being ridiculous," she whispered out loud. "Bianca is never going to promote you if you can't handle yourself professionally." With a shake of her head and a deep breath of renewed confidence, she crossed over.

GREG SCRUBBED HIS WET HAIR, RECREATING THE MESS OF BLONDE waves he'd had to cover up for years. It felt good to return to his natural color, and to have the money to hire some hairdresser on the spot to remove the brown dye and bring him back to his roots. He'd paid her double and along with a spectacular cut and color, she'd shown him how grateful she could be. Right now, staring into the mirror at the face of the man he used to be, he felt…unstoppable.

"Greg? Are you here?" Samantha's voice called from the stern side lounge, and his dick responded against his pants. He'd been waiting all day for this. Glancing at his watch he realized there would be no time for formalities. They needed to get from the upper bay, through the lower bay and out into open water if they wanted to be on schedule to meet Manuel in Bermuda. One overnight sail with his gorgeous dinner companion, and he'd be able to pay off his debt and make Victor a very happy man. Little did sweet Samantha know, she had a long night of pleasure ahead of her followed by a lifetime with Victor, which could be heaven or hell depending on how she liked it.

He made his way from the master suite up a few steps and into the lounge, stopping to adjust his shorts. He paused to admire his little prize. She had her back to him, as she stared at the lavishness of the yacht and some of the family pictures he had on display. Her hair was tied back in a long braid and seeing the hint of skin between her top and skirt made his palms itch. That tight little ass would be his and he couldn't wait. He flexed his fingers in anticipation.

Nothing until we're out on the water, he reminded himself before painting a delightful smile on his face and wiping his sweaty palms against his shorts.

"Sam! I'm so glad you're here." He approached and took her hand, placing a soft kiss on the back of it like he'd done at the hotel gala.

"Me, too," she confirmed, then stared at his features. "You dyed your hair? And you've grown a bit of a beard since I've seen you."

"It's for my wife," he chided. "I looked like this when she met me."

"Really?" She continued to stare, and he swore she was making the connection. He figured she would, eventually. He decided not to linger too long in her sight to keep her intrigued.

"I know this is a far cry from the suits I usually wear," he said while moving toward the chrome and wood bar which ran half the length of the room. Greg was pleased when she followed. "But after the day I had today, I needed the change; do you know what I mean?"

"You know, I do." She sighed and nodded in agreement. "I've had one of those myself for several days now."

"Let me fix you a drink. We can commiserate about our weeks." He didn't wait for an answer and handed her a glass of wine, noticing the fullness of her lips were so much like her mother's. Lips which had been denied him, but soon his fantasy would be fulfilled with her daughter. Sam took the glass, and with her other hand reached out and grabbed his wrist.

"What an interesting tattoo?" Her fingers floated across the skin on the inside of his forearm stopping at the numbers 25.034° N, 77.3963° W. "Coordinates?" She sipped her wine. "Where to?"

"My happy place." He grabbed a beer and motioned for her to come along before he lost his mind. Samantha's touch had lit the spark inside him, and he either needed air or her sitting on his face, and even he knew it was too soon for that. "Let's get up on deck and drive this boat out of the marina." They'd have all night to get acquainted.

"Oh, about that, I have a little phobia about open water." She pinched her fingers together. "Is there any way we can stay here and have our dinner meeting?"

"Unfortunately, no," he replied in a relaxed tone thanks to the extra hit with the hairdresser before she left.

"What?" She seemed genuinely afraid, and he totally got off on the smell of her fear. He knew exactly how to comfort her. *Soon my little mouse. The game is just beginning.*

"We're meeting one of my business partners and we can't be late, or he'll cancel the deal and then there will be some irrevocable consequences that I *really* don't want to have to deal with." He downed the beer, then poured his own scotch and marched toward the cockpit with her on his heels.

"Can't your partner come here? I don't want you to lose

your deal, but you must understand I just can't be on the water for any length of time. I get violently ill."

"Don't worry I'll take care of you."

"It's not a matter of being taken care of. I'm totally incapacitated. It happened once and I don't ever want it to happen again." She paused for a moment as if remembering. "How long before we get there? Maybe I can take something now, so I won't become ill. I keep prescription medicine in my purse, but I've never used it. I'd hate to pass out on you."

"We'll be there by tomorrow afternoon. Just in time for lunch." He didn't try to hide his lust as his gaze roamed over her entire body. "I have beds below deck if we, I mean you, need to lay down."

"Overnight? Where exactly are we going?" She stopped and placed a hand to her temple. "This wine is going straight to my head." He watched her blink a couple times to focus, the powder he'd sprinkled into her drink working as quickly as he knew it would. He'd known she wouldn't come willingly. Once they were out on the water, she'd have no choice but to do whatever he wanted. She swayed a little, and he gently guided her to a leather captain's chair next to his.

"You'll see soon enough." He tapped her cheek, so she'd focus on him. "Because my dear, sweet, Samantha…*you're* the deal."

CHAPTER 27

Dalton snuck on board the moment Samantha disappeared inside the yacht. There was no sign of Billy, so he decided to snoop around a bit. He was sure there were drugs on board, and maybe he could connect Billy to the fentanyl. Dalton had heard Sam call out, and within seconds heard Billy's voice. He'd also heard the nervousness in Sam's when Billy told her they were taking the boat out.

Dalton couldn't let him make it to open water. There was no time for him to call any other form of back-up. He'd filled Tony in on everything and trusted his partner would come through after telling Dalton he'd be calling in some favors with the Coast Guard. Dalton waited patiently and retraced their steps to the cockpit. Peeking through the cabin door he saw Sam slouched in the chair. With still no sign of Billy, he rushed in and knelt in front of her.

"Sam, hey, it's me." He checked the pulse at her neck. She was out cold. Billy must have drugged her. "C'mon, wake up. We gotta get you out of here."

"Not so fast, Lover Boy," a gritty, familiar voice said from behind him. Dalton turned and was immediately cuffed on the side of his head with the butt of a gun. He hit the ground at Sam's feet and struggled to get up before he was hit again. "I've been expecting you."

"I've waited for his moment," Dalton ground out while swiping the trail of blood away from his eye. "How's Florida been treating you, Billy?" He hitched his chin and smirked at the weary eyes of his opponent. "Or should I call you, Greg?"

"Better than New York has treated you, you dumb-fuck. And you won't live long enough to call me anything. You should have died on that boat. I won't make the same mistake again."

"Go ahead, take your best shot." Dalton wasn't sure why he said that. He couldn't help Sam if he were dead. "Let Sam go."

"I have plans for her, and someone very special who wants to meet her."

"Surely you're not stupid enough to think I'll let that happen?" Dalton taunted.

"You're about to die trying." Billy waved him forward, only this time it was Dalton who landed a blow. Billy shook the haze from his eyes and swung blindly giving Dalton another chance to make contact. He hit him square in the jaw. Billy stumbled back but didn't fall.

"You know you'll never get away with this," Dalton said and leaned right to avoid a punch.

"With what, killing you for real? No one cares about a coward, Dalton. You've had fourteen years to close this down and you did nothing. Because if you did, you knew you'd take the fall or worse, get jail time as an accomplice to murder. Let me help you take the coward's way out. I hear the sharks are hungry this time of year."

Billy drew his gun from behind his back and fired a shot, grazing Dalton's leg. Dalton's knee buckled and he dropped to the floor. Billy advanced, kicking him in the ribs several times. Dalton fought through the pain as he pulled himself up to balance on one leg as best as he could, continuing to match Billy blow for blow and eventually knocking the gun out of his hand. Dalton thought he was in a protective enough stance when Billy swept his injured leg and he fell hard onto the deck. Air exited his body in a whoosh, and he gulped quickly to refill his lungs. Glancing up, he saw Billy waving a small needle.

"I've come a long way," Billy said proudly. "I just realized, though, I can't kill you, at least not right now." He tapped the side of the syringe, then set it aside. "You're going to witness, firsthand, the man I've become. The kind of man who won't let anything happen to his family. You and this little bitch have become a problem."

"You're the problem," Dalton growled. He shook his head and blinked his eyes rapidly, fighting to stay in the game. He might be down, but he wasn't out. As long as no harm came to Samantha, he'd play Billy's game all night long.

"No, there's where you've got it wrong. I'm the solution. Before I pass along *my* little problem," he motioned with his head toward Samantha. "I'm going to live out a fantasy I've never been able to forget." Billy walked a circle around Dalton, stopping to secure his wrists and feet with a nylon cord. "I'm sure you remember. Nina was one very fine piece of ass. From what I can tell, Samantha has amazing genetics. I can't wait to explore that tight, sexy body."

"You bastard, don't you touch her."

"And what are you going to do about it?" He grabbed Dalton by the hair, forcing his face closer. "Oh, that's right! Nothing!" He pushed his head back with an evil laugh. "Except watch me enjoy a long-awaited fuck." Billy left Dalton and moved over to Samantha. "Come here, baby, you and daddy are going to have a little fun." Billy ran his hand along her jaw, down her neck and along the 'v' of her blouse. "All the way to Bermuda."

"Samantha!" Dalton yelled. She moved slightly and her eyes fluttered open. She screamed and tried to move away from Billy, pushing against his chest.

"Greg, what are you doing?" Her eyes focused beyond him, doubling in size as she gazed at the open water all around. "H-How did we get out here?"

"You see." Billy moved to expose Dalton in her line of sight. "Once Lover Boy showed up, I had to take us out sooner. But don't worry, we can go below deck if the water bothers you, or if you're feeling shy." He stroked his finger against her cheek, and she jerked her head away.

She stared at him long and hard. Dalton wondered if she was figuring it all out, until she lined her focused on him. "Why is Dalton tied up?"

"I can't have him stopping us from having fun, in case he's the jealous type."

She seemed dazed and confused from whatever it was Billy had given her. "This is a business meeting. He has nothing to be jealous about." Her eyes held a sadness which tore at Dalton's heart. Then she glanced up at Billy and said, "Dalton and I aren't together."

"You may not be dancing in the sheets, princess, but you spend an awful lot of time together."

Dalton shifted his ankles trying to loosen up the ties. Why didn't Sam understand what Billy was talking about? He feared she was in shock over being out on open water. How long was it going to take before she had a complete meltdown like the one she'd told him about? He had to break free so he could take care of Billy once and for all.

"Please untie Dalton so we can all go back to the marina. I'm really not feeling well." Sam placed her palms against her cheeks, closing her eyes when the boat pitched.

"Can't do that," Billy said matter-of-factly. "We're meeting my business partner, remember?"

"I think he'll understand if we meet with him virtually." Sam steadied herself once she was on her feet. Dalton watched as she attempted to look up. Her eyes pinched tight and when she opened them again, she was staring directly at him. Her lashes fluttered as she took in the full scene of what had happened. She took a hesitant step as the boat pitched again and Billy grabbed her shoulders to steady her. Dalton caught sight of the wicked grin on Billy's face before he leaned into Sam.

"Manuel is a hands-on kind of guy, and so am I."

———

"Stop it!" Samantha yelled and broke free of Greg's hold, rushing to Dalton. She had no idea why Greg would have him tied up. She'd noticed some blood on Greg, so he and Dalton had obviously been fighting, over what she couldn't imagine.

"What are you doing here?" she said to Dalton as she knelt by his side. Glancing down his body, she noticed the red stain on his pant leg and the blood surrounding it on the deck. "You shot him?" She glared at Greg, confused as to what had transpired while she was passed out.

Greg towered over them with hands on hips. "He came unannounced and uninvited."

"He's losing blood. We need to turn around." Samantha twisted her body to glance up at him, surprised when she didn't feel panic from the rocking vessel. The dark eyes staring back at her created a panic for an entirely different reason.

"Leave him. He's going to die in more ways than one."

"I'll call ahead for an ambulance." She pulled her phone

from her pocket, and he immediately grabbed it and tossed it across the deck.

"We're not going back to the marina, Samantha." He grabbed her arm and yanked her away from Dalton. This time his eyes held a glimmer of something evil and something…distantly familiar.

"Why did you shoot him?" She glanced between the two men, wishing for Dalton to be conscious enough to react.

"Dalton and I go way back." Greg extended his hands in a giant gesture before her face. "There's nothing important he needs to say to you. As a matter of fact, I need to stop him from filling your head with lies before you go on your way."

Her stomach clenched and it wasn't from the rolling waves. Dalton had been trying to warn her, and she should have listened.

"Don't worry, Dalton's always been a tough guy." Greg's voice cut through her thoughts. "Not as tough or as cunning as me, but I could always trust him to handle his own. It's a shame we parted on such bad terms, right Dalton?" Greg kicked Dalton's bloody leg, making him moan.

"Stop! Why are you doing this? Do you have a medical bag or something we could at least slow the bleeding?"

"You've got a good point. I do have this sick fantasy of having him be alive long enough to see the look on your face when you're satisfied by a real man."

Samantha felt her pulse quicken as she realized the danger she was in. She didn't have to understand everything to know what Greg had in mind. "Whatever history you and Dalton have I'm sure it has nothing to do with me and our business relationship."

"In a way it does." Greg held her gaze and she shivered as he continued, "You and I are about to take our business relationship to a whole new level." He advanced so fast she had nowhere to go. He backed her against the wall, one hand holding the back of her neck while the other worked at the gauzy material of her skirt. The moment she felt his hand on the back of her leg, she squealed, and uppercut him under the chin. He took a couple steps back and she ran to Dalton trying to untie his hands.

"Dalton, Dalton, please wake up." She frantically worked the knot loose but had no time to fully release him before Greg hauled her by the waist and back into a chair.

"You like to play rough, Samantha?" he said, his face close enough she could see where he'd bit his lip. Her heart pounded and she looked around for something to defend herself. "I like to play rough too." He pinned her wrists to the chairs, leaning close enough to slide his tongue up the side of her neck just below her ear lobe. She shuddered at the sensation.

"Mmm…you taste as good as I always imagined your hot-ass mother would." He groaned, "Fuck. Me." His tongue trailed along her jaw toward her lips.

"M-My mother?" She tried to turn her face away and he stopped until she made eye contact. "How do you know my mother?"

"Let's just say I *tried* to know your mother. I *wanted* to know your mother. She had no idea what she did to me. That smile of hers, and Christ that fucking body!" he yelled. "She'd prance around in her cropped tops and bikinis looking like some super model. Doc was one lucky sonofabitch."

"You knew my father, too?"

"Oh yeah, you were just a young girl and that mama of yours was so protective. Hell, I couldn't even appreciate the sight of the two of you together. She'd get her non-existent panties in a twist." Greg stroked her cheek, his finger coming to rest on her lips. "All I wanted was a taste of her, I wanted to lick her until she begged me to screw her all night long. I'd even offered to drug up your father so he wouldn't come between us. The bitch teased me for two fucking days." He paused as if collecting himself, and she saw his Adam's apple bob when he swallowed. He placed his fingers under her chin, tilting her head so she could see his devious smile when he added, "And now, I have you."

Sam's head felt as if it were in a vice as pieces of a memory long forgotten, shifted in her brain. What he said, the way he looked…she didn't know how, but it seemed familiar, yet she'd never met Greg before her job with Bianca. Had Greg raped her mother?

"For such a smart young woman, I'm surprised you haven't figured this out, especially now." He closed in until his mouth was only inches from hers. "My God, your innocence is such a turn-on, just like your mother." His lips assaulted hers as he leaned over her in the chair. The moment his tongue pushed into her mouth; she yanked her head back to break their contact.

"Stop it! Let me go. I don't know what's going on, but I won't tell anyone about this, not even Bianca."

"I don't give a shit about that bitch. She wouldn't believe you anyway. You're so lovesick over our detective friend, I'd tell her you came on to me and that you'd do anything if I continued giving you all of my business."

"She'd never believe that." Sam wiped her mouth with the back of her hand.

"She would if I told my wife, and my wife called Bianca." He paused. "I'm a shrewd businessman. I'll do whatever I need to, in order to close the deal. And right now, my deal is with my friend Miguel. Bianca will still have my business, but you will no longer be a part of it."

Samantha's eyes grew wide, and she covered her gaping mouth with her hand as recognition of his true purpose took hold.

"Are you getting it now, sweet little Sam? You and Detective Dreamy, here, are about to be collateral damage. Funny how I haven't been the only one keeping tabs on you. But now that the two of you have met, I can't take the chance on either of you ruining my life." He grabbed her arm, forcing her to walk with him. She tried to stay near Dalton, but he pulled her into motion. "Come, let me explain." His voice returned to the smooth, in control man she'd been working with.

Until he stopped and snorted some white powder.

He held up the tiny silver spoon in offering, and she shrunk away from him. "You'll take some later, whether you want it or not. That's how we play on the water."

Nothing made sense to Samantha. Any memory around her parents continued to be a black hole. Now she was at the mercy of a man who was apparently part of the past Dalton never talked about.

"As I was saying," Greg said close to her ear, "Thanks to your father, I was able to build this life and support my family. I never would have any of it, if I hadn't have killed him and then out of some freakish sense of guilt, felt the need to honor him." He shoved his tattooed forearm in front of her face, and she startled. "You asked about my happy place? These coordinates are where it all went down. Where my life changed forever."

"You, killed my father?" She felt bile hit the back of her throat and forced it down.

"I didn't intend to. I genuinely liked the man. If your mother had kept her mouth on my dick like I wanted and let me rock her world, none of this would have happened. It's a damn good thing I slaughtered them all, including Dalton's meddling martyr of a brother." Greg walked back into the cockpit and returned with a can of beer. He popped the tab and drank the entire can at once before tossing it into the ocean. "But I wasn't a kid killer, Samantha, and if

Dalton, here, would have stayed dead, I wouldn't be so concerned."

A familiar, sickening fear overcame Sam, and her eyes welled with tears she could no longer contain. "Why are you doing this?"

"He's not Greg Maddox," Dalton groaned as he regained consciousness. Sam sighed with relief, then brought her gaze back to Greg.

"Then, who are you?"

"Captain Billy Benning at your service." He over-exaggerated a bow. "Welcome to our happy reunion, Little Girl X.

CHAPTER 28

Fourteen Years Earlier
Samantha — Truth

wish we could get to the island already. All I see is water...everywhere. It's fun when we can stop and swim, but Mom gets worried about the current. Mom and Dad are really excited about having our own boat. I'd be more excited if I could have brought a friend. They both promised once the deal was done, we would go on vacation whenever we wanted, and I could bring as many friends as we had staterooms! Wait till I turn sweet sixteen!

"Sweetie, put more sunscreen on. Your shoulders are getting red," Mom said and tossed me the bottle.

"When are we going to stop and swim again? I'm getting hungry."

"Maybe we can ask Daddy...if he ever tires of fishing." Mom looked toward the back of the boat and waved to the captain before making a funny face at me.

The captain made me nervous, and I don't think Mom liked him either. He always seemed to be staring at us. Every once in a while, he'd have this crazy look in his eyes like he didn't know where he was, and he tried to make everything funny when he talked to us. Ewww, I wish he'd just sail the boat and leave us alone. I kept hoping Dad could sail it home on his own and we wouldn't have to have the captain with us at all.

"Look! Dolphins!" I yelled, jumping to my feet, and bouncing up and down. I pointed at the small pod and ran toward the back so I could see them leaping through the wake left by our boat. Dad had pointed to some earlier in the day, and I'd been disappointed when they didn't stay around long. Before our vacation adventure, I'd only seen dolphins at Bush Gardens. Watching them out in the ocean was so exciting. They followed us for a while, and I found myself feeling sad when they disappeared below the water. "Will they come back?" I asked the first mate, who I'd heard the captain call Riley. I wasn't sure if that was his first or last name.

"We're entering warmer waters now that we're about half-way to the Bahamas. I bet you'll be spotting more and more as we go. Keep your eyes open, squirt." He gave me a wink and pointed at the horizon.

Riley kind of reminds me of a movie star. His eyes are a mossy green color that changes with the light during the day. His brown hair is kind of shaggy like he hasn't had it cut in a while. The ocean breeze really messes with it and there have been a couple of days he wore a bandana like a pirate. He's actually funny, not like the captain. I've spent some time studying him when he doesn't know I'm watching. Mom doesn't know either, or she'd probably ground me in my cabin below deck.

"Can you show me how to fish like Dad?" I asked, thinking Mom was probably glad to get me out of her hair. "Will I have to bait the hook? Will there be more dolphins when the sun goes down? What about whales? Are they out here?"

"How about you let Mr. Riley show you what to do instead of hammering him with so many questions?" Dad's reasonable voice advised as he tossed his line back into the water.

"Sorry." I shrugged, feeling embarrassed. I had a million questions because I liked the sound of his voice and wanted him to talk to me.

"It's okay, squirt." He handed me a pole way taller than me. "It's hard to tell with dolphins when you'll see them. Kind of like with us fishing. Sometimes you just have to ride the tide and find out."

"Ride the tide…." My father echoed. "I like that."

"Ride the tide." I scrunched my nose and stared out at the rocking waves. "I just want to catch a big fish."

"They're out there. You going to be ready to reel it in? Your dad and I will have to make sure it doesn't pull you overboard."

"Oh, maybe I don't want a big fish!" I started to hand the pole back, but he and Dad were laughing.

"It's all right, honey. Mr. Riley will be right here. One of us needs to catch one because I'm getting hungry."

We all got quiet, and I think I know why Dad liked fishing. I became lost in my thoughts with an occasional survey of the water for more dolphins. Suddenly, Mom's scream broke through our silence.

"Ben! Ben come here!"

Dad set his pole in this long tube and ran toward the front of the boat. I tried to do the same, but my pole was too big. Mr. Riley helped me keep it out and focus on my line and the water.

"Just stay here, Sam. I'm sure your dad will have everything under control. We don't want to be in the way."

"I guess not. What do you think is the matter with my mom?" I didn't like the worry in his eyes even though I felt like he was watching out for me.

"I'm sure it's just grown-up stuff." He glanced back before taking my dad's pole and casting the line back into the water. "Let's keep fishing."

I couldn't stop wondering what was going on with my mom and dad. Mr. Riley was standing behind me so every time I tried to look, he was in the way. I was pretty sure he was doing it on purpose. I didn't like it and it made me worry even more. I was ready to tell him what I was thinking when there was a tug on my line and the pole almost slipped out of my hand.

"I think I got something! Help me!" I was so scared and excited I didn't know what to do. I was afraid I was going to get pulled into the ocean and I couldn't wait for him to take the pole away from me. Just as he was about to take control, we heard two gunshots.

I released the pole and took off running.

"Samantha, no!" Mr. Riley caught up to me, wrapping an arm around my shoulders as we raced to the bow. I was so scared, and I knew something horrible had happened.

I saw my mom and dad lying on the deck, covered in blood, and I began shrieking. The captain was standing over a man I didn't remember seeing on the boat since we left New York. I started to run to my parents, but Mr. Riley spun me around and pressed my face into his t-shirt so I couldn't see anymore.

"I want my mom and dad!" I screamed over and over into his shirt, making it all wet with my tears. He was holding me tighter as he walked me to a bench seat away from the blood.

"Stay put, okay?" He knelt in front of me, and his green eyes were so serious that I actually stopped crying and tried hard to catch my breath. "Let me see what's going on. You must stay here, Samantha." I nodded my head fast because I didn't want to go back to all that blood. Did the stranger hide out on our boat? Did he attack my parents and then the captain killed him? I prayed so hard that my parents weren't hurt badly.

"What the hell happened?" I heard Mr. Riley yell as he ran toward the captain.

Sounds muffled in my ears. All I could do was watch him run from body to body. I thought he was trying to save them all, but the captain was right behind him yelling back.

"Here's what we're going to do," I heard the captain scream. "We get rid of all the extra dead or soon to be dead, weight. We continue down the coast until we figure out what to do with the girl."

What to do with me?

"I won't let you kill her," Mr. Riley said, putting himself between me and the captain.

Kill me? I was so afraid my parents were dead now. I hadn't seen the other man move either.

"I'm no kid killer, give me a break," the captain said, walking closer. "I think we can make big money if we sell her, though. There's a market for this sort of thing. People are always wanting black market children."

The captain pushed Mr. Riley aside, descending on me. I kicked at him, but it made no difference. He was bigger and stronger and yanked me off the bench. I continued to scream and fight against him as we passed Mr. Riley.

"It'll be okay, squirt. Just go with the captain." Mr. Riley was kneeling next to my dad. I stopped screaming when Dad and I made eye contact.

"I need you to be strong, okay sweetheart?" Dad's voice was so weak, I could barely hear him over the sound of the rapid thumping between my ears. "Listen to Mr. Riley. Everything will be fine."

I nodded again, not believing anything could be okay after this. Dad wouldn't lie to me. I took one last look as Mr. Riley leaned closer when Dad grabbed his arm and spoke to him. I wanted to listen, but the captain dragged me below deck and shoved me into my stateroom.

"Shut your mouth and stay here. If you come out, you're going to be dead like everyone else, got it?" he seethed only inches from my face. His eyes were wild and crazy, and he smelled of beer. All I could do was nod. I didn't want to die.

When I was sure he was gone, I tried to open my door, but something was jammed against the knob from the outside. I rattled the handle and pounded on the door. Then I heard another gunshot.

"Mom! Dad! I'm down here!" I screamed so loud my throat hurt. "Come get me! Moooom!" I fell back on my bed and sobbed. The round window above my bed only opened out enough to stick my hand through. Even if I could break it, I was too big to fit.

I stayed on my bed for a while, listening for any sounds from the deck. When I got up to try the door again, the carpet squished between my toes. Water was flooding under the door as if someone were pouring from a bucket on the other side.

"Help! Help me!" I banged on the door. "I'm in here! Someone help me!" My palms pounded the door again and this time it flew open, and Mr. Riley was on the other side.

"C'mon, Sam!" He grabbed my hand and pulled me out of the room.

"You're, you're hurt," I said when we started to wade through water up to my knees.

"I'm okay. Don't worry about me." Once we reached the upper deck, he snatched a life jacket off a hook and fastened it around me. "I gotta get you off this boat, because it's sinking, okay?"

"Where's my mom and dad?" I scanned the area, but waves were starting to lap over the side of the boat. He didn't answer my question but kept hunting around for something. "Mr. Riley, I'm scared."

"Look, here's a lifeboat!" He picked up this small, yellow cube and pulled a cord which inflated the small craft.

"It's too small." My voice quivered as I gazed at him, then back to the tiny raft.

"Hey, it's the perfect size for you." He smiled at me, but it didn't calm me when I realized what that meant.

"No," I sob, "I won't go without you."

"You have to." He lifted me up and I fought him, clinging to his shirt so he wouldn't leave me. He slowly lowered me until my bare feet touched the bobbing rubber of the raft below. I wrapped my arms so tight around his neck, he had to pry me off. He kissed my forehead and said, "Remember what your dad said about being strong, okay?"

"Don't go...." My voice crackled as more tears fell.

"You'll be okay, Sam, I promise," he said, and I saw the tears in his eyes as he pushed the raft away from the boat. He watched me for a second, then disappeared below the deck once more. The current took me quickly and soon the sinking boat was out of sight.

I never did see him again....

CHAPTER 29

Dalton held his breath as he watched the blood drain from Sam's face. She stared at Billy as if finally recognizing him for who and what he was. Good. With her help, they could overtake him. As far as Dalton could tell, there were no others on board.

"I thought *you* killed them," she said, making eye contact with Dalton, her eyes growing wider as the dots she were connecting started to make sense. "But you didn't." He shook his head. Realization dawned, and a tear trickled down her cheek. "Oh my God, it was you. You're the one who saved me."

"Well boo-hoo," Billy whined in a mocking tone. "I hate to break it to you, but he isn't going to save you this time." He ran his hands down her arms and held them at her waist. Everything in Dalton burned from years of buried fury when Billy's palms skimmed the exposed skin of Sam's stomach before moving up to cup and knead each breast. Dalton worked feverishly to loosen the bindings Sam had started before Billy returned.

"Leave her alone, Benning," Dalton ground out.

"Shut the hell up, Riley. You're in no position to tell me what to do. I'm going to leave it up to our beautiful companion to decide if I should kill you now or let you live long enough to see her sail into the sunset with her soon to be husband."

"Husband, what are you talking about?"

"What I have here," he said pulling Sam tightly against him and keeping one hand on her breast as she tried to twist out of his hold, "is a prize worthy of the five-million-dollar debt that bonehead Rocco Patrone cost me."

"I knew you had something to do with killing Louie. What exactly are you and Rocco into?"

"Don't worry, Detective Riley, I've already taken care of that mindless bastard, Rocco. He screwed up with Manuel Salazar, totally fucked up with Louie because CeCe was never supposed to be injured. Once she was, he was supposed to take her out so she wouldn't be a pain in our ass on her mission for family justice. And now he messes up a third time when he was supposed to kill you and instead, killed your other partner."

"I already know about Rocco. What are you talking about, my partner?" Dalton's pulse beat so fast he could feel it in his neck. When he'd left the hospital, Nicole had been in serious, but stable condition, heading into surgery. "If anything has happened to Nicole, I'll send you to the gates of hell myself."

"Nicole?" Samantha whispered. "I really have been a fool."

"There, there, my angel," Billy soothed. "I told you Dalton wasn't worthy of you." He rubbed her back and every muscle in Dalton's body yearned to be free to protect Sam. "I'm here to give you everything you need." Billy gently eased her down onto the bench. By the glazed look in her eyes Dalton could tell she was being swallowed by the past trauma making its way to the surface at a rapid rate. He couldn't let her give up, not like this.

"Sam!" he yelled. "You have to fight, come on, Sam!" Dalton pulled his wrists apart to stretch the nylon cording, then reached to work at the knots around his ankles.

"Don't listen to Dalton. He's kept so much of the truth from you." Billy stroked her hair, letting his hand skim the side of her face down to her collar bone where he paused before dipping his finger between her breasts. "That's right, you're not going to be the hellcat that your mother was." Billy kissed her skin while keeping a firm grip on her shoulders. Dalton kept an eye on his nemesis as he continued to free himself. "I've waited a long time for this," Billy groaned, his hands moving to her hips, where he gathered the material of her skirt to her waist. "Oh, this is going to be the feast of a lifetime." Billy sat up, sliding both hands to her thighs. "Are you ready? I'm going to make you scream."

"Get your hands off her," Dalton ordered as he started to stand, surprised when Billy flew toward him in a blind rage and kicked him in the side of the head before he was fully on his feet.

"I told you to shut the hell up, Dalton. You're not ruining this for me. I'm taking what I want from her the rest of the way to Bermuda. And you're going to watch me get her off like you never did." Billy gave Dalton a swift kick to the ribs. "That's right, I know it was you who found the camera. As I'm sure you're aware, I watched the whole shitshow evolve."

"Camera?" Sam's shock registered through Dalton's pain.

"You're a sick sonofabitch, Billy," Dalton said through clenched teeth as his ribs burned with each breath.

"I was so envious of your position. Samantha desperately threw herself at you. You could have done anything with her, and she would have let you. There was that moment when I thought you were going all the way...but no, you had to play hero. I thought I'd taught you better than that. Very disappointing," he said as he returned to Sam who had pulled her skirt back down and huddled in the corner of the bench.

"Greg…Stop…." She frantically fought off his hands as he grabbed at the material of her skirt.

Dalton wiped the blood from his mouth with his wrists, noticing the binding was loose enough to slip out of. He glanced toward Sam, willing her to hang on as he slipped his hands free and finished untying his ankles.

"Greg's not here right now, so you're going to play nice with me," Billy said sweetly. "Do you understand? Victor won't want damaged goods, so don't put up a fight or I'll give you the needle."

"Please, don't." The distress in Sam's voice echoed in Dalton's skull.

He rose to his feet and propelled himself at Billy's back, grabbing the man and tossing him onto the deck. Calling on all the hatred he'd carried for fourteen years, he advanced before Billy could get to his feet. Dalton fisted his hand into Billy's t-shirt and pounded hit after hit against his face until he was bloody and unconscious. Letting go of the shirt, he rushed to Sam.

"Sam it's all right. Did he hurt you?" He placed his hands on either side of her face and felt every ounce of fear in her ocean blue eyes as she shook her head. "God, Sam, I'm so sorry." He pulled her in for a hug and she released wracking sobs and tears against his shoulder. He let her cry, and she held on so tight he didn't want to pull her away, but she needed to know the truth. "Listen," he said and waited until she met his eyes. "I saw it all. I should have told you. But your dad made me promise to keep you safe. All these years, I have never gone back on that promise."

"That's what he was telling you when Captain Billy took me away." She sniffed and wiped at her tears.

He nodded. "All these years I knew Billy was still out there and I've been following every possible lead, fearing what he might do someday if you ever remembered what happened. Only when I found out he was Greg Maddox, I realized all this time he'd been keeping tabs on you, too."

"That's why you came to my place."

"I didn't think you'd want to talk to me, but I had to try."

"Dalton, I'm sorry I didn't want to listen. I should have listened. It's all starting to make sense."

"I'm just glad I'm here. I won't let anything happen to you."

"I know." She wrapped her arms around his neck. "I'm glad you're here too."

A shadow blocked the setting sun, and Samantha's shrill scream rang through the salty ocean air. Before Dalton could react, he was yanked out of her arms and stood face to face with Captain Billy.

———

Samantha couldn't stop screaming as Dalton and Billy traded blows in front of her. She scanned for anything close she could use as a weapon to protect herself or to help Dalton. Not that he needed her help. He was holding his own and Billy seemed to be stumbling and losing ground.

Until he drew his gun and shot Dalton at close range.

Dalton grabbed his stomach as rich, red blood permeated the cotton of his shirt. The men stared in silence at each other before Dalton made eye contact with her. His lips formed the words, *I'm sorry,* and her trembling hands clasped over her mouth as he collapsed onto the deck.

"Nooo!" she screamed and jumped up to rush to his side, but Billy stopped her and planted a bloody kiss on her lips.

"Luscious." He licked his lips and forced them on her

again. "You sit your hot little ass right here and don't you move." He stepped away and then spun around, pointing. "I mean it. Right here so you can have a front row seat."

"Why did you kill him?"

"Oh, he's not dead yet. See? He's still breathing." Billy glanced at Dalton's body then went back to her. "I need to clean up this mess, and by that, I mean *him*. I suggest you think about how you want to say goodbye."

"What are you talking about?"

"Remember when I said I'm a smart businessman? I had a feeling we might run into some trouble, so I've been chumming the water since we left the marina. Yeah, that's right, you're going to be able to watch the feeding frenzy in just a few moments."

Samantha fought hard not to pass out as she fixated on Dalton's lifeless body, barely aware of what was going on. Years ago, he'd saved her when he didn't have to. He didn't have to honor his promise to her father back then, while she grew up, or even now. But he did, he always had. Whoever Nicole was, she was lucky to have his heart. Snapping out of her daze, Billy had already moved Dalton's body.

I can't let him die.

She followed the blood-smeared trail where Billy had dragged Dalton's body toward the back of the boat and picked up a small crowbar lying next to some rigging. Finns sliced through the dusk-dark water, catching her eye. Billy's back was toward her as she crept closer. Her chance to strike was now.

"No!" she yelled and hit him hard across the back. He was more muscular than she'd thought, and she felt the vibration through her forearms. Billy caught his balance as he fell forward, turned, and began to pry the bar from her hands.

"You stupid little bitch!" In one hard tug the iron broke free, and he tossed it into the ocean. "I asked you to do *one* thing!" His arms were around her in seconds and he tackled her to the deck.

"Get off me!" Samantha wiggled and kicked, doing everything she could to get out from under him. He stayed with her every move.

"I told you to stay put. What did I tell you would happen if you put up a fight?" Billy cast a grin full of pure evil, and she froze with his face only inches from hers. "You're going to get the needle and unfortunately I'm going to have to tie you down while I have my way with you."

"No!" She tried again to gain leverage.

"You're not going to be able to stop me, Samantha. I always get what I want, and this time there's no one here to rescue you." He stood and yanked her arm. "Get up!"

Samantha continued to fight as he dragged her across the deck. He'd have to loosen his hold eventually, and when he did, she would bolt. She needed something to protect herself. A man like Billy had to have more than one gun on board.

She'd do whatever she could to help Dalton survive this.

Once they were below deck, Billy slung her into one of the captain's chairs so hard that she practically bounced out. She gripped the arm rests for support and stared into his wild eyes. She gasped for breath as much as he did. Every nerve ending sparked in anticipation of the right moment to run.

"You're lucky I've got my shit together." Billy opened a drawer and pulled out a velvet pouch. Laying out a syringe, a rubber band, a lighter and a container of powder he licked his lips. "Samantha, you're about to be in for the ride of your life. You're going to be so spent when I'm through with you, Manuel will have to carry you aboard his yacht. Which might not be a bad thing. Then you can rest and recharge in preparation for your new life."

Sam watched him carve two lines and snort each one, not really paying attention to what he'd said. He lit some powder on a spoon and filled the syringe. Billy then licked his finger and rolled it in the tin of powder, stepping toward her with the syringe in his other hand.

"Suck this off my finger, like a good girl, because you'll be sucking it off my cock soon enough." He moved his finger closer to her lips and she turned her head. "Play nice Samantha. The needle is coming, and so will you." He leaned in closer and whispered in her ear, "I can't wait to hear you beg for more."

"I don't want it." She tried to dodge his finger until the hand that held the needle settled on the side of her face to stop her movement.

"You will when I'm done with you." He shoved his finger in and out of her mouth then worked quickly to tie the rubber band around her arm, while she spit furiously hoping to keep the drug out of her system. "Don't be a wasteful bitch. That's my primo product from Manuel. You'd better learn not to disrespect him since he's taking you to your future husband."

"I'm not going anywhere." Sam pulled her knees to her chest and kicked Billy in the stomach right before the needle penetrated her skin. He hit the floor, the needle flew from his hand, and Sam ran up the short set of stairs and into the main living cabin. Behind the bar was a display of trophy fish and in the center was a crossbow.

"Oh my God, yes, thank you!"

Adrenaline pumped through her as she rushed to dislodge it from the wall. She didn't even know how it worked, or if it worked. There was an arrow already loaded and one in the quiver. Billy charged into the room just as it broke free from its hooks.

"Whoa now! You think you can use that? Just set it down before you hurt yourself and I have to explain to Manuel how wild you are. Then again, maybe I should keep you to myself." He chuckled low and full of menace. "I always enjoy a hearty challenge."

"I will kill you," she said and didn't recognize her own voice. This man killed her parents. Fear and the need to survive fueled all the courage she needed to do whatever unthinkable acts she had to.

"Think about it." Billy stepped closer as she raised the bow. "Dalton is as good as dead. If you kill me, you'll be that orphan on the ocean all over again."

The bow lowered in her hands as she remembered floating for days, all alone except for the dolphins. She never wanted to feel that loneliness and all-consuming fear again. She forced a swallow as her arms began to shake from the weight of the weapon. Her mind seemed to work against her, sending flashes of endless ocean, boiling sun, and the feeling of being so small and helpless.

Catching herself, she raised the bow back in his direction. "I'll call for help."

"I disconnected the radio," he countered, but she wouldn't let her disappointment show. "I know where I'm meeting Manuel. And he knows the route, so if I don't show up and you're all alone, he'll just come retrieve you himself. Manuel always has his security team with him. And you, my dear, will only have one arrow—that is, if you kill me with one shot." He stepped toward the bar, and she threw a bottle of liquor at him, but missed and it smashed on the floor.

Sam wasn't going to let him play on her fears.

"You're not going anywhere and you're not a killer, Samantha." He took a couple steps toward her. "But I am. Only I don't need the crossbow to kill Dalton. I'm just going to flip him over the edge." He took another step. "Put the weapon down and let's enjoy our time together."

She pulled the trigger.

The arrow released. He jerked forward, clutching his thigh, and victory sparked hot in her chest.

But he didn't fall.

When she looked, there was no arrow at all.

"You missed." He hobbled forward and she ran.

As she rounded a corner toward Dalton, her foot slipped in the still slick trail of his blood. She fell, the crossbow bouncing out of reach. She rose to her feet but the pain in her ankle made her pause.

"You're pissing me off, Samantha!" Billy roared from behind her.

She bent to pick up the bow. Her fingers closed around it, but Billy swept her legs out from under her, and she fell again. He yanked her across the deck.

"I. Told. You. To Play. Nice." He stopped to catch his breath. "Damn it, this hurts."

Sam still had the bow. Her shaking hands fumbled the last bolt from the quiver, and she shoved it between her teeth while she repositioned the weapon.

"I've had enough of these games. I'm going to fuck you right here in front of Dalton's dead body and then maybe I'll throw you both to the sharks just like I did with mommy and daddy." As he turned her over, she kicked him hard in the knees. "You bitch!" he yelled as he fell to the deck.

Samantha got to her knees and slammed the front of the bow against the deck, using it like a brace and threw her weight back. The string inched, then jerked, then finally snapped into the latch.

She dropped the bolt into the groove and raised the bow.

Billy was already coming.

But she was faster.

The bolt punched into Billy's neck just above his collar bone.

He lurched back, choking on his own breath. The railing

met him with a hollow thud. Then he pitched over it, disappearing into the black water.

All Sam heard was the splash of the sharks feasting on his horrible soul.

Samantha dropped the bow and curled into a ball of tears on the deck. All the grief she'd never been able to shed poured out in body wracking hysteria.

Billy was right, she was alone on the ocean once again. There was no radio, and she had no idea how to drive a boat or how to read a nautical map. This time, someone worse than Billy was on his way to find her.

How much time did she have? The pain and crippling fear of what she went through as a child began to suffocate her. Growing up, she never had a reason to question what she'd been told. Her aunt and uncle protected her and gave her a wonderful life.

Sam felt something touch her arm and looked down to see a bloody hand. She screamed as she pushed it away.

"Shhh…Sam, it's okay," a weak, raspy voice said, "It's me."

"Dalton?" She lifted her head. "Oh my God, you're alive!" She crawled closer to meet him and their foreheads touched. "Billy said you were dead. I thought I was alone."

"Not getting rid of me that easy." He laughed then sucked in a breath. "It's not good, Sam. I need a doctor."

"W-what can I do?" She sat up straighter to look him over. His t-shirt was saturated. "You've lost so much blood."

"We need to put pressure on this. Towels, rags, whatever you can find."

She cried out in pain when she stood.

"What's wrong? Did he hurt you?"

"I slipped." She glanced down at the pink stains on her skirt. Dalton's blood. "It's just a bad sprain. I'm more worried about you."

Sam moved as fast as she could gathering bottles of water, the med kit and towels from the master suite. She returned to a very pale Dalton. For a moment she became that scared little girl.

"Don't leave me," she said but her ears heard her eleven-year-old self. He stirred and opened his eyes.

"This time, I won't."

She cleaned the wound, hating the sounds he made as she sterilized it. There was no exit wound, which scared her more. Sam followed his directions and packed several washcloths against the wound. She ended up ripping some gauze from her skirt to be able to wrap it tight enough around his waist.

From the slew of bottles she'd taken out of the medical cabinet, they'd found an antibiotic, which he downed more pills than she was happy about. Sam propped him up and sat next to him. His fingers weaved into hers and squeezed.

"Dalton, I'm scared. Billy's associate Manuel will be coming. If we don't leave, I think he will kill you and take me."

"Not going to happen." Dalton winced in pain when he tried to move. "Tony knows where I am."

"What? How? There's no other boat on the ocean." She turned her body so they were facing each other. The pain was evident in his features and while she was relieved Tony was aware, she feared Dalton didn't have much time.

"I called him before I got to the marina. Told him to stay back." Dalton paused to catch his breath. "Shoot the flare gun. He'll find us."

Once more, Sam did as he instructed and eagerly returned to his side. She sat facing him, holding his hands, and occasionally taking a cool washcloth to his face. This man would forever have a place in her heart, and she refused to believe he would die.

A pod of dolphins surfaced and breached in front of the setting sun.

She leaned in so her forehead touched his. She felt his strength, his energy, his truth all in that simple touch. "Thank you for everything you have ever done. Now I have closure."

He surprised her by reaching forward and pulling her close.

"We both do." he replied.

EPILOGUE

4 months later....

The doorbell rang and Bianca excused herself from the group discussion. She returned with Samantha in tow followed by a familiar looking young man. Dalton smiled and walked over to embrace her.

"Hey there, squirt." He kissed her cheek.

"Hey there, yourself." She wrapped her arms around his neck and then let go. "I can't remember if you met officially at the barbecue, but this is Matt Johnson."

"The audit guy?" He winked and she rolled her eyes. "Nice to officially meet you, man." He extended his hand and Matt returned a firm handshake. Dalton liked that. His father had always told him you can judge a good man by the firmness of his handshake.

"Same here. Sam speaks very highly of you." Matt reached back to casually put his arm around Sam's shoulder, surprising Dalton when she leaned into him.

"I've heard a little about you as well."

"Don't even think you guys are trading notes on all of my quirks," Sam warned, waving a finger between them.

"I love all of your quirks." Matt kissed her temple. "Especially that one where you—"

Samantha gasped and Dalton let loose a roar of laughter. "Oh, I like this guy already." He clapped Matt on the back.

"All right," Bianca interrupted. "Now that we're all here, please come inside and enjoy some drinks and appetizers before dinner." She ushered everyone further into the house.

"How's the healing going?" Sam asked Dalton while Tony made their drinks at the bar.

"I'm learning to appreciate physical therapy."

"He's lying," Nicki blurted out before sipping her whisky.

"Maybe a little." He wrapped an arm around her waist, something he'd never done within their friend group. "Thankfully, I have you to talk me off the ledge."

"It's more like stop you from punching the poor trainers, or the wall, love," she said, and his heart soared. It had taken almost losing her, and then his own life, to make him realize how much he truly loved her. They were more than just a hookup. He couldn't imagine his life without her in it.

"You're Nicole?" Sam asked with a genuine smile.

"Yes. Samantha, right? I'm so glad you weren't hurt." The two women exchanged a hug.

"I have Dalton to thank for that, for a lot of things."

"Not true, you held your own and rid the world of a killer. I'm proud of you."

"Speaking of which, next time you have some rogue mission going on in the background, I'd appreciate some kind of heads up," Tony ordered.

"That's why it's a rogue mission. And I did call you."

"Yeah, at the eleventh hour and I needed to sell my soul to get my buddy at the Coast Guard to help on his day off."

"Successful mission all around then." Dalton raised his

glass. "Most importantly, you got me to the hospital in time." He winked at Sam. "Don't forget the surprise arrest of Erik Wilson, the not-so-nice doorman."

"Yeah, what a rap sheet he had." Tony shook his head. "He also happened to be in possession of some Gamma 10, which made our job a lot easier."

"Isn't that a date rape drug," Matt acknowledged, then quickly explained to everyone's shocked and curious expressions, "I've heard about it on the news lately."

"And the big take away?" Dalton clapped Tony on the back, "You were able to capture Manuel Salazar, so that will stop the fentanyl trail for a while anyway."

"That's true. I've got a team mapping out his other associates. I do believe that's a war we will continue to fight. Speaking of fighting, I'm trying not to hold against you the fact you're keeping me stuck with RJ longer than I should be. I'm beginning to think you've extended your leave on purpose. That hurts, man." Tony hit his fist to his chest as if he were wounded and everyone laughed.

"Trust me, I want back in action more than you want me riding shotgun. We'll talk privately about my leave extension." Dalton shot Tony a look that only he understood.

"What happens to Billy's...I mean Greg's family?" Sam asked, breaking the awkward silence. "I can't believe Becca had any idea what her husband was doing."

"We used Billy Benning as the killer in order to close the case," Tony replied.

"That's right," Dalton added. "Becca will know the truth because she met him when he was Billy Benning. No one else will know that, and this way she and the children will retain all of Greg Maddox's assets once he is declared a missing person. His children will never have to know what an evil man their father was."

"Victor Perez, on the other hand, remains a mystery," Nicki added.

"To think I could have ended up being held captive by that man," Sam said with a shudder, and Matt pulled her closer. "I'd thought he was so nice when I met him at the gala. I never suspected anything was wrong."

"He pulled all his projects and there's no forwarding contact information. It's like he just disappeared," Bianca said before sipping her drink.

"He's become a ghost," Nicki added. "I suspect he will go into hiding for a while. It may be years before he surfaces again."

"The FBI is involved and hot on his trail in Venezuela. Now that we know Rocco participated in the human tracking ring, too, we can bust anyone in the Patrone family he'd convinced to help him." Tony paused. "Again, due to your rogue mission."

"Team effort," Dalton responded with a wink toward Nicki this time.

"Forever," she said and raised her glass.

"Wait! What is this?" Bianca grabbed Nicki's wrist, almost spilling the contents of the glass. "Is this what I think it is?" She pointed to the diamond on Nicki's ring finger. "Dalton Joseph Riley, don't you give me that look. When were you going to tell me?"

"You notice everything, Bianca. It was only a matter of time." Nicki grinned from ear-to-ear and Dalton couldn't love her more. "It happened last night."

"Congratulations!" Sam said, giving Dalton a hug. "You two look great together."

"Thanks, I can say the same for you and Matt. He suits you."

"Yeah, I guess I should have been paying more attention."

"I'd like to propose a toast to Nicki and Dalton!" Bianca

raised her glass. "And you all can thank me later. I love you both!"

"We love you too," Dalton said with a clink of his glass on hers.

"So, when is the wedding?" Bianca asked.

"Are you guys headed anywhere to celebrate?" Tony added.

"Wedding next year," Nicki offered up, "We have so much to figure out and Dalton needs to be healed and ready to dance all night...among other things." She gave him a light hip check.

"Okay, Okay," he said with a chuckle. "Now that we all know there's no celebrating happening right now. I can tell you we are taking a trip."

"Where are you going? Someplace fun, I hope?" Sam inquired.

"Home," Dalton responded and noticed the shocked expressions of everyone in the room. "It's time."

"That's a big step for you," Tony said, placing his hand on Dalton's shoulder.

"It is. After everything that has happened," His eyes were drawn to Sam's and then Nicki's. "I want to introduce my parents to their future daughter-in-law and tell them the truth about what happened to Justin." He paused to swallow the lump in his throat. No matter how much he'd rehearsed this, the emotional punch hit him hard every time.

"For fourteen years I've fabricated a lie that Justin was traveling the world being a journalist. I paid people to send post cards to my parents a couple times a year." He cleared his throat. "It's time to come clean. If you're up to a road trip to the outer banks, Sam, I'd like to introduce them to you, too."

"Me? Why?" She genuinely appeared surprised, and he hoped she'd still come.

"I lead them to believe Justin caught up to me and convinced me to turn my life around. In part, that's true. But the reality is, it was you and my promise to your father, along with avenging my brother's death that made me enter law enforcement."

"You really did change your life. I understand so much now." She wiped at a tear before it could tumble down her cheek, and Dalton took her hand.

"I think when they meet you, and listen to the whole story, they will understand too." He squeezed her hand when he continued, "You're like the little sister I never had, and I can see them being as protective of you as I am. You may have found an adoptive family whether you want one or not."

"Are they anything like you?"

"They are far better than I could ever dream to be." He thought of the family life he had when he was younger and how much better it would have been if he had listened to those who loved him. With the death of Billy Benning, he was able to put all of that in the past and could finally focus on his future. A future which was brighter than anything he could have ever imagined.

"Then how can I say no?" She smiled and his heart soared.

"You're serious." He glanced from Nicki to Sam, who nodded repeatedly with a smile. "You have no idea how much this means."

"It means a lot to me, too. When do we leave?"

"Tomorrow morning." He gazed around the room, feeling love and friendship and a renewed sense of self.

All because of a promise and Little Girl X.

ABOUT THE AUTHOR

Kit Witek writes atmospheric fantasy mysteries and romantic thrillers where love is dangerous, legends breathe in the dark, and secrets never stay buried. Her stories blend haunting atmosphere, simmering tension, and slow-burn emotion, leaving readers spellbound until the final page. She also writes cozy mysteries as Barbara Witek.

When she's not plotting twists or dreaming up brooding love interests, she can be found sipping something steamy, walking woodland trails, or indulging her love of moonlight, crystals, and candlelight. She believes in loyal dogs, strong coffee, slow burns, and the power of a well-kept secret.

A small press bound by the belief that every voice matters.

Sign up for our newsletter to learn about new releases and more.

Buy directly from us to save on ebooks, book bundles, and special editions.

Follow us on social media:

facebook.com/oliverheberbooks

instagram.com/oliverheberbooks

tiktok.com/@oliverheberbooks

bsky.app/profile/oliverheberbooks.bsky.social

youtube.com/@OliverHeberBooksPublisher

oliverheberbooks.substack.com

amazon.com/oliverheberbooks

9 7989004 31529